T0244657

PREPARE FOR THE WORST

VANESSA LAFLEUR

North Carolina

Published in the United States by BQB Publishing
(an imprint of Boutique of Quality Books Publishing, inc.)
www.bqbpublishing.com

Printed in the United States

ISBN 978-1-952782-74-9 (p)
ISBN 978-1-952782-75-6 (e)

Library of Congress Control Number: 2022939393

Book design by Robin Krauss, www.bookformatters.com
Cover design by Rebecca Lown, www.rebeccalowndesign.com
First editor: Olivia Swenson
Second editor: Andrea Vande Vorde

For my students

A special thanks to Terri Leidich and everyone at BQB publishing for their support in bringing my vision to life; to Olivia Swenson for her expert advice and encouragement; and to my family, friends, and students who cheer me on and inspire me to keep writing. I couldn't do this without all of you.

PART 1

WHO CAN BE TRUSTED?

PART 1

WHO CAN BE TRUSTED?

CHAPTER 1

CHARLIE

November 22, 2090

Four days. I hadn't found a trace of Rochelle or a clue to her whereabouts in ninety-six hours. After leaving her with Molly on that gravel road outside of town, I had foregone sleep to aid with every phase of the search. Too tired to stay awake while sitting down, I paced from Alexander's kitchen into his living room and back again. Each time I passed, I stopped at the window above the big kitchen sink, slid aside the thin curtain, and scanned the front yard lit only by the porch light and the moon.

"The Defiance has taken control of Dallas and continue their southward march to Austin. Militias have formed to stop their progress, but they're outnumbered and disorganized in comparison to The Defiance." I switched off the radio before the reporter could deliver any more bad news about the country's gradual fall to Defiance rule.

"You have to eat something, Charlie." Alexander, twenty years old and mayor of the small Nebraska town of Maibe, poked at the contents of an open Styrofoam container on the kitchen table. A closed one sat in front of my empty chair. On his way home from the weekly council meeting, he stopped at the diner and picked up two hamburgers with fries. Although he'd tried to convince me to take my usual notes to write the meeting report for the newspaper, I couldn't imagine attending without Rochelle. And I dreaded the questions the remaining three council members would ask.

"I'm not that hungry." The response had become automatic whenever food was offered. For the first forty-eight hours after I'd lost Rochelle, Alexander and I had driven up and down miles of gravel roads north of town. We stopped at every farm to talk to the people living there and walked around the abandoned ones but came up empty in our search for a red truck. For the last two days, I'd been unable to shake the sickening realization I would never see Rochelle again and it was all my fault.

"Please." Alexander sighed, rubbing the back of his neck. "I'm going to see Kinley in a little while and she always asks how you are. You should really call her—or better yet, stop by the house with me."

Walking over to the table, I flipped open my container and shoved two fries into my mouth. "Tell her I'm alive, and I won't rest until I find Rochelle. I don't expect her to forgive me."

"She's not mad. Just worried. About you, about Rochelle, about Todd." The dark shadows under his eyes and the way he leaned heavily against the table indicated I wasn't the only one who hadn't slept in days.

The only good news we'd received was that Todd was slowly improving. If he hadn't been in such bad shape, I never would have left without Rochelle, but I couldn't have convinced her to choose her life over her best friend's. Molly had created a situation that could only work in her favor.

For a moment, I imagined the safety of the library at the Aumont house, the kitchen smelling like coffee and freshly baked bread, the warm comfort of my bed. Alexander lived in an old farmhouse big enough for a family of ten. It was clean, warm, and gave me plenty of space, but it wasn't the same. As much as I wanted to go home, the memory of disappointment in Kinley's eyes and the anger on Kat's face when I told them I'd failed to protect Rochelle twisted my stomach into a knot.

"I can't face them without Rochelle."

"We'll find her." Alexander stood and clapped my shoulder. "If you change your mind, I'm leaving after I change into a clean shirt." I didn't respond and he didn't push further on his way out of the room.

Alone, I looked down at two uneaten meals, then carried them to the refrigerator, trying to decide whether it had been yesterday or the day before when I'd last changed my shirt. The phone rang with an ear-piercing peal, and I banged my head on the edge of the freezer door.

"Can you get that, Charlie?" Alexander shouted from upstairs.

Rubbing the back of my head and hoping it wasn't Kinley, I pulled the ringing phone from its cradle and pressed it to my ear. "Alexander Brewster's house. Can I take a message?"

"Keppler? Why are you at Alexander's?"

"Aumont?" I gripped the phone so tight I thought it might snap in half. "Where are you?"

"I'm at the hospital. I need Alexander to come and get me." Her voice shook and she cleared her throat. "I don't want to upset Kinley and if she sees me . . ." She took a sharp breath and I heard another voice, softly comforting her.

"We'll be there in ten minutes." I looked up as Alexander hurried into the room, still sliding one of his arms into his button-down. "Just stay right there, okay?"

"Okay. Thank you." The phone crackled and clicked on the other end.

"Charlie, what's going on? Who was that?"

"Rochelle. Hospital." It was all I could manage to string together as I pushed Alexander toward the door, stuffing my feet into my shoes on the way out. We ran to the truck, and Alexander started it up and pressed the pedal to the floorboards. I willed him to drive faster.

When we pulled into the hospital parking lot, I jumped out before we stopped moving and sprinted through the door to the emergency department.

Ahead, a thin figure lay on a cushioned bench, knees curled to her chest, face tucked into her arms. I ran to her. "Aumont?"

Slowly, Rochelle lifted her head and sat up, squinting against the fluorescent lights.

"Aumont, you got away." I collapsed onto the seat next to her, careful not to touch her as I registered the purple and black bruises spread over the left side of her face. Her eye was so swollen she couldn't open it. She was filthy from head to toe, hair a tangled mess around her face, and the blue jacket she wore didn't belong to her. "I never should have left you. I'm so sorry."

"You had to." She gripped my shoulders. "Todd? Is he . . ."

"He's safe. Recovering here in the hospital."

Her eyes teared up and her shoulders relaxed as she released mine. Her voice dropped to a whisper. "And the pendant?"

"I have it." I wished Rochelle had never learned it existed. The wedge-shaped plastic pendant, if united with the other seven, created a key that could unlock research leading to a miracle vaccine or the world's next pandemic. Molly and The Defiance wanted the one left to Rochelle by her father, which led to Rochelle's kidnapping.

She took a deep breath and lunged forward, squeezing me so tightly I couldn't breathe. "Molly knows about your connection to The Defiance and Griff. She figured it out. But I won't let them hurt you. I promise I'll fix this."

Her words slithered through my veins like ice. "It'll be okay, Aumont. Just catch your breath."

"Be careful, you'll hurt her," an unfamiliar female voice scolded me.

Two teenagers approached. The girl had short dark hair and a pretty face, wore jeans and a light jacket, and carried a wad of wet paper towels in her hand. A boy with curly blond hair sauntered beside her.

"It's okay, Lareina." Rochelle forced a smile. "Keppler is a friend." She squeezed my hand. "Keppler, this is Lareina. She picked the lock and we stole a truck to get away from Molly . . ." Her voice trailed off as she watched my face contort in confusion. "I'm sorry. My head hurts and it's hard to explain."

Lareina nodded and put her hand on Rochelle's shoulder. "I'm sorry, Keppler. I'm a little on edge right now." She turned her attention to Rochelle and sat down beside her. "I called Kinley and she'll be here any minute."

"No," Rochelle protested in a sudden gasp. "If she sees me, she'll flip her lid. She's going to . . ."

"She'll be so relieved." Lareina gently pressed the paper towels to Rochelle's face. "We can't let her worry a minute longer."

Lareina? The girl Max had a crush on in second grade? How did Rochelle run into an old friend while she was being held hostage? I glanced at the boy, who shrugged as if to say he was just as lost as I was.

A loud commotion came from the entrance and then Alexander, Kinley, and Kat rushed toward us. At the sound of Kinley's voice, I sprang to my feet, prepared to be scolded or questioned, but she rushed past me.

"Oh, Rochelle." Gently, she cupped her cousin's face in her hands. "What happened?"

"I was . . . I just . . . I thought I would never see you again." Any feigned bravery vanished and Rochelle's voice dissolved into sobs.

"You're okay." Kinley sank into my recently vacated seat and cradled her cousin in her arms. "You're safe now. We'll get you to the doctor and then we'll go home and get you cleaned up."

"No, you have to stay away from me." Rochelle didn't lift her face from Kinley's shoulder. "Molly said she'll hurt you to make me help her."

Kat stood next to Alexander, gripping his arm, eyebrows furrowed as she studied her sister.

Lareina squeezed Rochelle's shoulder as she made eye contact with Kinley. "I told her Molly wouldn't dare follow us back here. She wouldn't risk it."

"That's right." Kinley tried to smooth Rochelle's tangled hair. "Alexander's here, and he won't let Molly get anywhere near us ever again." She looked up at Lareina and gave her an understanding nod. "I have no idea how you managed to find Rochelle, but thank you for bringing her home. We owe you so much. Whatever you need."

Lareina's stiff shoulders relaxed a little. "It's just good to finally be home."

I took a step toward Kat, but she gave me the same angry scowl as the last time we stood in the hospital. Before I could try another apology, a nurse I recognized as one of Kinley's friends walked over.

"Kinley, you can bring Rochelle to the exam room. Dr. Brooks will be right in."

"Thank you." Kinley stood and held her hands out to her cousin. Rochelle pulled herself up, but her knees buckled. I dove forward to catch her elbow.

"I'm sorry." She leaned heavily against me, failing to regain her balance. "I get dizzy sometimes."

"She hit her head and I don't think she's had anything to eat or drink in a while." Lareina hovered nearby. I didn't know her, but the suspicion in her eyes mirrored my own distrust of her.

"Here, I've got her. Ready?" Alexander slipped an arm behind Rochelle and hoisted her into his arms as easily as if she were a feather pillow.

Kinley patted my arm. "Wait right here. You and I need to talk." She glanced over at Lareina. "Don't worry, we'll make sure you have a place to stay and everything you need." Taking Rochelle's hand, she led Alexander to a hallway at the other end of the waiting room.

Kat folded her arms over her chest and scowled at me. "I can't believe you just abandoned us. I've been awake for days, worrying about Rochelle, trying to comfort Kinley every time she argues with Audrie over the phone, and taking care of everyone all by myself." The forceful anger drained from her voice and tears sprang to her eyes. "I thought you cared about us. If you're part of our family, why weren't you there when we needed you?"

"I just…" My mouth went dry and my stomach hurt. No matter what I did, it was always the wrong thing. "I'm sorry I wasn't there for you." It wasn't enough, not nearly enough. "I'm going to fix all of this." My feet sidestepped her and took a backward step toward the door.

Kat watched me through betrayed eyes. "If you leave here, don't even bother coming home." She turned on her heel and strode after Kinley and Rochelle.

I sank to the cushion of a waiting room chair. People like me weren't meant to have a family. The best thing I could do for the family I didn't deserve would be to find Molly and trade my life for Rochelle's. If she wanted the pendant, I had it. If Griff wanted me dead, I deserved it.

"She'll be okay." The blond boy held his arms open to Lareina, who blinked away tears. "And Aaron will be okay too. Everything will be okay."

Lareina nodded and leaned into his embrace. "This isn't how I imagined we'd find her, Nick. But now…"

He wrapped his arms around her and rested his chin on the top of her head. "You're home and we're safe. For real this time."

I watched the relief and the uncertainty wash over them as they considered the possibility of a new life and a fresh start in Maibe. I'd had that once, but I fought it every step of the way and never let myself appreciate everything I had until it was too late. I believed my own lies that I could escape my past and hide from my mistakes. The Aumonts had given me everything, and I'd repaid them by dragging them into the darkness with me.

Nick and Lareina sat huddled together a few seats down. It didn't matter how they'd found Rochelle, only that they'd done the one thing I couldn't and brought her home. They belonged in Maibe more than I did. I didn't belong anywhere.

Leaving Nick and Lareina lost in their own world, I stood and made my way to the exit. Molly thought she was in control, but I wouldn't let her hurt my family again. I would go back to The Defiance camp and turn myself into Griff along with the pendant. Before he killed me, I would assure him Rochelle knew nothing about any of it, and then Molly would be useless to him.

CHAPTER 2
ROCHELLE

November 23, 2090

"It would be better for everyone, Kinley." My aunt Audrie's voice drifted through the heating vent in Kat's room. "Something clearly has to change because this arrangement isn't working."

"You aren't listening to me." My cousin's voice rose in frustration. The furnace turned on, and the rest of her words vanished into the rumble of hot air.

For a few seconds, I remained on the carpet with my ear pressed to the floor. Kat had left me tucked into my bed ten minutes earlier, promising to be right back with some ice for my eye. I had to know what was happening downstairs. Audrie had arrived an hour earlier and spent all of that time arguing with Kinley. From Kat's brief explanation, I understood Audrie had called every day I'd been missing, accusing Kinley of being an irresponsible guardian, and no one had seen Keppler since I'd talked to him at the hospital.

Knowing I wouldn't hear more until the furnace finished its cycle, I sat up and rested my throbbing forehead against the cool wall.

"Rochelle?" My sister's frantic voice yelled my name. "Rochelle, where are you?"

"In here." Slowly I lifted my head and faced the doorway

where Kat appeared, carrying an ice pack with a towel wrapped around it.

"Why aren't you in your bed?" My sister rushed into the room and knelt down next to me. "Kinley said you're supposed to rest."

"I'm fine." My eyes drifted to the vent and Kat rolled her eyes before sitting next to me.

"Last night you started crying every time you were alone for a minute. I guess if acting like a three year old is your definition of fine . . . All right, you've convinced me."

"I'm well enough to hold Todd's hand. That's all I'm asking." I had begged my cousin to let me go see Todd, but she countered all of my arguments with *You need to rest*. "Why can't Kinley understand that?"

"Rochelle, she has barely eaten or slept all week because she was imagining all the terrible things that could be happening to you." Kat shook her head. "And you didn't hear the awful things Audrie said to her on the phone that she's now down there saying in person. Give her a break."

Crying with one eye swollen shut should cut the amount of tears in half, but somehow my good eye made up for the impaired function of the other. I felt as if I had been transported to a year earlier, confined to my bed as I struggled to recover from my difficult battle with the fever. It was a battle my grandma and Kinley's parents and an estimated fifty percent of adults in America had lost. It had forced my cousin to leave her prestigious medical school in Omaha and return to Maibe so Kat and I wouldn't be sent to a home for children. At the time, I thought that would be the biggest challenge we ever faced.

"I'm sorry. Please don't cry." Kat sighed. "Everything is so messed up. I mean, I'm defending Kinley, which is weird, and I'm comforting you. I want to go back to Kinley making me cry and you fixing it, so please get better."

Sniffling, I dabbed at my face with the sleeve of my shirt. "Believe me, I'm trying."

"I would believe you more if you were in bed with ice on your eye." My sister placed her hands under my elbows and helped me to my feet. "Come on. Back to your room."

My throbbing left eye, the sharp pain in my head, and aching body had me leaning heavily on Kat as we walked across the hall to my room, where she tucked me back into bed.

"I got to the kitchen just in time to get the cinnamon rolls out of the oven." She refolded the towel around the ice pack and gently held it to my eye. "Alexander and Sid would have just let them burn while they talk football." Sid was Audrie's work partner whom I hadn't met.

Struggling to focus on my sister's irrelevant chatter, I took her free hand in mine. "Please, Kat. Help me get dressed and sneak out to see Todd."

My sister lifted my hand to hold my own ice pack. "If I were going to sneak anyone anywhere, it would be me to the grocery store to get the ingredients I need to make a real meal. But Kinley is five minutes from a nervous breakdown and I won't let either of us push her over the edge."

Feeling helpless, I sank back into my pillows. There had to be someone in the house who would help me. "Did Alexander find Keppler yet?"

Kat sighed and shook her head. "We have enough problems without worrying about Charlie. He'll show up when he gets hungry." Her eyes met mine and the tight muscles in her face relaxed. "Speaking of food, you'll be happy to know I'm making grilled cheese sandwiches and tomato soup for our Thanksgiving dinner."

"It's Thanksgiving?" It was my fault that Kat's favorite holiday had been ruined and that my family and friends had spent four days worrying nonstop. Any other day, that guilt would have twisted my stomach into a knot, but all I could think about was seeing Todd.

"I won't disturb her if she's sleeping." Audrie's voice was our only warning before my door opened. "Rochelle, good, you're awake." She sat down on the edge of my bed, made to hug me, then saw my bruises and patted my leg. "I heard how brave you were. I couldn't have handled things better even with all of my training. I'm so proud of you."

A smile spread over my face. She thought I could handle myself, while Kinley didn't think I could handle making the smallest decision without her help.

Noticing my cousin standing in the doorway, looking like a child who had been scolded for getting her church clothes dirty, I felt a new power with my aunt present. "It was the only choice I had to help Todd, and now I want to go to the hospital to visit him."

"We already talked about that, Rochelle." Kinley spoke before my aunt could, making an effort to keep her voice even. "Neither of you"—she looked from Kat to me—"are leaving this house."

An unfamiliar annoyance burned through the throbbing in my head. "Quit telling me what to do." A surge of adrenaline carried me to my feet, making Kat and Audrie rise too. "You're not always right and you're not always in charge. I'm going to see Todd."

Kat squeezed my elbow, warning me I'd gone too far, but I couldn't back down.

Kinley took a step toward me. "I thought I washed all of the dirt out of your ears last night." The force of her words sent me tumbling back into Audrie's arms. "The answer is no, and it's not going to change. You were missing for four days, you're hurt, and this is the only way I know how to keep you safe."

"Take a breath, Kinley. Just calm down." Audrie stroked my

hair while I hid my face against her shoulder and tried not to cry. "She's been through enough as it is. Maybe we could get her something to eat and then I can take her to the hospital to see her friend."

"Right, because you know what's best for them." My cousin's voice broke. "Bad things only happen when I'm in charge because I only care about myself."

Audrie sighed. "Kinley, that's not what I said."

"You didn't have to." I looked up in time to see Kinley collapse into the chair by my bed. "I do my best, but it's never good enough." Her lip quivered and she squeezed her eyes shut.

As fast as it had come, the fire went out of me, doused by my cousin's attempt to not cry in front of us. "I'm sorry, Kinley. I didn't mean any of that." Sliding away from my aunt, I stood on wobbly legs. "I just miss Todd and I don't feel so well."

Kinley stood and held her arms open, wrapping them around me when I stumbled into them. "You deserve all of my patience right now but I'm tired and I'm scared and I'm so sorry." The two of us fell back into the cushioned chair, welded together. "We're going to figure this all out. I love you and I'm just trying to do what's best for you."

"I love you too." I couldn't find the strength to lift my forehead from her shoulder. "I'll listen to you from now on. I won't talk back."

"I know. You're a good kid." She kissed the top of my head then slid her arms away and lifted my chin. "Now let me see you. How does your head feel?"

"It hurts a little. I don't really feel like myself." Kat sat next to Audrie, watching me with the same scrutiny she had when I didn't know it was Thanksgiving. My aunt stared at her hands folded in her lap. "Is that bad? Am I going to be okay?"

"It's perfectly normal." Kinley turned my head to examine my eye. "You're going to be okay and Todd is going to be okay, but you both need a lot of rest right now."

"And we'll take good care of you." Kat crossed the room with a box of tissues and handed Kinley the ice pack before sitting down beside me.

Squeezed between my sister and my cousin in an armchair meant for one, the burning fears and guilt in my chest were extinguished. I was home, exactly where I wanted to be. Kat dried my face with tissues and Kinley eased the ice pack against my eye.

Audrie watched us and I wondered if she felt left out. "Kinley, about our conversation. I have no doubts that you love your cousins and you would do anything to protect them. My point is you shouldn't have to do that. You're nineteen years old, you're trying to build your own life and your own career, and you should have some fun while you're young."

"She'll be twenty in a few days." Kat reached across me for Kinley's hand. "And we have a lot of fun. Right, Kinley?"

"That's not exactly what I mean." Audrie looked at Kinley then shifted her eyes to Kat and me. "What Kinley and I have been discussing is the possibility of Rochelle, or maybe even both of you, coming to stay with me in New York. You'd be able to attend a real school, it would get you away from the commotion around here, and Kinley would get a break." My aunt swallowed hard as she observed the three of us still huddled together. "She would always be your cousin, but I would take over as guardian."

"You mean you want Kinley to sign those papers?" Kat looked over at our cousin. "To give us up?"

The thought of being away from Kinley again, of leaving Maibe and living more than a thousand miles away from Todd and Max and all of the people I loved, made me nauseous. "Are we really in danger here?" My eyes pleaded with my aunt to give me the answer I wanted. "Will Molly be able to come back?"

"Unfortunately that will always be a possibility, kiddo." Audrie leaned forward with her elbows on her knees. "The good news is there's already been a move to secure borders near Defiance territory, and the news of recruiting farther north is only increasing that effort. That being said, we have to be extra careful, so we're going to make a plan to keep all of you safe for the next few weeks while we work on a long-term solution."

I nodded as Kat squeezed my hand, silently echoing my own discomfort with the thought of moving away. "That doesn't have to mean leaving though, right? Kat and I can't leave Kinley here alone. We all take care of each other. We have to be together."

Audrie nodded. "I understand this kind of change sounds scary, and I wouldn't separate you before the holidays, but maybe we could go downstairs and discuss all of this over lunch."

I nudged my sister, urging her to at least hear Audrie out. After all, she was our aunt and we were the only family she had. Maybe she would be satisfied with just coming to visit more often.

"Okay. It doesn't hurt to talk about things." Kat stood and looked back at Kinley. "I can get our gourmet grilled cheese and tomato soup started."

A relieved smile spread over our aunt's face. "I'll help you, kiddo."

"Rochelle and I will be right down." Kinley's hand had been gripping my arm the entire time as if I'd disappear if she let go. "I just need to wash my face and take care of a few of her scrapes."

"Okay." Audrie wrapped an arm around my sister, and they made their way out into the hallway.

I turned to my cousin, noticing her ashen complexion and puffy eyes. She'd been with me all night, always there to comfort me when I had a nightmare, and it sounded like she hadn't slept much before that. "I'm sorry I messed things up so bad. Audrie can't do anything unless we agree. Right?"

Kinley sighed and forced a smile. "I won't give you up without a fight. No matter what you do, I will always want you. And Kat . . . and Charlie."

"He'll be home soon." I wasn't sure about that but hoped I was right. "He probably just needed a little time to himself."

"He spent the last four days living at Alexander's. He blamed himself for what happened to you and I didn't do anything to discredit that." She shook her head. "Poor kid. As if he didn't have enough trust issues."

"He'll come home. He has to." A chill crawled up my spine at the thought of him all alone with the pendant, waiting for The Defiance to come for him any minute. I wished I could tell him the TCI was on high alert and securing borders. We would make a plan and, as long as we followed it, everything would be okay again. By not giving up the pendant, we'd won.

"Of course he will." My cousin looked down at my wrists, scabbed over from days of ropes binding them. "There's some cream in the bathroom that'll help those heal. Let's go get ourselves cleaned up and find out how fast we can convince Audrie to go home."

CHAPTER 3
CHARLIE

November 23, 2090

"You have your pendant now. You don't need Rochelle." Griff and Molly stood in front of me, examining the pendant I had just handed over.

"You should be worried about yourself." Griff clutched my shoulder and pulled his fist back.

"Let me go." I struggled away from his iron grip. "Let me go."

My eyes shot open and my head lifted off the workbench in Max's garage. I looked around wildly.

"Geez." Max stood next to me but was leaning away as if I'd taken a swipe at him. "Do you always wake up like that?"

"What?" Groggy and confused, I rubbed my hands over my face. When I left the hospital, I had walked to Max's, considered talking to him, figured he was still mad at me after how I'd reacted to him calling me *hermano*, and made my way to the last shelter I could think of.

"Why are you sleeping in my workshop?" He pulled an apple out of his coat pocket and tossed it behind his back, catching it in his other hand.

"I needed to think, so I was working on your time machine." While Max believed he would invent something life changing, I went along with his crazy ideas because keeping my hands busy kept my mind calm. "What's the apple for?"

Max tossed it into the air again. "This is for the possum."

I glanced around the cluttered garage. "You have a possum?"

"Last night when my *tio* took out the trash, he told me he heard some scuffling in here, so I figured I had a possum again." He closed one eye and made a funny face. "Last year the possum almost mixed two jars of liquid that would've caused a minor explosion."

Cold and stiff, I braced my arms against the workbench to sit up straight. "Yet you waited until now to come and check on it?"

"Not check on it." He took a bite of the apple. "Trap it. Plus, it was too cold before now."

"No kidding." I slapped my numb hands against my legs.

Max cringed and held the apple out to me. "Sorry, do you want some?"

I shoved his arm away. "I don't want your possum food."

He shrugged. "Why didn't you tell me you were here? I would've helped you with the time machine. You could've slept inside. My *tia* likes you. She would have found an extra pillow somewhere."

Shoving my hands into my pockets, I looked down at my shoes. "I figured you were still mad about what I said on Saturday."

"I think you have that backwards." Max pulled up a rickety stool and sat down beside me. "You were the one who was mad about what *I* said. I've been trying to call you, but Alexander never answered his phone."

Nodding, I studied my worn sneakers. I hated apologizing, but Max hadn't known what calling me his brother meant to me. "What I said to you was pretty rotten, but Griff always said he and I were brothers. You know how that worked out."

Holding the apple between his hands, he considered my explanation. "I've never met the guy, but I'm pretty sure my definition of brother is different from his. What did I ever do to make you think I'm anything like him?"

I shrugged. "Nothing, I just . . . freaked out in the moment."

"Don't worry. I'll forgive you this time. You didn't know any better, being raised by wolves and all." He leaned back against the bench and grinned.

Despite my misery, I felt myself smile. "*Hermanos* then?" I held out my hand.

"You know it." He gripped my hand and shook it. "So, did you solve time travel?"

"No."

"That's okay. Someday . . ."

"Delgado, I need to borrow money for a train ticket." I stood, unable to sit still any longer. "Actually, borrow is the wrong word. I won't be able to pay you back."

"What do you need a ticket for?"

I reached into my pocket and pulled out the pendant, hand trembling. "Molly won't stop until she has this. So I'm going to take it to Kansas City and hand it over to Griff in exchange for them leaving Rochelle alone."

Max stared at me, one eyebrow raised. "That is the worst plan I've ever heard. And you said I wasn't taking things seriously? We both know what's going to happen if you show up in Kansas City."

I kicked a stool and it toppled with a satisfying clang of metal against concrete floor. "I'll get exactly what I deserve and save the people I wish could have been my family."

"They are your family. Alexander has been searching for you all night and Kinley is panicking because you didn't come home. How do you think they'll feel if you just take off and they never see you again?"

I groaned. "Do you have a better plan?"

"Yeah. Go home." He was so calm and unphased. "Get something to eat, get some sleep, and then let Rochelle and me help you come up with a real plan when we have all of the facts."

It sounded so simple and so logical. "Last night at the hospital, Kat told me not to come home."

Max shrugged. "Kat kicks me out every day. I just give her a little space and I'm back the next day in time for dinner."

"This isn't the same thing. She has every right to hate me. I left Rochelle out there with Molly."

"You saved Todd's life. I've been worried about Rochelle the past four days too, but now she's home and everything is okay again."

"Nothing is okay." I paced on tingly feet. "Molly is part of The Defiance, Griff knows where I am—you didn't see what she did to Rochelle—"

"Keppler." Max put a hand on my shoulder, walked me back to the stool, and righted it. "Sit down. And please explain that last sentence. Kinley hasn't let me see Rochelle yet."

Everything had happened so fast, I had forgotten he wouldn't know about what Rochelle had told me at the hospital. Sinking back onto my stool, I described the night I had exchanged Rochelle for Todd, the four sleepless days of dead ends trying to find her, and finally the chaos at the hospital.

Max nodded. "So, we have some things to figure out. The first thing we have to do is go see Rochelle. She'll never forgive herself if you don't come home, and I have to make sure she's okay."

"You just told me she was okay a few minutes ago."

"Kinley said she was at home and resting. That sounded like okay until you told me she was all beat up. I'll just tell my *tia* I'll be a little late for Thanksgiving dinner. She loves Rochelle; she'll understand."

"I can't go back to the house." No turning of my neck or rolling of my shoulders could relieve the stiffness. "Remember what Kat said?"

"And remember what I said? We both know Kinley is in charge and Rochelle would never kick you out. That's two against one."

What Kat said mattered to me, and I didn't want to give her

any more reason to hate me, but I couldn't explain that to Max. I couldn't even explain it to myself. "Are you sure Kinley will let me in?"

"I'm sure." He clapped my shoulder and nudged me toward the door. "And on the slight chance I'm wrong, I'll help you convince her to reconsider."

CHAPTER 4
CHARLIE

November 23, 2090

I pushed open the door into the kitchen's familiar warmth and aromas of coffee, cinnamon, and freshly baked bread. Alexander turned as if ready to fight off anyone entering the house but relaxed when he saw it was Max and me—then did a double take and stood so fast he almost tipped his cup of coffee.

"Charlie, where have you been?" He turned to Max. "I thought you said you didn't know where he was!"

I caught sight of the man sitting across from Alexander and forgot about my fear of being rejected by my family. When Max and I had secretly accompanied Rochelle to meet with her aunt for the first time, we thought we were gathering information on Audrie, but this guy had been in the café too. That meant Audrie knew Rochelle hadn't come alone. What else did she know? He locked eyes with me, but his posture remained relaxed.

Max nudged my arm with his elbow and I forced myself to breathe normally.

"How was I supposed to know the possum in my garage was actually Keppler?" Max pulled out a chair and sat down across from the man I knew he recognized as well.

Alexander's eyebrows furrowed, and he shook his head before turning back to me. "What were you thinking? Kinley told you to stay put." Reflexively, my shoulders hunched, ready for him to hit me. He never had, but I deserved it and I wouldn't fight back.

The man eyed my defensive posture curiously. I took a deep breath and made myself straighten. "Sorry, Alexander. I had some things to work out."

Max leaned forward with his elbows on the table. "You look kind of familiar. Do I know you from somewhere?"

The man laughed, a full, genuine belly laugh, before extending his hand across the table. "Sid Dotson. Audrie's partner."

"Max Delgado. Future inventor." They shook hands. "If you're Audrie's partner, that makes you . . ."

"An agent of the Threat Collection Initiative." A cool-guy grin spread over Sid's face. "It's not really as exciting as it sounds."

A loud ringing drew everyone's eyes to Sid, and he pulled a device out of his pocket. After a glance at the screen, he stood. "Excuse me, I have to take this one." He slipped past us and disappeared into the laundry room.

"He has his own mobile phone?" Max whispered. "How do I get a job with the TCI?"

Before I could remind him that playing around with unauthorized technology would get him sent to reform school, approaching footsteps drew my attention to the other side of the room.

"Well, look who finally showed up." Audrie strode into the kitchen followed by Kinley. "Looks like everyone's home, safe and sound." Her eyes studied me suspiciously over a fake smile, and I knew she was disappointed to find me here.

Sid rushed back into the room, stuffing his phone into his pocket. "Audrie, we have to go. That's the call we've been waiting for." He picked up his coat and tossed another one to his partner.

I elbowed Max to break his fascinated trance.

"Perfect timing. I just said my goodbyes." She thrust her arms into her coat and turned to Kinley. "I'll call as soon as I can and we'll arrange a time I can visit for a few days, get a long-term plan hammered out. Follow all the precautions we discussed and call me immediately if anything happens. Take care of the girls." For a second, I thought she would try to hug Kinley, but she just patted her shoulder awkwardly and followed Sid out the door.

With Audrie gone, Kinley's focus zeroed in on me. Max inched toward the next room. She didn't even give him a glance as he slipped away. "Charlie Keppler, where have you been?"

Kat appeared at her cousin's side. "Translation, you stink. You could have at least showered before you walked in like you still live here."

Kinley gave her a sharp look. "Knock it off, Kat. He does live here."

"Not by my definition. All I want is to go buy groceries so I can make a decent meal, and he's the reason we're all imprisoned in the house."

"It's Thanksgiving, remember? The store is closed." Kinley turned to me. "You're a complete mess." She scrubbed at something on my forehead with her thumb. "No more living at Alexander's. He can barely take care of himself."

"Kinley. I'm standing right here." Alexander, ever patient, gave Kinley a look of mock offense.

Unable to bring myself to meet the eyes of either of my guardians, I stared down at my shoes.

"I know you care about Charlie, but he has more structure here," Kinley said to Alexander. She sighed and squinted. "Speaking of structure, I need to stop by the hospital and convince Lareina and Nick to come back here for dinner and check on Emma..."

"I'll do that, Kinley." Alexander stepped forward, placing a hand on her shoulder. "I can tell by the look on your face that your headache is worse every time I see you. You need to lie down for a while."

"I have too much to do." Kinley walked to the refrigerator. "I should get back to Rochelle." She pulled the freezer open and reached for an ice pack.

"Wait. Listen." Kat nodded toward the next room and in the quiet we heard laughter. "She's visiting with Max and this is the first time I've heard her laugh since she got home." She glared at me. "He might be annoying, but I know he'll take care of her, unlike someone."

"Kat, I'm sorry," I blurted. "I know I messed up, and I'm sorry."

"For letting Molly kidnap Rochelle, or for abandoning your family when we needed you?" She adjusted the collar of her sweater with a quick flip of her fingers. Her eyes bored into me. "You don't belong here."

The words hit me like a slap and I took a step back.

"Katia Rose Aumont." Kinley gripped her cousin's elbow and pulled her away from me. "What's wrong with you?"

"I've been trapped in this house all week." Kat's lip quivered and tears filled her eyes. "I just need to get out of here."

Alexander placed both of his hands on my shoulders, looking at me with care even while talking to Kinley. "We could all use a little breather. How about I take Kat with me to check in on everyone at the hospital? I have a couple other errands to run too. I won't let her out of my sight, and then we'll all have a civil conversation when we get back."

"Please, Kinley." Kat gripped her cousin's arm. "I promise I won't leave Alexander's side."

"Fine." Kinley massaged the spot between her eyebrows. "But if you can't reach out and touch him, then you're too far away. Understood?"

"Understood." She rushed into the laundry room for her coat.

While Kinley walked Alexander to the door, I surveyed dishes piled in the sink, a skillet and soup pot still on the stove, and half full coffee mugs on the table.

"Are you okay?" Kinley wrapped her warm arm around me in a side hug. "Kat was really out of line there."

Exhaustion and guilt pulled my shoulders toward the floor. "She's right. I shouldn't be here, but Max made me come."

"Remind me to thank him." She slid her hand under my chin and raised my eyes to meet hers. "Charlie, listen to me. A thousand times, I've tried to imagine myself in your shoes and decide between Todd's life now or Rochelle's later, and I would have just had a panic attack." Her tired eyes glistened with tears. "You did the best you could, and your quick thinking saved Todd's life. I'm so proud of you, and I'm sorry I didn't say that five days ago."

"You didn't even think about it when I asked to stay with Alexander." I swallowed the lump in my throat and realized how abandoned I had felt.

"I was scared and upset and not thinking clearly." She sank into the nearest chair and held Rochelle's ice pack to her own forehead. "If it helps, I've been worried sick about you since you left, especially when you disappeared last night."

"I didn't mean to give you more to worry about." I sat down next to her.

"I know. From now on, promise you'll talk to me. If you need some space, just tell me where you're going. If you know Rochelle is digging herself a hole too deep to get out of, give me a heads-up. I have a hard time trusting people's intentions too, but you can trust me."

"Okay." It was a half-truth I wished could be whole. I trusted Kinley as long as she knew me as the kid who ran away from an abusive home and just needed a second chance. Only Rochelle and

Max knew about my former commitment to The Defiance, and I intended to keep it that way.

"That's settled then." She extended an arm and pulled me into a hug. "I'm going to check on Rochelle and then go lie down. And you'll feel better after a shower. We can talk about everything else over dinner."

We walked together to the dining room and then parted ways. Downstairs, I took a quick shower and changed clothes before hurrying back up to the library. Pausing just outside of the door, slightly ajar, I took a breath and tried to ignore the cold outline of the pendant squeezed in my hand.

"They were shooting at us and the truck wouldn't start." Rochelle's voice rose with excitement and disbelief. "Then Nick tried one more time and I heard the engine and Lareina was holding my head down, so I couldn't see anything, but I felt us jerk forward, then back, and we were out of there."

"That is so much more exciting than the time I went storm chasing." Max's voice bounced across the room. "You win. That is the greatest adventure of all time."

I pulled the door open all the way. Rochelle and Max, side by side on the couch, turned to me.

Max's eyes went wide with excitement. "Rochelle verified it. Audrie's partner is the guy from the café." He kept his voice hushed as if ears listened all around us. "She must have known we were spying on her the entire time."

Rochelle shrugged, an ice pack pressed to her eye. "Neither of them brought it up. Audrie was too preoccupied with everything else. She thinks I'll be safer if I move to New York with her."

My resolve to remain calm failed. "She's just trying to get the pendant. You have to tell her about it, Aumont. You have to get rid of it before it gets you killed."

She lowered the ice pack, revealing deep purple bruises around a swollen eyelid. At least she could partially open it today. "It's okay. Kinley, Audrie, and Alexander have all promised me we're safe—"

"We were never safe." My voice came out harsher than I intended. "They don't know everything we know."

"They know enough from what you told Kinley." Her expression softened when she saw me cringe. "It's okay. I know you had to."

"Then tell Kinley the rest." I held the pendant out in front of me as if it would bite. If Kinley found out we actually had the pendant that Molly kidnapped Rochelle to get her hands on, she would make Rochelle give it to Audrie.

Rochelle shook her head. "She has enough to deal with. This is my responsibility."

"Then tell Audrie." I took a step closer. "Those are your two options."

"No. If my dad wanted her to have it, he would have given it to her." Panic flashed through her one good eye. "I have to find out whether she'll use it to locate the vaccine or just lock it away so The Defiance can't get to it. This is important, Keppler."

"We're out of time." My voice dropped to a hiss. "None of them have any idea what The Defiance is capable of. If they want to come here, no one is going to stop them."

Rochelle slumped in her seat and swallowed hard. "We'll figure it out."

"How can you say that?" I looked away from her bruised face and raw wrists. "Look what Molly did to you. If she had another day, another week . . ." I shook my head. "We're helpless against them. Don't you understand?"

"All right. All right." Max sprang to his feet, standing between Rochelle and me. "That's enough."

"It's fine, Max." Rochelle stood a little unsteadily and dropped her ice pack. "Molly doesn't want me dead. She wants me to join her. If she contacts me again, I'll play whatever game I have to and finish what my dad started."

"Are you listening to yourself?" I couldn't stand to see her volunteer to put herself in that psycho's clutches again. "Everyone is disposable to Molly. You saw what happened to Todd. Do you want that to be Kinley or Kat—"

"Keppler." Max interrupted in an unusually serious tone. "She has a concussion. This isn't the time." He took Rochelle's arm and guided her back to the couch.

I opened my mouth, then shut it, then opened it again. I needed Rochelle to understand, but maybe Max was right. I sank to the coffee table.

"Do you want me to hold onto the pendant?" Max's voice was absent of its usual excitement. "They expect one of you to have it, not me. And then, when we're all rested and thinking clearly, we'll decide *together* the right thing to do. Is that a reasonable plan?"

Rochelle took a deep breath before nodding.

I dumped the pendant in Max's outstretched hand. "Okay. But we have to find someone we trust enough to help us."

He patted my shoulder. "We will. Once everyone gets some sleep, everything will be back to normal."

Normal? Nothing would ever be normal for any of us ever again. My fragile sense of security had been shattered with Rochelle's news that Griff knew where I was, and now she would forever be looking over her shoulder, aware of just how evil the world could be.

CHAPTER 5
ROCHELLE

November 26, 2090

Why didn't my dad give the pendant to Audrie? Did he not trust her or had he just run out of time? Had he trusted Eric Bennett, Molly's father, or did he suspect his betrayal? Was he just trying to help his friend, and had I fallen into the same trap with Molly?

These thoughts tormented me as I sat next to Todd's hospital bed. He'd been asleep when I arrived. After Kinley took Emma, Todd's older sister, to get lunch, I sat alone, listening to the beeping medical equipment and watching snowflakes drift outside the window.

Todd was getting better, but he spent more time asleep than awake. The day before, we'd talked for about an hour before he was exhausted. He had verified Molly's story that his train was raided in Kansas and he'd been in a Defiance work camp for the months he'd been missing. When he fell from a roof he was helping to construct, he had laid in a makeshift medical tent for three days and thought it was all over when they loaded him onto the bed of a truck.

He coughed a little, but his eyes didn't open. I found myself studying him, noticing all the ways he had changed during his time away. His hair covered his ears and eyebrows, longer than it had ever been. His collarbone was pronounced where his hospital gown hung on his frail frame, and his eyes sunk into gaunt cheekbones. Healing pink scrapes crisscrossed purple bruises all over his face.

Another cough followed by a groan prompted me to take his hand. Todd's eyelids fluttered and his gentle hazel eyes, unchanged, brightened when they saw me.

A smile spread over his face. "Shelley, you came back." His hand squeezed mine. "Is your head feeling better?"

"A lot better." I had woken up that morning headache free. My eye was still black and blue, but the swelling had gone down. I finally felt like I could think clearly, and I had more control over my emotions. "How are you feeling?"

"Ready to get out of here." Without letting go of my hand, he tried to sit up but only made it halfway before falling back to his pillow. "I had it yesterday, Rochelle. I sat up all by myself. I even walked to the window with my dad's help."

"You're just not all the way awake yet. Here." I pressed buttons on his remote, raising the top of his bed. Then I readjusted his pillows and helped him lean back comfortably.

"Rochelle, I'm sorry." Todd's voice broke through the silent misery that surrounded us. "I just hate sitting here all the time, thinking about how rotten people can be, how awful the world is."

I'd learned he didn't want to talk about his experiences at the work camp, but he had nightmares about it.

"You'll be out of here soon. The doctor told your dad and Emma if you keep getting better at this rate, you'll be home by this time next week."

Todd laid his head back on the pillows and stared at the ceiling. "Lily tells me what they don't say. I'll be weak for months. It'll take at least six weeks for my arm and ribs to heal. I'll need help doing things I've been doing myself since I was five. I don't like everyone giving up all of their time to take care of me. You guys don't deserve to be punished for my mistakes."

I wished Todd's little sister would be a little less honest about her knowledge of his recovery, but she was scared too. Plus I remembered feeling like a burden when I had been sick. "After you took such good care of me last year, I owe you. You'll be better in no time."

A soft knock pulled our attention to the door as Lareina peeked in. "Hey guys."

"Hey, Lareina. Come in." Todd rubbed his eyes with the back of his hand. "Welcome home."

"Thank you." She stepped into the room, head ducked in humble surprise, the same way she reacted when anyone in Maibe recognized her. "Rochelle, I wanted to let you know you're supposed to walk home with me. Kinley needed to run some errands, and I convinced her we could get home safely together. I plan to stay a few more hours until Nick gets here, but if you're ready to go sooner, I'll be right down the hall in Aaron's room."

"A few hours is perfect. Thank you." It was an unexpected gift knowing I wouldn't have to leave with Kinley in minutes. I needed the extra time with Todd. "How's Aaron doing?"

The doctors hadn't been able to save Aaron's leg, and they weren't even sure the antibiotics would fight his infection. Though Lareina was sleeping at my house, I only saw her at some meals or in passing at the hospital.

"He's more alert today." She smiled. "He had a whole conversation with Kinley about enrolling in the medical training program. That's how I convinced him to come here with me, you know. He wants to be a doctor more than anything, and I told him Maibe had a small hospital." Her smile faded. "He has months of recovery and physical therapy ahead, but Aaron Swanson has a one-track mind."

"That's a good sign, Lareina." I raised my eyebrows at Todd.

He nodded. "It helps to have a distraction from this place."

She stepped to the edge of Todd's bed. "How are you doing?"

"I'm ready to get out of here, but I don't quite have the doctors convinced yet." He smiled. "Soon though."

"Good." Lareina took one of his hands and one of mine. "Guys, about what happened to get you here—"

A loud crash in the hallway prompted Lareina to spin around, eyes glued to the door.

After a couple of tense, silent seconds, Todd sighed. "They drop things sometimes. One of my student nurses, Amy, is kind of a klutz, but she also brings me ice cream, so I'm not complaining."

Lareina took a sharp breath. "I should get back to Aaron. I don't like to leave him alone."

She was on edge, and I didn't know how to help her. "Maybe we can come down and visit tomorrow. Todd is supposed to walk a little to get his strength up, and I bet we could make it down the hall."

Lareina nodded. "Aaron would love that." She took a step backward, toward the door. "By the way, I used your return address on a letter from him to his family, so if you get mail from California . . ."

"I'll get it to you guys immediately."

"Thanks. I'll be back in a couple of hours. Get well soon, Todd." She slipped out the door and eased it shut until it clicked behind her.

"Is she okay?" Todd whispered as though she could hear him.

"I don't know." I stood and stretched my arms behind my back, hoping the movement could stave off the intensifying throb inside my head. "I'm not sure if any of us are okay."

"Now I feel kind of rotten about complaining." Todd scratched around a scab on his forehead. "A guy like Aaron loses a leg and all he can think about is studying. I'm all in one piece and feeling sorry for myself."

"You just need something to focus your energy on." I glanced around the room and spotted the sketch pad and pencils Emma had left on the cabinet under the window. "I have an idea." Feeling reenergized, I crossed the room and brought them back to Todd. "Draw me something. I haven't seen a Todd original in months."

"Rochelle, I don't know." He flexed the fingers on his right hand. "It's been such a long time."

"There is no way Todd Tatem could forget how to draw." I flipped the brand-new sketch pad open, laid it across his lap, and held out the pencil. "So what if your left arm is in a cast. Your drawing hand is fine."

He took it but his forehead creased with concern. "You're squinting. How bad does it hurt?"

"I'll be fine if I sit down." He knew me too well for me to lie.

"The chair is too far away." He slid over a few inches and nodded to the empty space beside him.

"There's not enough room. I don't want to hurt you."

Todd made a face that made me laugh. Memories of sitting shoulder to shoulder while he sketched convinced me to slip off my shoes and sink back against his pillows. He adjusted his sketch pad.

"Much better." He leaned over and kissed my right temple. "Now, what am I drawing?"

"The two of us ice skating under the Christmas lights."

Todd laughed. "You couldn't start off with something easy like a bridge or a skyscraper?" His pencil glided over the paper, making little gray lines that would soon become the picture I imagined.

My head slid to his shoulder and I closed my eyes against the dull ache in my head. "I missed you so much."

"I missed you too. I had dreams like this all the time." His shoulder trembled gently with every pencil stroke. "I was sure I made it home, and then I would wake up. I still get scared none of this is real."

"Don't worry, it's real." The warmth of the room and comfort of Todd's presence lured me toward sleep. "And I'll never let you leave town without me again."

"Rochelle?" Todd's arm stopped moving. "All of this pendant stuff. It's not over, is it?"

Opening my eyes, I lifted my head to face my best friend. "I don't know. If Aunt Audrie's right, then we just have to be extra cautious, but if Keppler is right . . ." I didn't have to tell Todd it was all top secret. He had always been my confidant.

"I'm here for you, but you have to be careful."

"Yeah, I know." I glanced at the rough lines already becoming the outline of a person. "I just want to do the right thing, but I don't know who to trust."

"I'm with you. Life is confusing." Todd returned to his drawing and a rare sense of calm settled over me like a fuzzy blanket. He understood me, and I could do anything with him by my side.

He finished half of his drawing before he drifted to sleep. I dozed next to him until Lareina returned to walk me home. Careful not to disturb him, I tucked Todd's blanket around him, put his sketch pad on the bedside table, and kissed his forehead before slipping out of the room.

"I wish I didn't have to leave him here." I blinked back a tear as I walked down the hall next to Lareina.

"I know what you mean. But his sister will be here before he wakes up." She wrapped an arm around me. "And soon he'll be home."

We walked in silence out the front door and into the chilly afternoon air.

"Aaron's nurse, Violet, used to be at the home for children with me. She was four or five years older but she remembers me."

Lareina's voice held a mixture of disbelief and determination. "She said the whole town is in shock because of what happened with Molly. They all think after losing her parents so suddenly to the fever, she had a nervous breakdown. And since you were her only friend, she was obsessed with dragging you into her misguided plans."

I took a sharp breath of winter air. It didn't surprise me that people were talking, but I could at least set the record straight with Lareina. "It's a little more complicated than that." I paused to think about how to tell her. It had been hard enough explaining Molly's obsession with the pendant and Dad's involvement with it to Kat and Kinley even after Keppler had explained it once.

I told her about Molly's dad and his research team, how my dad supposedly got involved, and finished with Molly's intentions to collect my pendant for The Defiance.

"So do you have one?" Lareina turned to me, eyes wide. "A pendant?"

"No." It was the same lie I had told when explaining the circumstances surrounding my kidnapping to Kinley and Kat. "That's what I kept telling Molly, but she wouldn't believe me."

"And the pendants are like a key to this research that can be used for good or evil?" Her expression brightened with understanding, then contorted with concern. "Won't Molly just keep coming back until she gets the pendant she thinks you have?"

"It's a possibility." I echoed Audrie's words. "That's why we're being extra careful. My aunt is a TCI agent. She's coming up with ways to keep us safe."

"TCI?" The letters escaped in a strangled gasp. She whirled to face me, all color drained from her face. "And she knows about all of this?"

"Of course she knows." I gripped my friend's arm to steady her. "She's my aunt and it's her job to save the world." If only I could convince myself that her idea of protecting the world was the same as mine. "I know it's a lot. We probably shouldn't talk about it here."

Lareina forced a smile and a nod, a tinge of pink returning to her cheeks. "Let's just get back to your house where you're safe." With a hand on my arm, she propelled me quickly across the street and over a snowdrift.

I didn't understand why my story had made her even more jumpy. Hopefully, given time, she would find Maibe to be as safe as I wanted it to be.

CHAPTER 6
CHARLIE

November 28, 2090

Slowly, I pushed the basement door open, stopping it at the halfway point so it wouldn't creak. The dining room was empty and dishes clanked in the kitchen. I had spent the last several days hiding out in the basement or the library, burying myself in my writing so I wouldn't have a panic attack thinking about the moment I would have to face Griff. I had no doubt he would come; it was just a matter of time.

I felt like a character in an Edgar Allan Poe story, stuck in my own head and spiraling into insanity. Even interacting with people I cared about, people I would have to give up, was too difficult. Rochelle spent most of her time with Todd or resting anyway. Kinley came to check on me and make sure I ate something, and Kat, as far as I could tell, still hated me. On top of that, Nick and Lareina were in and out of the house, and I wasn't sure whether I trusted them. What did it mean that they showed up to rescue Rochelle at the exact moment she needed them?

Stepping over the squeaky floorboard, I tiptoed to the library where I'd left the notebook I needed. Fearing Kat would hear me from the kitchen, I backed through the half-open library doors, stumbled over something, and crashed to the floor.

"Oh. Are you okay?"

I sprang to my feet to face Lareina, standing behind the desk.

On the floor lay the toppled stool, moved from its usual place in the corner.

"I'm sorry." She leaned forward, palms flat against the desk's wooden surface. "It was meant to alert me if someone came through the door."

Ignoring the throbbing in my elbow, I faced the latest stranger Rochelle claimed as family. Lareina and Rochelle had been friends when Lareina spent a year at the Maibe Home For Children. Although they hadn't seen her in almost ten years, Rochelle, Kinley, and Kat had welcomed Lareina as if nothing had changed. I couldn't bring myself to trust her so quickly. "I'm fine. I just came to get..." My notebook was laying open on the desk in front of her.

Following my gaze, she slammed it shut. "I just saw it on the window seat and I was curious." She slid it away from her. "I was looking for some paper."

Swallowing my annoyance, I scooped it up.

"You're a really good writer. I started reading three different books, but none of them took my mind off things like your stories."

From our brief encounters, I knew she was paranoid, had nightmares about whatever happened before she arrived, and worried about her friends as much as Kinley worried about Kat and Rochelle. "Thank you. I can get you your own notebook."

"No, never mind." She walked over to the window seat and sat down. "I'd never be able to actually write the whole story. I'd never make it past the first paragraph."

"What were you going to write about?" The question was out before I could help myself. Something similar to my own anxiety reflected in her eyes.

"My journey to Maibe. I thought if I put it on paper, I could stash it away and stop thinking about it."

"That bad?"

"The reason I can't sleep or feel safe." Her brown eyes

scrutinized me, giving me the impression she'd read more than I meant to reveal. "Kat offered to make me tea, as if that's going to fix it. She doesn't understand what it's like out there. None of them do." Lareina's eyes met mine. "But you're like me. You're afraid too."

"After everything that's happened, I'm worried about what'll happen next." I turned toward the door. "That's it."

"Charlie, wait." Lareina bounced to her feet before I took a step. "Rochelle said you want to be a journalist. That you're always looking for a story to tell."

"She's exaggerating." I forced a smile. "And I'm pretty busy."

"Is it because of all this pendant stuff everyone keeps talking about?" Her whispered words froze me in place.

"What do you know about that?" My heart stopped beating as I imagined Lareina as the next spy sent to torment my family.

"I've just overheard some things. That's why Rochelle was locked up, right? Because The Defiance wants it too?"

"They want it *too*?" I closed the space between us. "Who else wants it? How do you know anything about it?"

She glanced around the room then squeezed her eyes shut. "There are these men in gray suits. The TCI? Bad guys, I think." I couldn't tell if she was lying to me, but she clearly knew more than what she had just revealed.

"You have to tell me everything you know, right now." I glanced at the door, keeping my voice low so Kat wouldn't hear.

"Why? What do you know about it?" She took a step away from me. "Never mind. I'll just ask Rochelle when she gets home."

I gripped her arm and pulled her back. "Leave her out of it. She's in enough danger as it is."

"Don't tell me what to do." She pulled her arm away from me and stumbled back onto the window seat.

"I'm sorry." I sank to the edge of the desk, my thoughts

scrambled by what she had just revealed and my curiosity piqued by what she hadn't. "I'll write your story. But you have to promise not to tell Rochelle anything about it until I decide whether it's safe for her to know."

Lareina eyed the door, probably planning her escape options. She looked back at me. "Fine. But if I tell you everything I know about the pendant, then you have to tell me what you know. And there are some things that happened on my way here that I'm not ready for Rochelle or the others to know about yet."

"You can ask me questions and I'll answer them the best I can." The last thing I needed was for her to find out about my affiliation with The Defiance, but I could answer questions cautiously. "Your secrets are safe with me."

"Okay, we'll start with chapter one tomorrow and see how it goes. I'll tell it in order, exactly as it happened, and if you do anything to indicate I can't trust you, I'll find someone else to write it."

"Deal." My chest ached with anxiety over what she knew, but that was a problem for tomorrow. Before I turned, I held out my notebook. "You might as well finish reading. Tell me what you think."

A real smile spread over her face. "Thank you."

Feeling equally apprehensive and hopeful about the information Lareina could provide, I walked out of the library and closed the door behind me. Before I could take another step toward the basement, a loud crash came from the kitchen followed by a scream from Kat.

I ran into the kitchen to find Kat on the floor, flour covering the linoleum around her. "You missed lunch by an hour," she snapped. "I don't have time to serve you at special times."

"That's not . . ." The kitchen was a mess of pots and pans,

spatulas and spoons, and cooking ingredients. Kat held one towel-wrapped hand in the other. "Are you okay?"

"Do I look okay?" She folded the towel back to reveal her bleeding hand. "I'm trying to cook for my family, plus Lareina and Nick, plus Alexander and the Tatems. Not just today, but for the foreseeable future."

"Isn't that kind of your dream?"

"Not anymore." Her voice faded out with hurt instead of rising in anger. "I can't do it. I don't even have time to clean up after one meal before I start making the next one. I cut my hand slicing celery for the soup and I can't even get the flour out of the cupboard because now I can only use this hand . . ."

"Kat. Take a breath." I sank to the floor in front of her. "When you're really a chef, you'll have assistants to do all of the boring stuff like dishes, right?"

"I guess."

"If you want, I'll wash dishes and slice vegetables." I waited for her to make eye contact, but she didn't. "Maybe we should take care of your hand first."

"You shouldn't be so nice to me after I've been so unfair to you." Kat blinked her watery eyes.

"I deserved it. I left Rochelle behind, and that's unforgivable—"

She shook her head. "That's not it. None of us could have talked her into leaving Todd behind." A tear trickled down her flour-smudged cheek. "I would have forgiven you for that once I got past the original shock, but then you left. Rochelle was gone, Kinley was panicking or arguing with Audrie, and you left me all alone."

"Come on, Kat, don't cry." It was bad enough dealing with her when she was mad at me, but I couldn't handle crying.

"Or what, you'll run away?" She rubbed her eye with the back of her hand. "If you're going to leave, then just do it. I have enough problems without trying to guess which days you're part of this family."

"That's not what I meant. I'm sorry. I just don't know the rules of being in a family."

"There aren't rules." Kat cringed and then her expression softened. "I'm sorry for all of the things I said. You won't leave again. Right?"

All I could tell her was the only truth I knew. "I don't want to leave. This is the only home I've ever had."

Her blue eyes burned into mine. "But?"

"But I will if it's for the best."

"Great. As if four days without you and Rochelle weren't bad enough." She squeezed her eyes shut and took a deep breath. "You could disappear any day, and Audrie wants to take Rochelle and me away from Kinley." Despite her best efforts, tears broke through again. "I don't want to lose my family. Everything was finally good again and—"

"It'll be okay." I slid across the floor until I sat beside her with my back against a cupboard door. "Kinley is never going to give you up."

"What if she doesn't have a choice?" Kat sniffled.

"What if you ruin your day worrying about all of this and none of it happens?" The irony of my words weren't lost on me. I'd spent days fearing Griff would show up, giving up precious time with the people I cared about. "Let's just focus on right now. We'll take care of your hand and then get dinner ready. I know how to make macaroni and cheese and sandwiches."

Laughing, Kat cupped my face with her floury hand and kissed my forehead. "That sounds like a good start. But don't forget about the celery."

My head flooded with warm chaos and I couldn't reply with

anything coherent, let alone clever. A thousand pounds lifted from my shoulders to know Kat was no longer mad at me, but the giddy feeling that replaced it made me feel light enough to float.

"Right. Celery." Unable to stop smiling, I stood and helped Kat to her feet.

CHAPTER 7
ROCHELLE

November 30, 2090

"So, Nick was sitting on the ground looking up at Aaron and me. He was in pretty bad shape and scared to trust either one of us, but he decided we were his best option. Ever since then, the three of us have been trying to survive together." Lareina sat cross-legged on the bed in our spare bedroom upstairs.

My sister and I sat next to each other on the foot of the bed, listening attentively to her answer to Kat's question about how long she had known Nick and Aaron. It reminded me of when Lareina would spend the night and tell Kat and me stories about all of the different places she had lived.

"And you have a crush on Nick. Right?" Kat ignored my elbow nudging her arm. "I've seen you two holding hands with your fingers laced together."

Lareina laughed and shrugged. "That's very observant. Nick and I are friends, but we also disagree on a lot of things. He recently lost his family to the fever, so we were both alone, and I told him we'd be safe in Maibe. That's kept us together for now, but I don't know what happens next."

My sister drew her knees up to her chin. "Did you ever figure out why that detective followed you out of San Antonio?" It wasn't a polite question, but I felt Lareina had strategically left out details, and I was curious too.

Lareina's smile vanished and she swallowed hard. "Because I was a thief. Stealing is a serious crime, even if it's the only way you get to eat."

"Other than that though . . ." Kat tipped her head to view me in her peripheral vision. "Going wherever you want with no one to tell you what to do? I could live with that." As the excitement of the past week faded away, Kat and Kinley had resumed their usual arguing. Kat wanted to return to her volunteer role at the home for children, but Kinley didn't want her walking there alone. Unfortunately, Alexander and Kinley were both too busy to accompany her.

"There are a few other things to take into consideration." Lareina nodded toward the window where a cold wind whistled outside. "You have no real shelter, no warm meals, no one to help you if you get hurt, and no shower for weeks or months at a time."

My sister's nose wrinkled and I wrapped my arm around her. "See? Living by Kinley's rules isn't so bad. Just give her a break right now and then next week, Alexander will put it in his schedule to take you to the home for children."

"Do you go there every week?" Lareina asked.

Kat nodded. "When Kinley lets me. I like helping in the kitchen and talking with the kids." She huddled closer to me. "I still remember how scary it is to be in their shoes."

"Me too. Maybe I could come with you and help? Do you think Kinley would let you go then?"

"She would." My cousin walked into the room and placed a pile of clean laundry on the dresser. "As long as the two of you stay together and get home before dark."

"If you really want to go . . ." My sister sat up, studying Lareina. "They're expecting me tomorrow."

"Nick is spending the day with Aaron." Lareina nodded. "Yeah, I'll go."

Kat sprang forward and hugged Lareina, then rushed to Kinley and hugged her.

"Problem solved." Kinley laughed and wrapped her arm around my sister. "By the way, you all need to go to bed. It's late."

"Kinley's right. I'm exhausted." Lareina yawned.

"Rochelle and Kat, I need to talk to you for a minute." Kinley ushered us into the hallway. "Lareina, is there anything we can do to make you more comfortable?"

Lareina shook her head. "Now that Aaron's doctors are sure he's recovering, I'm looking forward to a good night's sleep."

Separating from Kat and Kinley, I went into the bathroom to wash my face and brush my teeth. When I walked into my room, they were sitting on the foot of my bed with matching serious expressions.

"Is everything okay?" I froze in the doorway. "Did something happen to Todd? He's still getting out of the hospital tomorrow, right?"

"He's okay and coming home on schedule." Kinley's lips drew into a thin line. "What we have to talk about is Audrie's visit. I was on the phone with her before I came upstairs and she's coming to stay with us next weekend."

"That's not such bad news." I sat down next to my cousin. "We're going to show her that you take good care of us and you have everything under control. And we're going to give her the family time she needs." Audrie wouldn't do anything to hurt us. She just needed some reassurance that we were safe.

"Hopefully." Kinley sighed. "I'm going to need help from you guys though. I'm making a list of chores, and you both need to be on your best behavior." She turned to Kat. "Please, no arguing while Audrie's here."

"I can do that." Kat looked down at her feet. "I'll even start now."

"Thank you." Kinley looked ahead through the door to Kat's dark room. "Tomorrow, I'm going to offer Nick the chance to move into my old house across the street." Since losing her parents, Kinley hadn't crossed the threshold of her childhood home. Alexander sometimes went over to make sure everything was working or to bring her something she needed. "Eventually, Aaron can move in there with him, and we should have plenty of room for Lareina to stay with us as long as she needs to."

"Are you and Alexander going to sign papers for them like you did for Charlie?" As always, Kat asked the question I hadn't even thought of.

"Charlie was only fifteen and on the radar of people who thought he was a delinquent." Kinley shook her head. "Aaron is already eighteen, and Nick and Lareina will be in a few months. They'll be all right if we help them get on their feet."

"Are you sure about your house though?" I knew my cousin was already struggling to balance the changes and uncertainty we faced.

She pulled me closer. "I think it's time. That house has been sitting empty for a year, and it's just going to fall apart without someone living in it. At least this will put it to good use." She stood and stretched her arms behind her. "We should all get some sleep. We can talk more tomorrow."

Kat hugged both of us and disappeared into her room. I stood, glimpsing my face in the mirror over my dresser. After a week, the bruises had faded to shadows, but the continuous threat of Molly's return only intensified.

"Rochelle, are you okay?" Kinley stood at my shoulder. "You do that sometimes. Zone out with that lost look on your face."

"I'm all right." I walked to the other end of my bed and sat down on the edge. "Just tired, I guess." I wanted to believe Keppler was right about turning the pendant over to Audrie, but then she would know I lied to her about not having it, and there would be no going back.

"And your head is better? It didn't bother you even a little today?"

I swung my legs onto the bed and sank into my pillows. "No, Kinley. My head is fine." That much I could be honest about. My physical symptoms had vanished.

Kinley nodded and pulled the blankets up to my chin. "You know, if something's bothering you, we can talk about it."

More than anything, I wanted to discuss Keppler and the pendant with her, but I couldn't give her another worry. "I know. Everything will work out okay with Audrie. She just wants to spend some time with her family. We're all she has left."

Kinley nodded and smiled. "Goodnight, Rochelle."

"Goodnight." I turned my face into the pillow as Kinley turned off the light and closed the door.

For the next hour, I watched the minutes tick by on my alarm clock. I wouldn't have been worried about Audrie's visit if I didn't have the pendant. It wasn't that I thought she would use it to harm people like Molly would, but that she wouldn't use it to help. I didn't want the TCI to lock it up and never investigate the vaccine possibility. I didn't want my aunt to think I lied to her because I didn't trust her or, even worse, abandon us when I turned over the pendant because that was the only reason she had contacted us in the first place. Unable to sleep, I decided reading would be a good distraction, so I tiptoed through the dark hallway and down the stairs, careful to be silent in the living room where Nick slept on the couch.

Light glowed faintly through the curtains on the French doors, so I knocked before entering. Lareina sat on the window seat with an open notebook on her lap and a steaming mug in her hand.

"Rochelle?" She flipped the notebook shut. "I thought you were asleep."

"I have too much on my mind to sleep." Clicking the door shut behind me, I walked over to the window seat and sat down next to her. "Is that why you're down here too?"

She nodded and slid the notebook to the cushion behind her. "I've always felt safe in libraries, and Charlie is letting me read some of his stories. They're really good."

"His writing is pretty impressive." I smiled. "If Kinley ever lets us attend council meetings again, you should read his reports. He has a way of turning our discussions into a compelling story." My cousin had been adamant that we would always be home by five o'clock until she decided otherwise, and I didn't intend to argue with her.

"Do you trust him?" She took a sip from her mug. "Even though you haven't known him for long?"

I nodded. "We've been through a lot together. He would never do anything to hurt me." My mind drifted to him begging me to turn the pendant over to Audrie. I'd been avoiding him so we wouldn't argue about it.

"But?" She tilted her head, eyebrows raised.

"But him and I have differing opinions on something right now." I sighed. "We both think we know the right thing to do, but it involves telling my aunt something that I'm not ready to tell her."

"Your aunt the TCI agent? The one who wants to take you away and tear your family apart?" Clearly she had been talking to Kat and Kinley.

"She's just trying to take care of us." I felt a need to defend my aunt. "She's coming to visit next weekend. Once you meet her, you'll understand."

Lareina nodded, looking unconvinced. "So you trust her, but you don't want to tell her what Charlie thinks you should tell her?"

"What I have to tell her is something I've been lying to her about for a while. I'm afraid if I tell her the truth now, she'll think I betrayed her and she won't want me in her life anymore."

"I understand what you mean." She ran a finger along a thin necklace chain partially hidden by her T-shirt. "Rochelle, I'm not telling you that you shouldn't trust your aunt, but I think you're right to be careful. I've heard some things about the TCI."

Sitting forward, I met Lareina's eyes. "Like what?"

She clutched her mug in both hands. "They kill innocent people to get what they want."

A gust of wind slammed against the window behind us and we both jumped.

"Maybe it's not true." I pulled my knees up to my chin. "And even if it is, it doesn't mean Audrie would do something like that. An organization can be corrupt without every person in it being bad. Right?"

"I suppose." Her tone was doubtful. "Maybe you should do your own research. Find out all there is to know about the TCI. I can help you if you want."

Why had I never considered that? Because I trusted my aunt. Because I believed she was telling me all I needed to know. "That's a good idea. Let's get started after this weekend." Kat had announced we'd be hosting a late Thanksgiving dinner to celebrate Todd getting out of the hospital, Lareina coming home, and Aaron recovering.

Lareina smiled. "It's been a long time since I've had something to celebrate. I definitely made the right choice by coming home. I just hope I can keep doing that. Keep my life on the right track." She stared into her cup, and I couldn't tell if she was contemplating past mistakes or holding something back. Then she looked up at me. "I can make you some hot chocolate if you want to stay up and talk for a while?"

"That sounds great. Thank you." There was no guarantee I would fall asleep if I went to bed, and Lareina needed me more than I needed sleep.

"I'll be right back." She hurried to the kitchen, and I walked to the couch for a blanket.

Pausing at the mantle, I examined the framed family photos. The past few years, I had lost far too many of the people I loved, and I couldn't handle watching anyone else walk out of my life. I had to protect my family and hold them together, Audrie included.

CHAPTER 8
CHARLIE

December 3, 2090

Without hesitation, she sprang forward, catapulting herself away from shelter, safety, and the two people who had almost been her family.

I tapped my pen against my notebook and glanced over my most recent section of Lareina's story. So far I'd written about her dangerous escapes from Detective Galloway, meeting Nick and Aaron, foolishly walking through Austin during an outbreak of the fever, and jumping from a train to avoid involving her new friends in her life on the run. I knew somehow she would find them again. But I wanted to know what happened to the pendant. So far I knew how it came into her possession and that she'd managed to hold onto it for almost two months. But she was adamant I had to hear and write the story in order. When she finished, I would have my answers.

Whether I could trust Lareina, I still wasn't sure. I believed she was telling me the truth, but I'd spent several days writing about how she had manipulated everyone around her. It also bothered me that she had used Rochelle's name while lying and stealing, though I understood why she would want to keep that detail concealed from her old friend. Her first question for me had been, predictably, about the pendants. I did my best to explain all I knew about their purpose.

After a late Thanksgiving feast, everyone except me had

gone across the street to clean and rearrange Kinley's old house for Nick, and eventually Aaron, to live in. My only company was a mournful song wailing from the kitchen radio someone had left on. Then again, everything on the radio sounded sad, from the music to the news of the entire state of Texas falling to The Defiance. New reports told of communities quarantined due to outbreaks of the fever and states not already in Defiance territory securing their borders. Every other advertisement urged people to stock up on necessities before the country went to war. Kat was already complaining about the weekly ration of one bag of flour per family at the grocery store. Even Lareina's story was an unwanted reminder of how dark the world was outside of Maibe.

On Friday, Lareina had returned from the home for children with a job. They had been searching for an overnight caregiver since July, and Lareina was the perfect candidate. The home for children offered a room of her own and a weekly paycheck in exchange for assisting with dinner and bedtime and then taking care of the kids overnight. She planned to move in the next day.

As much as Kinley was dedicated to helping the three newcomers, I could see her relief that they would be safely out of the house before her aunt paid another visit. According to Audrie, it was bad enough that Kinley kept me around. I glanced through the bay window at the quickly fading light of the gray afternoon. It had been two weeks since Molly turned our lives upside down, and I hadn't heard from Griff. I knew he would contact me, but I didn't know exactly what to expect. A phone call? A letter? Griff stepping out of the shadows when I walked outside?

The screen door slammed, making me jump and then freeze. At the sound of pots and pans clanging, I took a breath, deciding it must be Kat. Turning back to my writing, I searched my notes for anything I had missed. I would give Lareina my draft later, and if she approved I'd hear more of the story.

A light knock came from the closed French doors and Todd's older sister, Emma, slipped into the room.

"Charlie, what are you doing over here all by yourself?"

I closed my notebook and shrugged. "Just catching up on some writing." I was behind on my homework in both of Emma's classes and hoped she would think that's what I was working on. "How is everything going across the street?"

"We have the house clean and ready to move in. Kinley teared up a few times when we packed up her parents' stuff to store in the basement, but that was to be expected." Her eyes sparkled. "We're going to cheer her up with a surprise birthday party. Do you have a minute to help me?" She nodded toward Rochelle's sewing room.

I stood and crossed the room. Kinley's birthday had been right after the real Thanksgiving, but she'd refused any talk of celebration with all of the madness of Rochelle's kidnapping and return.

Inside the sewing room, Emma loaded my arms with three cake pans before hoisting a large rectangular container into her arms. "I have the coffee started and apple cider heating up on the stove." She led the way to the dining room table and opened the containers, revealing cookies, cinnamon rolls, and a cake with Kinley's name on it.

"She'll be surprised." I glanced through the patio doors to the house across the street. It was odd to see it lit up against the encroaching darkness.

"Charlie, are you okay?" Emma stood with her hands on the back of a chair. "You were really quiet at dinner, and you haven't been yourself lately."

"I'm all right." I shrugged and looked at the desserts on the table. Of all the people I could tell the truth about my connection to The Defiance and Rochelle's pendant, Emma would be the most understanding and forgiving. But I couldn't ask her to keep that kind of secret from Kinley and Alexander.

"I know the past few weeks have been hard and that Kinley and Alexander have been distracted. But I'm here if you need someone to talk to."

"I said I'm fine." I immediately regretted my tone. "I'm sorry. I didn't mean . . ."

"I know." She gently squeezed my arm. "Everyone's a little on edge because of Audrie's visit. Is that bothering you too?"

It was bothering me far less than my role in putting everyone in danger. I sank into the nearest chair. The truth was, I couldn't sleep, every out-of-place sound I heard was Griff coming for me, or Molly for Rochelle, and I avoided people out of fear I would snap at them.

"I just keep thinking maybe everyone would be better off if I hadn't come here." It took all of my self-control to stop myself from asking her to talk some sense into Rochelle.

"No, Charlie. Don't think that for even a minute."

"But I don't want to mess everything up for the Aumonts." I looked up at Emma. "I'm the reason Audrie is questioning Kinley."

Emma pulled out the chair next to me and sat down. "Oh, sweetie. I know things are a little rough right now, but it's not your fault. None of us would ever give you up, and I know, even if she could go back, Kinley would make the exact same decision to sign that paper."

"Even if the consequence is losing Rochelle and Kat to Audrie?"

"That isn't going to happen." She leaned forward and hugged me. "Let's just take it one day at a time."

"Okay." I managed a smile. "Do you need help with anything else?"

We carried plates and silverware to the dining room and put

twenty candles on Kinley's cake. By the time we finished, a flurry of voices entered the kitchen.

"It was the first day of school, and Max promised he would bring his new puppy for show-and-tell the next day." Lareina's voice was alive with the memory.

Kat laughed. "Then the puppy conveniently ran away that night before any of us ever saw it."

"I actually had a puppy, guys. He slipped under the fence and got dognapped." Max walked backwards into the room followed by Kat, with Nick and Lareina right behind.

"Are you sure he didn't run away by choice?" Todd appeared in the doorway with his arm around Rochelle for support as he limped into the room. He had only been out of the hospital for a few days, and it didn't take much to exhaust him.

"Guys, don't be mean. I remember how upset Max was when he told us the puppy was gone. He couldn't fake those tears." Rochelle helped Todd to the nearest chair. "That's what convinced me to sneak away at recess and help him look around the neighborhood."

Todd laughed. "And I came along to keep you two out of trouble. Now that I think about it, the three of us spent a lot of time in the principal's office together. I probably should have learned my lesson, but every time Max and Rochelle had a new scheme, I got pulled in."

"That's the real definition of friendship." Max slid into the chair between Todd and me. "Right, Keppler?"

"Unfortunately." I wondered whether he carried the pendant with him or had it hidden at his house.

Emma's hand ruffled my hair as Max gave me a sideways glance. "Everyone find a seat. They're coming in now."

"Coming to Maibe was a great plan." Nick took Lareina's arm and guided her to two empty chairs. "I love this place."

I'd been here for almost a year, but I didn't fit in like Lareina, who had been away for ten. I didn't grow up with them or re-member the good times they remembered. Even Nick, who had only known my friends for a few weeks, could relate to their experiences in a way I never had. It was another reminder that I really didn't belong in Maibe.

Rochelle pulled a chair close to Todd, and Kat hurried over to sit next to me.

"I was wondering where you were. Did you stay here to help Emma with the surprise?" she whispered.

"Sort of."

Kat tilted her head to study me, then smiled and picked up my hand from the armrest, lacing her fingers through mine.

"Alexander, this is ridiculous." Kinley shuffled into the room with his hands covering her eyes. "I'm going to fall and break my neck before we get to the surprise."

"Then it's a good thing we're here." He pulled his hands away.

Before Kinley could blink, we broke into a round of *Happy Birthday* and then Alexander and Emma made her blow out all twenty candles. Once everyone had a slice of cake, the conversation returned to old times. Kinley, Emma, and Alexander drifted into the kitchen for a cup of coffee. Rochelle and the others took their conversation into the living room where Todd could lie down. I remained in the dining room with an untouched piece of cake in front of me.

"Do you feel left out too?" Lily's voice made me jump, and my elbow clattered against my plate.

I smiled at Todd's younger sister. "Yeah, I guess I wasn't here to remember any of the stuff they're talking about."

"I was only four, so I don't remember either." She pulled a deck of cards from her pocket. "You should try your cake. I made the frosting."

Obediently, I picked up a fork and scooped a sliver of the cake into my mouth. "That's the best frosting I've ever tasted. But don't tell Kat I said that."

Lily grinned and sat down next to me, shuffling the cards in her hand. "Do you want to play a game? I'll teach you the rules."

"Okay." I agreed because Lily reminded me of my little sister, Isabelle. They didn't look alike—Isabelle had golden curls and gray-blue eyes to Lily's straight brown hair and brown eyes—but the curiosity, gentleness, and optimism were the same. If only I could find my sister and bring her to Maibe, share with her the amazing family I had found.

"Why does everyone look so worried all the time?" Lily's voice brought me back to the dining room.

"The older you get, the harder life gets." I watched her deal the cards back and forth between us. "And no matter what we do, it never gets better because we don't have a choice. Everything is entirely out of our control."

She frowned at me. "We get choices." She placed the rest of the deck on the table. "We could have chosen cinnamon rolls or cookies, but we both chose cake because I made good frosting."

If only dessert was my toughest decision. How could I convince Rochelle that Audrie was the best option for getting rid of the pendant? In every other situation, she trusted too much. "What if your choice was broccoli or brussels sprouts?" I purposely chose two foods I knew she despised.

Lily laughed. "That happened a few weeks ago. I told Emma I'd eat the broccoli if she put cheese on it and she did. So I got to make a choice, and I found a way to make it even better."

"That was pretty clever." I picked up my cards, inspired by Lily's outlook. What if I could make Griff believe I wasn't his enemy? What if I could rejoin The Defiance and protect the people I cared about from the inside?

Lily picked up her cards and rearranged them thoughtfully. "I know how to negotiate with Emma. I've been practicing my entire life."

I hadn't known Griff my entire life, but when I took his pendant, I believed he trusted me enough that I wouldn't be his first suspect. Hadn't we been best friends, even brothers, before the pendants got in the way? If only I could have left under different circumstances. Then I could have used my friendship with Griff to protect my family. If I had been thinking clearly, I wouldn't have been so quick to betray him. If only I could have always lived in Maibe, or at least known it existed like Lareina. If I'd known I had a better option, I never would have joined The Defiance in the first place.

CHAPTER 9
CHARLIE

December 5, 2090

"If I had known Galloway could track me with those shoes, I never would have taken them in the first place." Lareina sat on the couch, wrapped in a blanket with her eyes half closed. "That would have saved me a lot of trouble and changed the whole story."

I looked up from the notebook on my lap and leaned forward in my chair. "You're sure it was the shoes he was tracking and not the pendant?" A sudden panic pounded inside my chest.

We sat together in the quiet warmth of the Aumonts' library. Lareina had come over at lunchtime, long after Kinley went to class and Rochelle and Kat went to the Tatems to take care of Todd while Emma finished her homework. There was no one in the house to overhear our conversation.

"Pretty sure." She rested her head back against the couch. "It's going to take me a while to get used to this new job. I thought the kids would sleep most of the night, but I have a baby who cries unless you hold him, three kids who have chronic nightmares, and a toddler who came down with the stomach flu."

"That's . . . awful." I stood and faced Lareina. "But what makes you pretty sure it was the shoes and not the pendant?" If the TCI or The Defiance were able to track the pendants, it would change the entire game.

"Because if Galloway could track the pendant, he would have found me at Oak Creek. Times two." She sat up and gave me an understanding smile. "Don't worry. That'll make sense in the next few chapters."

I sank back into my seat, relieved by Lareina's verification of information I should have already known. If the TCI could track the pendants, Audrie would have just located Rochelle's and left. If The Defiance could track the pendants, Molly would have found what she was looking for without telling Rochelle it existed. My ability to think logically had been corrupted by fear and lack of sleep. "Maybe we should stop for today. You're tired."

Lareina rubbed the side of her face. "I'm fine. You're the one who keeps interrupting the story with questions that don't matter."

"Everything I'm asking is important to the narrative."

"My narrative or yours?" She leaned forward with her elbows on her knees.

Ignoring her question, I flipped through the half-filled notebook. "Can we go back to Detective Galloway for a minute?"

Lareina sighed. "What else do you need to know?"

"You said he was after Susan because of the pendant and after you for the same reason, but before all of that he was just a regular detective who let you off with a warning not to steal again?"

"That's correct."

"He told you he didn't want the pendant, but he worked for people who expected him to retrieve it." I paged through my notes as I tried to phrase my real question. "So who did he work for? The Defiance, the TCI, or someone else?"

Lareina sighed. "That doesn't really come until the end, but I'll jump ahead this one time. The last time Nick and I saw Galloway, he was having an argument with four men in gray suits. They were upset because he hadn't yet recovered the pendant, and they identified themselves as working for the TCI." She avoided eye contact and played with the edge of her blanket.

"And you think they're the bad guys?" The way her demeanor changed when talking about them gave me the impression she feared them.

"Nick and I know they're the ones who murdered Av—I mean Susan's parents, and of course Galloway killed Susan under their orders." She squeezed her eyes shut and swallowed hard. "I'm helping Nick research what happened to her family so he can get some closure."

What did Nick have to do with the girl Lareina met in San Antonio, and why would he need closure? What had Lareina and Nick witnessed and how did they permanently escape Galloway? Where was the pendant she had been carrying throughout the entire story? The questions exploded in my head and tingled in my fingers.

Lareina smiled but her brown eyes remained wide and sad. "That's why we shouldn't jump ahead. You already know too much and I don't want it to impact the way you tell the rest of the story."

"It won't." I flipped my notebook to a blank page and picked up my pen, eager to get my answers. "Let's start where we left off. You mentioned something about a place called Oak Creek?"

Lareina leaned back in her seat. "Yes. When I opened my eyes . . ."

Her sentence was cut off by a knock on the door. No one was supposed to be home for hours.

I closed my notebook. "Come in."

The door eased open and Rochelle stepped into the room. "Hey. Lareina, I didn't know you were coming over. How did everything go at the home for children?"

"Great." She smiled. "I'm a little tired but I already love my kids."

"I thought you were staying with Todd all afternoon," I blurted.

"Emma got home early and Todd is sleeping." Rochelle cautiously approached with a folder in her hand. "We stopped by the library." She stepped around my chair and sat down next to Lareina. "Look at all of this information we found on the TCI, and that was only a half hour of research."

Lareina took the folder and flipped it open to reveal a stack of printed papers.

"Most of it just explains when they were established, what they do, and some of the old cases they've worked. Nothing surprising." Rochelle spoke quickly, glancing at me. "There are some records of the TCI being investigated by other government agencies for unprofessional conduct though."

"I'm glad you're finding the information you need." Lareina closed the folder and handed it back to Rochelle. "Just let me finish a few things with Charlie and I'll help you sort through all of it."

"Great." Rochelle stood and looked at me, eyebrows raised. "Kat, Max, and I are going to make cinnamon popcorn and watch a movie. You're both invited."

Taking a deep breath to remain calm, I forced a smile. "Thank you. We'll be there in a few minutes." I waited for her to close the door before springing to my feet. "You're the one who encouraged her to investigate the TCI? If she finds anything negative about them, then she won't want to . . ." I stopped before I could bring up Audrie or the pendant.

"Won't want to what?" Lareina stood and faced me. "Turn her dad's pendant over to the TCI?" When I didn't answer, she continued. "Charlie, does Rochelle have her dad's pendant?"

"No." I stared down at my socks. It wasn't a lie. Max was keeping the pendant until we made the plan we were supposed to have had weeks earlier.

Lareina cleared her throat. "But she knows where it is?"

"It's none of your business."

"I disagree. First of all, you promised to answer my questions. Second, I spent months trying to keep my pendant away from the TCI and you want to just hand one to them. Third, Rochelle is my friend so her safety is my concern. Do you need more reasons? Because I can do this all day."

"Fine." I turned away from her. "We know where it is. And until Rochelle gives it to Audrie she'll never be safe." Spinning around, I met her eyes. "You think the TCI is bad? Do you know anything about The Defiance?"

Lareina shivered. "I never want to run into one of those psychotic, brainwashed idiots again."

"I'm glad you feel that way." The sarcasm in my voice wasn't lost on Lareina, but she didn't know my secret. "Because if Molly gets Rochelle's pendant, then the fate of the world will be in the hands of those brainwashed psychos."

"Then we need a Plan C." She took a sidestep. "I should be talking to Rochelle about this anyway."

"Say a word about the pendant or the TCI to Rochelle, or any of the Aumonts for that matter, and I'll tell all of them you used Rochelle's identity."

"It wouldn't change anything." She took a big step back and sank to the couch. "Rochelle would forgive me."

"Are you sure?" I hated what I was doing. Preying upon her fears of being rejected by her family when I knew how deeply those fears sliced through my own heart. "Do you want to risk it when you've only been here for a few weeks?"

She covered her face with her hands then looked up at me, eyes narrowed. "You know, I'm a little disappointed. Here I thought you were an aspiring journalist."

"What is that supposed to mean?"

Her composure held firm despite my agitation. "Isn't it your job to investigate a story from every angle? Rochelle's research is valuable whether it gives you the answer you want or not."

"What do you want me to do?" I sat down in my chair. "Let Rochelle get kidnapped again, or worse, because we can't agree on who the bad guys are?"

Lareina shook her head. "I want you to find all of the answers and consider all of the possible solutions before you decide the world's fate." She leaned forward. "You've made it clear that the TCI and The Defiance both want the pendant, but if these scientists were so secretive and created the pendants to hide their research, how did all of these other people find out about it?"

"The Defiance knows because Molly's dad was head of the research team." The last thing I wanted was to bring up Griff and explain how I knew about his connection. "The TCI knows because the scientists were working for the government."

She puffed out her cheeks and let the air out. "What part of the government?"

"How would I know?" Lareina was observant and intuitive, and I was beginning to think she had better investigative instincts than I did. "What I do know is the pendant is dangerous and I don't trust Audrie. So, if Rochelle gives it up, she's safer and there's a good chance she'll get Audrie out of her life."

"I want to protect Rochelle as much as you do, but it's a little selfish to put the whole world at risk just because you think this will keep her safe."

"If it's selfish then I'll be selfish." I sighed, deflating a bit. "Look, if you can come up with a reasonable third option, I'm all ears."

Lareina nodded. "I won't say anything about the pendant, but I won't stop doing my own research either. And I won't stop encouraging Rochelle to look for answers to her questions."

"Do what you want." I took off my glasses. "Just don't push

her to do something dangerous, because she'll risk her life if she thinks it'll save even one person."

She stood. "Maybe we should take a break from writing for a few days. I know you're dealing with a lot right now, and I think I'm more exhausted than I realized."

As much as I wanted answers, my concentration was broken and I knew she wanted to get away from me. "Sure. Stop by when you're ready to continue the story." I watched her leave the room, knowing I may have lost my chance to ever find out what happened to her pendant.

CHAPTER 10

ROCHELLE

December 6, 2090

"When Audrie gets here on Friday, you have to tell her about the pendant right away." Keppler pulled the ladder away from the house and guided it to the ground until it rested on its side.

I looked up at the strings of lights along the gutters over the front porch and looped over the railings. We had spent the afternoon putting them up before the snow came in overnight.

"Aumont, are you listening to me?" Keppler stepped out of the already shin-deep snow and stomped his boots on the sidewalk in front of the porch.

"Yes. I hear you. Just like every time before." Due to his incessant warnings to give up the pendant, I had spent the week avoiding him whenever possible. "You have to stop with the gloom and doom." I stuffed my gloved hands into my pockets. "Everyone's safe. We haven't heard from Molly. Maybe everything will just blow over."

"Now that she's gone, she's even more dangerous." He shook his head and picked up the ladder. "We don't know what she's planning or when she'll be back, but she will be back."

"We also don't know what Audrie's planning. Remember, she doesn't get to decide what to do with the pendant. She works for the TCI."

"And their goal is to protect the country from threats like research capable of turning the common cold into a deadly virus."

But not to pursue the vaccine that could save millions of people from deadly viruses we already had. A gust of wind sliced through our coats and we both shivered.

"We should get inside." I shoved all of our extra supplies into a bag. "Kat needs our help with all of the cleaning." Between preparing for Audrie's visit and taking final exams, Kinley had been more stressed than usual. We were trying to ease some of her load.

"Don't change the subject, Aumont." Keppler started toward the garage with the ladder, and I followed.

"I'm just being logical. I don't want to make any rushed decisions when the consequences affect the entire world."

"We've been weighing this since the summer." He navigated the ladder through the door and lowered it to the floor where it leaned against the wall. "The longer we wait, the closer Molly and The Defiance come to hurting you and your family. Molly is far worse than Audrie."

"Then why didn't my dad just give it to her in the first place?" I tossed my bag of supplies on a shelf of gardening tools. I would put everything away when I could feel my fingers. "He must have had a good reason for hiding it instead."

"He was best buddies with Molly's diabolical dad, so maybe he didn't make the best decisions." Keppler kicked the ladder so it fit flush against the wall.

"That's not fair." My cheeks grew warm despite the cold. "You didn't know him. You didn't know either of them."

Keppler turned to me, eyebrows furrowed in frustration. "What I do know is he jumped into something that put himself and his family in danger and left a mess for you to clean up. He's dead because he was reckless, and you're acting just like him."

My shoulders stiffened. "He wasn't reckless, he wanted to help people. But you're right about one thing. I'm just like him and I'm going to do the right thing. I'm going to make him proud."

"Proud." Keppler spat the words. "He's dead. He can't be proud; he can't see you. He'll never know what you decide. He made his choices and if you want to live, you have to make better ones."

"That's not true." My lungs burned as if I'd had the air knocked out of me. "None of it." Taking a deep breath, I forced myself not to break eye contact. "While Audrie is here I'll decide if I can trust her with the pendant." I turned to leave so he wouldn't see me cry.

Keppler's hand clamped onto my elbow and turned me back to him. "That's not good enough. I know you'll change your mind, and there isn't any time left." I tried to pull myself free, but he gripped my arm tighter, his face flushed. "Say you'll give her the pendant."

"I already gave you my answer." He had never been anything but protective of me, but something else shone in his eyes now. "Let go of me."

His eyes slid from my face to his hand on my arm. He took a weird gasping breath, let go, and took a backward step. "Aumont, I'm sorry..."

"Forget it." I turned and rushed out of the garage and into the warmth of the laundry room. Taking my time, I removed my coat and boots then tried to dry my tears, but they returned the minute I walked into the kitchen.

Kat turned from what she was stirring on the stove. "It's about time. Where's Charlie?"

"Still in the garage." I took a breath and blinked hard. "Putting everything away."

"What's wrong?" My sister took a step toward me then reached back to stir as if connected to the pot by an invisible thread. "Come here."

I obeyed and she wrapped an arm around me. "Brrr. You're ice cold. Good thing I'm making hot chocolate."

Nodding, I brushed the back of my hand across my cheek.

"Rochelle, why are you crying?" Kat's blue eyes scrutinized me. "Did you get hurt hanging the lights?"

"No. It's just . . . That's something I used to help Dad with." It was part of the truth, and part of the reason Keppler's words had hit me so hard. I hoped it would be enough because I couldn't explain more.

"I miss him too." Kat let go of her spoon to hug me with both arms. "It'll be weird celebrating Christmas without him, but it's better than not celebrating at all like last year."

"You're right." Last December we had all been recovering from a year of loss and illness, so there didn't seem to be much to celebrate.

"It's okay if you need to cry. Just don't do it alone." Kat slowly released me. "Why don't you go check on Todd and I'll be there in a few minutes with hot chocolate and cookies."

Todd had spent the entire day at my house while his dad was at work and Emma studied at the library. She only had two weeks to finish her first semester of classes that would allow her to teach in January when Maibe's middle school reopened. Although he had made immense progress in his recovery, he spent most of the day sleeping, still trying to get his strength back.

"Is he awake?" I took a step toward the next room.

"He was a few minutes ago." Kat smiled when she heard my voice brighten. "I told him you'd be in soon."

I hesitated. "What about Kinley's list?"

"We still have two days and I already have Audrie's room ready." Kat turned back to stirring the milk and cocoa. "We'll be done ahead of schedule. Now go warm up."

"I'm going." Thankful for Kat's understanding, I hurried to the living room where Todd sat on the couch with a blanket over his legs. "How was your nap?"

He smiled, familiar dimples sinking into his unfamiliar gaunt face. "Great. Your lights look good from here. I'm in the holiday spirit for sure." He nodded to the big window across the room that looked out onto the front porch.

I smiled and crossed the room to sit down next to my best friend.

His hand found mine then let go. "Shelley, you're freezing. Here." He did his best to wrap a blanket around my shoulders with one arm in a cast.

I huddled closer to him. By the time Kat brought two steaming mugs and a plate of cookies, I could feel my fingers.

Todd lifted his cup to his lips. "You have no idea how many times I wished for a cup of your hot chocolate while I was away." That's how he always referred to his time in The Defiance work camp. He didn't bring it up often, but he had started sharing details with me about the cold nights, sparse food, and senseless beatings.

Kat ruffled his hair. "I'm making your favorite peach pie for the church booth at Friday's festival. I'll make an extra one for you."

"You're the best." Todd grinned and squeezed my hand. "I can't wait. I'll be all rested up so we can have a good time. We might have to save ice skating for next year, but we can check out all of the homemade stuff at the booths, eat some good food, sit under the lights, and listen to carols . . ."

I smiled and rested my head on his shoulder.

Maibe's annual winter festival hadn't happened the previous year thanks to the fever, but this year, Kiara, my fellow town council member in charge of town events and morale, decided it would be a good way to end the year. Last I heard, she hoped to have the food booths run by the churches, local businesses sponsoring game booths, and vendor booths with local products, plus sleigh rides, a snowman-building contest, and—my favorite—ice skating. I didn't know how much was actually panning out because I hadn't been to a council meeting since I'd been kidnapped by Molly.

Kat walked over to the Christmas tree and pushed the clicker on the electrical cord with her foot. The white lights sparkled through the branches and she nodded with approval. "We should all hang out together! I convinced Charlie to go with me, and he even agreed to go ice skating." She was so excited I didn't have the heart to tell her he probably wouldn't be in a very festive mood.

"Don't forget, we have to spend most of our time with Audrie." I held my warm mug between my cold hands. "We don't want to be rude." Despite my pendant problem, a part of me was excited to talk with my aunt and reintroduce her to the town she grew up in.

"I'll be on my best behavior." Kat rolled her eyes. "But I'm not going to let it ruin my fun. I have to get back to making dinner. If you guys need anything else, just yell."

After Kat left the room, Todd and I sat in silence sipping our hot chocolate and enjoying the warmth of the room and festivity of the decorations Kinley and I had taken so much care to set up.

Todd took a cookie from the plate and offered it to me. I shook my head. "Are you okay, Rochelle?"

"Yeah, just a little tired." I couldn't find the words to explain the hollow feeling where my heart belonged. "Life has been exhausting since Kinley found out Audrie is coming."

"I'm sure Kinley will be back to normal soon." Todd wrapped his arm around me. "It probably doesn't help that Alexander won't be around this weekend."

Alexander had one of his leaders of Nebraska meetings in the far western part of the state. He would be gone Friday afternoon until Tuesday morning, unable to support Kinley when she needed him most.

"I think she knows she'll miss him and she covers it up with anger. You know Kinley. She likes to be in control of everything. Even her emotions." I glanced at the newspaper on the coffee table. The front page headline announced that The Defiance had taken control of Texas, and states bordering their territory were mobilizing for war. More bad news right before the holidays.

"Rochelle, are you going to tell me what's really bothering you?" Todd's voice was soothing and reassuring. Nothing I said, nothing I did, none of my problems would ever make him love me less.

I sighed, wrapped my blanket more tightly around myself, and leaned into him. Then I told him what had happened in the garage.

"He has no right to say any of that to you." Todd shifted too quickly and winced as he placed a hand over his ribs. "You say the word and I'll go talk to him right now."

"No." I turned to face him, putting a hand on his shoulder. "You're supposed to be resting and Keppler is just scared."

"The doctor said I'll be less stiff if I walk around. Plus being scared is no excuse to . . ." Todd looked at me and his expression softened. "Rochelle, I agree with Charlie about one thing. You need to get rid of that pendant."

"I know. But how?" I slumped forward with my elbows on my knees. "I don't want Molly to create super viruses. That's easy. But I don't want Audrie to do nothing if the pendant is also the key to a vaccine that'll save millions of lives. What if I just need to pursue it myself?"

"Pursuing this yourself has to be your last resort—I think you know that. Besides the fact it would give all of us nervous breakdowns, where would you even start?" Todd relaxed back into the pillows.

I groaned. "I have no idea. I just can't let the pendant go to waste. That's probably why my dad didn't give it to Audrie, right?

It's not that he didn't trust her, but he disagreed with her plan for the pendant. He knew he could do better and save the world."

Todd's hand enveloped mine. "I don't know what your dad was thinking, Shelley. But I do know he was trying to do the right thing, and he's so proud of you for doing the same."

My head slid to Todd's shoulder. "If only he could send me a message and tell me what I should do."

"I'll help you figure it out. Are you sure you don't want me to talk to Charlie?"

"No. He wasn't trying to hurt me. I'll talk to him after we've both calmed down." I closed my eyes, feeling sleepy from the warmth and familiar comfort of Todd next to me.

CHAPTER 11

CHARLIE

December 7, 2090

"Okay, hold it steady." Max carefully slid a wire into a panel on the side of his time machine while I sat in front of a second open panel, waiting to fish it through. "I've got it." My fingers gripped the wire for a second, and then like the six times before, it slipped back through the narrow opening. "No." I slapped the metal paneling and kicked the wall.

"It's okay." Max walked around into view. "We'll get it eventually. We've made it this long without time travel. What's another day?"

"I don't care about time travel. There's nothing good in my past and I don't even want tomorrow to come." During my hour of helping Max with the invention that would never work, I had told him about my fight with Rochelle. I'd avoided disapproving looks from Todd until Emma came to pick him up. During dinner, I tried to keep up a conversation with Kat while Kinley worried about Audrie's visit and Rochelle remained silent, sliding food around her plate.

I hadn't told him about my stop at the home for children on my way to his house. After reading through what I'd written of Lareina's story, I made myself see the situation from her perspective. I hadn't told her about my time with The Defiance so she couldn't do the same, and she was only trying to make the right decision with the information she had. It was my intention to apologize and convince her to continue our writing project, but she wasn't there. So I left a note and all of my conflicts remained unresolved.

"Maybe we should take a break." Max pulled two folding lawn chairs from along the wall and set them up close to the heater.

"I'm not like my dad." The pain in Rochelle's eyes when I'd squeezed her arm played over and over in my head. Even more disturbing, when I closed my eyes, I was back at home, watching my dad drag my mom into the room with an iron grip on her arm and then shove her so hard she hit her head on the wall as she tumbled to the floor. "I didn't mean to hurt her."

"I know you'd never hurt anyone on purpose. Especially not Rochelle." Max patted my shoulder. "I get it, you're trying to protect her, but you can't. Todd learned that the hard way and Kinley is still trying to figure it out."

His presumptuous attitude annoyed me. "That's ridiculous. Everything Kinley does is to protect Rochelle and..." And Rochelle spent plenty of time sneaking around and lying to her cousin.

"Rochelle has always had this thing about saving lost puppies, stray kittens, and even people." Max sat down, elbows on his knees. "She doesn't want anyone to get hurt or upset, or to worry. And she will hide things from us if that's what it takes."

Disgusted, I started pacing from one end of the garage to the other. "So you're telling me to just play along with her. To let her walk into danger and get kidnapped again, or worse."

"No." Max stretched his feet toward the heater. "I'm telling you to work with her. Like the night we met you. I told Rochelle I wanted to dig up thistles, and she thought it was a bad idea. But she knew if she said no, I would go by myself and get in trouble, so she played along and came with me."

"And then you both got in trouble." I stopped in front of him. "What would have happened if I didn't show up?"

"We would have had a long, cold walk." Max's grin faded. "What I'm trying to say is Rochelle already knows about the pendant. She'll do the right thing at any cost, and the best thing we can do is join her and help her weigh the risks and avoid as many as possible."

I plopped into the other chair. "If you give me the pendant, I can just slip it to Audrie this weekend. Maybe hide it in her room and she would believe she found it herself."

Max pressed his hand to his chest where the pendant rested under his shirt. "Believe me. I'm on your side. First, because I think you're right, and second, because Rochelle already has Todd, so it's only fair that you get an ally too. But Rochelle has to be the one to give up the pendant or she'll never be able to put all of this stuff behind her."

"I've been trying . . ." Exhausted, I slumped in my chair. "Can you talk to her? We have to get rid of that thing before something terrible happens."

"And you're sure Audrie is the right choice?" Max played with the chain around his neck that held the pendant.

"Better than The Defiance or Molly. I don't like her, but she'll keep the pendant away from them. And as long as none of them can complete the collection, nothing bad can happen. Plus, if Rochelle gives Audrie the pendant, she'll stop trying to tear the family apart. I know once she gets what she wants, she'll leave for good."

"Are you still going to the festival with Kat on Friday?" He leaned over to adjust the knob on the heater. "We could pull Rochelle aside and have a quick pendant meeting. Just the three of us."

"Yeah, I'm going." Kat was pretty excited about ice skating and the food she was making. The tightness in my chest relaxed a little. I'd interviewed Kiara to write an article about the upcoming celebration, and I didn't even have to embellish the story to sell the event as appealing. "If Audrie wouldn't be there, I'd be excited too."

"Is she really that bad? I mean, maybe if you just give her a chance?"

"She hates me. I even asked Kinley if I could stay with Alexander for the weekend, but he has his stupid leader meeting. Kinley doesn't want me three miles out of town all by myself."

Max leaned back in his chair. "You can stay here if you want. I bet after a whole weekend together we'd solve time travel for sure."

"Thanks, but I should probably stick around to give Kinley moral support." I really appreciated Max's offer and wanted to take it, but the look in Kinley's eyes when I asked to stay with Alexander revealed fear of being Audrie's only target.

"I understand, but if you change your mind, you can have my bed and I'll sleep on the air mattress that deflates overnight." He shrugged. "I've got your back."

"Thanks." The weight on my shoulders felt a little lighter with Max's agreement to help with Rochelle.

Max stood. "Do you want to stay for dinner?"

I glanced at the clock above the work bench ticking toward five o'clock. "I can't. Kinley wants everyone home before it gets dark."

"Oh yeah." He thought for a moment. "Come over tomorrow and we'll finalize what we want to say to Rochelle. We can meet everyone at the festival. That way you won't have to be home when Audrie arrives."

"Good idea." I stood and walked to the door with Max. "I'll come by after lunch."

We made small talk on our way to Max's house. At the back door, Max went inside and I continued down the driveway to my truck parked along the street. Not my truck. A truck that belonged to a man I had called reckless and accused of endangering his family.

Chest burning with guilt, I got inside and started the engine. An envelope rested on the passenger seat. It hadn't been there when I parked a few hours earlier. I glanced through the windows, looking for the person who had placed it there. The snow-covered neighborhood was quiet with lights coming on inside houses to fend off the encroaching darkness.

With shaking hands, I held the envelope in front of me, reading my name in the familiar blocky handwriting that turned my bad week into a nightmare. With no other choice, I ripped it open and unfolded the note inside.

Charlie,

We need to talk. I know you didn't betray me and I'm sorry for overreacting. I apologize for not believing you. Please accept the enclosed ticket and meet me at your old house. I have information about your family and a plan to bring you home. It's best that we meet in a neutral place, but I will come and find you if necessary.

Your brother,
Griff

I shook the envelope until a train ticket fell into my lap. It would allow me to board a train out of Maibe at ten o'clock on Friday night and take me back home to Orville, Kansas.

If I didn't face Griff, he would come to Maibe looking for me. On the other hand, I wanted to know what he knew about my family. Could he tell me where to find Isabelle? Maybe it was just a trick to ensure I would come. I scanned the quiet neighborhood once more, but no one appeared.

Had Griff sent a messenger to slip the letter into my truck?

Molly could have told him what I'd be driving and where to find the truck unoccupied. What if Molly had delivered the letter herself? What if she had gone to the house to find Rochelle? I shoved the note and ticket into my pocket and shifted the truck into drive. Speeding down the snow-packed street, I fishtailed in the main intersection and spun halfway around, only stopping when my front bumper collided with a pile of snow along the curb. Fortunately, the streets were deserted.

Cautiously, I backed up and turned the truck toward home, this time keeping my speed reasonable for the wintry roads. Pulling up in front of the Aumont house, I rolled to a stop in the middle of the street. The front path ended at the patio doors looking into the brightly lit dining room. Inside, Rochelle set the table while Kinley spoke to her and Kat carried a covered dish of food from the kitchen. They were all safe.

Exhausted by my five minutes of panic, I pulled into the driveway, cut the engine, and rested my forehead against the steering wheel. If I left on Friday night, Kinley and the others would worry about me, I wouldn't be there to support them during Audrie's visit, and they would probably spend a lifetime wondering why I just disappeared. If I stayed, Griff would come looking for me, potentially hurt my family, and maybe even bring more of The Defiance with him.

A lifetime of worrying about what happened to me would be merciful compared to what my family would experience if Griff came to Maibe. Max and I would still have plenty of time to convince Rochelle to give up her pendant and then I would slip away. I had twenty-four hours to prepare for the worst.

CHAPTER 12
ROCHELLE

December 8, 2090

"This is going to be so much fun." Kat stacked containers of cookies on the counter next to her meticulously wrapped pies. "I can't believe I talked Charlie into ice skating."

I sat at the table and listened to my sister chatter, wishing I could overhear Emma's conversation with Todd in the next room. He had spent most of the day dozing, and confessed to me his throat was scratchy and he had chills. I didn't think Emma would let him go to the festival and I didn't want him to go out feeling miserable, but I didn't want to go without him.

"I think Audrie will have fun too." Kat turned to me and brushed a crumb from the sleeve of her sweater dress. "We'll make her join our team for the snowman-building contest and the snowball fight. She'll see that Maibe is the best place for us to live."

Half an hour earlier, I had driven the truck to the train station to pick up Audrie. Once home, she hugged Kat and me then went upstairs to get ready for the festival she seemed excited to attend. Keppler had left for Max's after an awkward lunch during which he avoided eye contact with me. I wanted to talk to him, but I didn't want to start another argument.

I glanced at the clock. "It's already after five. I thought Kinley would be home early."

Kat shrugged. "She's been late all week. Probably trying to catch up."

"Come on, Emma." Todd followed his sister into the kitchen. "I'm not sick. My temperature is a little warm because I've been sleeping under a pile of blankets. Once I'm outside for a few minutes, it'll drop to hypothermia levels."

"That's not one of your best arguments." Emma turned to face him. "You'll be miserable out there if you're not feeling well now, and I don't want you to get any sicker than you already are."

Todd looked at me then back at his sister. "But I promised Rochelle. I've already missed so many things."

Emma wrapped one arm around him and gave me an apologetic look. "Sorry, but you're going to miss one more. Dad will stay home with you, and Lily and I won't stay out any later than we have to."

The back door slammed and Kinley limped into the kitchen, still wearing her coat and boots. Her face was flushed from the cold and eyes dull with exhaustion.

"Kinley, what happened?" Emma knelt to examine Kinley's knees, both dirty, one soaked through with blood.

"I slipped on the ice." My cousin squinted and rubbed her forehead. "I was in a hurry to get home."

"Are you feeling okay?" I guided her to a chair and helped her out of her coat.

Kinley kicked off her boots, uncharacteristically leaving them dripping in the middle of the floor. "I'm fine. Why wouldn't I be?"

Emma's hand reached past me and rested on Kinley's forehead. "You're burning up." She glanced over her shoulder at Todd. "Even after you walked home in the cold."

"I'm negative for strep and influenza A and B." She coughed into her sleeve.

"But you have a scratchy throat and a headache." Emma sighed. "That seems to be going around."

Kinley nodded. "I just need to sit for a minute."

"No way, kiddo. You're not going anywhere but your bed." Audrie stood in the doorway wearing a green turtleneck sweater with black-and-white checkered pants that made her look like the models in clothing magazines. "You're not fine. You look miserable."

Kinley stood a little shakily. "I've been at work and class for the past nine hours. Give me a chance to wash my face and change..."

Audrie pressed her hand to Kinley's forehead and tenderness crossed her face. "You're sick. You know better than anyone that you need to rest."

My cousin's head dropped in defeat.

"Audrie and I can cover your shift." Kat stepped forward. Kinley was supposed to sell pulled pork sandwiches and slices of pie at the church booth for a few hours of the festival.

"That sounds like a good solution." Audrie put her hands on Kinley's shoulders and nudged her toward the next room. "Go to bed and you'll feel better tomorrow."

Kinley trudged away, and I turned to Todd sitting at the table with his head in his hands. I had been looking forward to attending the festival with my aunt, but my heart pulled me in a different direction. "You guys go ahead. I'll stay here with Kinley and Todd."

Before Emma could protest, Audrie stepped in front of her. "Are you sure? I was looking forward to spending some time with you."

"Me too. But Kinley needs me right now and we take care of each other. You go with Kat." I threw my arms around her. "We'll still have the rest of the weekend."

She hugged me back and it felt warm and real. "I understand. Take good care of your cousin."

Kat loaded Audrie's arms with baked goods before dragging her out the door in her excitement to meet Max and Keppler.

"Get some rest." Emma kissed the top of Todd's head then hugged me. "Tell Kinley I'll keep an eye on Kat." She picked up the remaining pies and then Todd and I were alone.

"Sorry, Shelley. I really wanted to take you to the festival."

"We'll have plenty of time for all of that when you're better." I tried to smooth Todd's hair where it stuck up from sleeping all day. "We still get to hang out for the rest of the evening, and that's all I wanted anyway."

Hand in hand, we walked to the living room. "I'm going to check on Kinley. I'll make you some tea for your throat when I get back." I accompanied Todd to his favorite chair then hurried up the stairs. "Kinley?" I peeked into her room but she wasn't there.

"Rochelle? If you don't get going you'll be late."

I followed her voice to the bathroom where she sat on the floor next to a bottle of peroxide, band aids pasted over her knee and three places along her shin.

"I'm staying home to take care of you and Todd."

"You don't have to do that. I know you wanted to go to the festival, and Kat . . ."

I sank down next to her, sitting back on my heels. "I didn't want to go without Todd, and Emma promised to look out for Kat."

Kinley sighed and pressed her hands over her face. "Rochelle, I'm so sick. I don't know how this happened."

I didn't have the heart to remind her she'd only been getting three hours of sleep at night. "I'll heat up some of the chicken noodle soup Kat made for lunch and then you'll get some sleep and you'll feel better in the morning."

She dropped her hands to her lap and tears glistened in her eyes. "I've had such a bad feeling about this weekend since Audrie called. How could Alexander leave now? I need him here, but his stupid meeting is more important."

I leaned back against the bathtub and stretched my legs out alongside hers. "It is hard he isn't here right now."

"He has these big plans about him and I getting married someday. But what's the point if I'm at work all the time and he's all over the state trying to become governor of the universe? Let's face it. We haven't had time for each other since the sixth grade."

I tried not to smile. "You're only twenty. You don't have to figure out your life yet."

"It feels like I've lived two lifetimes already." She sighed and shook her head. "Plus, I don't want to be alone when Audrie wins custody of you and gets Kat and Charlie taken away from me in the process."

"Why would she get custody of me and not Kat?" I scrunched my knees up in front of me.

"I've been saying she wants both of you so Kat won't feel bad, but for whatever reason, Kat and I don't meet the requirements to qualify as her nieces." Kinley shook her head. "If she fights me for custody and wins, I won't be able to keep any of you."

Again, I wanted to tell Kinley the truth about the pendant and propose it could have something to do with Audrie's choices, but the entire situation gave me a headache. It would only give my cousin one too. "Whatever her reasons, she can't convince me to leave you guys. You're my family. And I know if we just give her a chance, she'll understand."

"She's your family too, and I'm not so sure she'll give you a choice. I'm no match for her, Rochelle. She's a real adult with an established life, steady job, and prominent career. And I'm—"

"The only one who has the patience and understanding to take care of all of us." I pulled my feet under me and stood. "You're the only choice, and anyone who talks to you for five minutes will know it." As much as I admired my aunt and wanted her to be a part of our family, I couldn't ignore the way she treated my cousin. If I could help them to find common ground, maybe everything could work out.

Kinley's breath caught somewhere between a sob and a laugh as I extended my hands and pulled her to her feet.

"I'm really glad you stayed in tonight. I don't know what I would do without you."

What I couldn't tell her was how often I had imagined moving to New York with Audrie. It was the opportunity of a lifetime, a chance for an adventure, and—if Molly had been right about our generation being left behind—my only prospect for a future. "And you'll never have to find out." My arm looped around her and I led her down the hallway. "Because I'm not going anywhere."

CHAPTER 13

CHARLIE

December 8, 2090

Kat giggled as we raced around the temporary ice skating rink as fast as we could, swerving in and out to avoid other skaters. Her gloved hand gripped mine, the icy air brushed my face, and my only worry was keeping my balance. It was bottled freedom, pure joy, and minutes ticking by too fast. Kat took my other hand and we spun to a stop a few feet from where Max stood in the trampled snow.

He raised one arm in the air. "Thirty seconds. That's a new record."

"I told you we could do it." Another couple raced past us, and Kat pulled me closer to the snowy border. "I wish we could have a holiday festival every Friday."

I hated that I was about to ruin that for her. We had built a snowman with Audrie, enjoyed hot chocolate and cinnamon rolls with Emma and Lily, and walked under the thousands of white lights hung all across Maibe's fairgrounds.

"It would be okay if this one could just last a little longer." I gripped her hand tighter than I intended, but she didn't protest. If only I could stop time and remain in that moment. If only . . . One of my feet started to slide forward.

She wrapped her arms around me before I lost my footing. "We can go around again. There's still time."

"Hey, Kat." Lily ran up to us with skates in her hands. "Emma said we have fifteen minutes before we have to help clean up at the booth." She plopped down on the bench and pulled off her shoes.

"You better get out here then." Kat let go of me and I was back on my lonely road to doom. "Are you coming, Charlie?"

I had minutes left in Maibe, but I couldn't say goodbye. I couldn't risk anyone trying to stop me or follow me. "I should probably take a break, but thanks for being patient with me." I sat down next to Lily as she laced up her skates.

Kat laughed. "You learned fast for never skating before. I'll find you skates that fit better for next year."

Next year. My chest ached as I nodded. There wouldn't be a winter festival with Kat next year. There wouldn't be Christmas with my family this year. I didn't even know where I would be tomorrow.

"Ready?" Lily jumped up and pulled Kat onto the ice.

I watched them glide away from us, Lily a little unsteady and counting on Kat for balance.

Max sat down next to me. "Too bad Rochelle couldn't come. I can't believe Todd and Kinley are both sick."

"Yeah." I pulled off one skate and shoved my foot back into my shoe. So much for our pendant conversation. Maybe Rochelle would still change her mind. I hadn't apologized after our fight, hadn't even spoken to her, and I was about to leave without saying goodbye. "You should talk to her about the pendant as soon as you can. I don't think she'll speak to me."

"Of course she will." His eyes narrowed as he picked up on the intensity of my tone. "I'm sure we'll have a few minutes to talk to her tomorrow. There's still plenty of time."

"Right." I kicked off my other skate and pulled on my shoe. "Delgado? When the day comes that I have to face Griff, will you tell them all it's okay? Tell them I'm thankful I had a real family for a while."

Max's eyebrows furrowed to a deep V. "You just said *when.* Don't you mean *if?*"

I should have been more careful with my wording. All afternoon, I had been giving him directions for what-if scenarios, the best I could do to leave last messages for the ones I cared about. *If I have to leave, keep the truck running for Kinley. If Griff comes for me, never let Kat forget her food is the best I've ever tasted. If I disappear, tell Rochelle there's nothing she could have done to prevent it.* He had agreed, but every time I mentioned my potential departure, his shoulders stiffened and the muscles in his face tightened.

"It just feels inevitable." I shivered, even under my heavy coat. "You have to remember everything I told you. It's important."

"No worries." He knocked his knuckles against his head. "I have it all in here. But I think you have to quit dwelling on the worst-case scenario. That almost never happens. Unless you know something—"

"No, of course not." I stood and shoved my hands into my pockets.

"Well then, relax." Max stretched his arms over his head and leaned back against the bench. "It's been weeks since Rochelle escaped from Molly and nothing bad has happened."

"I'd rather prepare for the worst. Just in case." A train whistle blared in the distance, reminding me my time was running out. "Can you make sure Kat and Lily get to the booth safely? If I don't get back in time to do it myself?"

"Sure." Max eyed me suspiciously. "Where are you going?"

"To get us all hot chocolate. Before everyone starts cleaning up." For a second I thought he would see through my lie, but Max, ever trusting, just nodded. I wanted to say more, some kind of goodbye or thank you, but instead I waved at Kat and Lily as they skated by, then turned and walked away.

As I walked under the glaring strands of lights into the thinning crowd around the food booths, my mind tormented me with all I had left unfinished. If only I had more time. If only I had never told Rochelle about the pendant when I found it in her dad's truck.

"Hey Charlie!"

I glanced in the direction of Lareina's voice and spotted her standing in line with Nick. They both waved and then she jogged over. "Hey. I got the note you left for me." She paused to catch her breath. "I'm sorry too. I know you're trying to protect Rochelle and the last thing I want is for her to get hurt, but we have to look at the bigger picture, or at least what we can see of it."

The only part of the picture that mattered to me was keeping Rochelle with her family and out of danger, but I nodded.

Lareina smiled and adjusted her hat with both hands. "Yesterday, when you came by to talk to me, I was at the library with Nick." She paused and glanced around. "We haven't gotten to this part in my story yet, but there's something you should know. Susan, the girl who gave me the pendant, lied about her name. While I was at Oak Creek, I found out she was actually Ava Welch."

Nodding, I tried not to reveal any emotion. Welch was one of the scientists on the research team. I had read the news reports with Rochelle and Max about the dead-end murder investigation that only became murkier when the daughter's body was found weeks later in San Antonio. It was another piece of the puzzle I should have put into place when I heard the details of Lareina's story. "Nick and I found Ava's uncle, and we're going to Lincoln to talk to him tomorrow. We're hoping he can shed some light on how Ava's dad got involved with the research team and who commissioned them in the first place."

When we read the news reports, I had assumed The Defiance had killed the Welch family for their pendants. But if a detective working for the TCI had killed the daughter . . . "You're hoping he'll say it was the TCI?" It was easy to follow Lareina's line of investigation.

"I'm hoping for answers." She slid her hands into her pockets. "After everything I witnessed on my way here, I have to know the truth about the pendants."

I admired her for seeking answers to her questions after I had spent a year avoiding the truth, but there was one fuzzy detail I needed her to clear up for me. "Lareina, what happened to your pendant? Did the detective take it from you and turn it over to the TCI? Is that why you've centered your investigation on them?" After writing about her many close calls, it was the likely ending I had imagined for her story.

She looked down at her boots. "I have to tell the story in order, and we're not there yet." Her eyes met mine, and I wondered what emotions she read from my expression. Disappointment, probably. It was going to be hard to leave without knowing what happened to her pendant. "Once Rochelle's aunt leaves, I'll start coming over again."

"I understand." As much as I wanted to finish Lareina's in- credible story—one I wouldn't have believed if I hadn't experi- enced my own unbelievable circumstances in Maibe—I couldn't stay and open the door for Griff to come looking for me. Maybe I was never meant to learn the truth.

"I got us the last two pretzels." Nick handed Lareina one of the small bags and wrapped his arm around her. "Hey, Charlie."

"Hey. It looks like they're closing things down." I had to get going or I would miss my train.

"I guess the festival is over for this year." Lareina looked up at the strands of lights. "I should get back to the home for children. The director was nice enough to cover my shift for a few hours so I could enjoy the festival."

Nick nodded. "And we have a busy day tomorrow." They looked at each other with knowing glances.

"I should go too. I promised everyone hot chocolate." I took a few backward steps then stopped. "It was a good idea to encourage Rochelle to do her own research. She deserves the chance to make an informed decision. Just remind her she also has to look out for herself." Before either of them could reply, I headed toward the hot chocolate booth before circling behind it and looping back toward the train station.

As I passed through the fairgrounds gate, I stopped, feet planted in the snow. Laughter and the jingle bells from the sleigh rides compelled me to return to my friends, but there was no turning back. I walked away from my family and the only place I'd ever wanted to stay.

CHAPTER 14

ROCHELLE

December 8, 2090

"'m fine, Rochelle." Kinley picked up her open text book from the couch cushion as I covered her with a blanket. "If I'm just sitting here, I might as well accomplish something."

"You're shivering." I closed the book and placed it on the coffee table. "And you're supposed to be resting. Do you want me to make you another cup of tea?" I had spent the evening coaxing Kinley and Todd to swallow chicken noodle soup and stirring honey into tea.

"Studying makes me feel better." Kinley looked at the book, too far away for her to reach. "I hope I did okay on my test today. If I failed . . ."

"I'm sure you aced it. Now, stop worrying and close your eyes." I kissed her forehead and returned to my armchair pulled up next to Todd's chair. He sat with the side of his face pressed against the back cushion, watching the weather man on TV report a gloomy weekend of freezing fog and icy conditions.

"Maybe it's not such a bad time to be sick." He pulled the blanket up where it had slipped off his shoulder.

I took his icy hand and squeezed it. "See. You'll get all of the bad stuff over with and then life can be nothing but good."

"You should read some more." He smiled and nudged *The Great Gatsby* toward me. "At the rate we're going, I'll be caught up in literature by Valentine's Day." I had spent most of my time with Todd reading the books he'd missed and helping him complete the reports Emma had assigned. He assured me he had math under control, which was a relief because, despite being at lessons for the past six months, I didn't know what I was doing.

As I reached for the book, a commotion of voices clamored in from the kitchen.

"It's about time," Kinley groaned. "They should have been home an hour ago."

"Rochelle? Kinley?" Kat rushed in, scanning the room desperately through eyes puffy from crying.

"Kat, what's wrong?" Kinley sat up too quickly and pressed a hand to her forehead.

"He's gone." Kat stepped toward me as Max and Audrie entered the room behind her. "Emma and Lily are still looking for him, but Audrie made me come home."

My heart sank. *Keppler.*

"Once a runaway always a runaway." Audrie stood with her hands on her hips, clearly annoyed. "I told you the kid was trouble."

"Wait, Charlie's missing?" Kinley swung her legs off the couch to face our aunt. "What did he say? Why wasn't he with you?"

Max stuffed his hands in his pockets and looked down at his socks. "He said he was going to get hot chocolate, but he didn't come back."

"I knew I should have been there." Kinley stood on wobbly legs, and Kat gripped her elbow to steady her. "We have to call the police."

"Why? Do you think he got kidnapped?" Audrie laughed, a brittle sound. "At the festival? In Maibe? He'll be back when he gets cold or hungry."

Max raised his eyebrows at me and nodded his head toward

the next room. As Audrie and Kinley argued, I followed him into the library.

"I should have stuck with him." He pressed both hands to the top of his head. "All day he's been telling me what I need to do when the time comes for him to face Griff, and I was supposed to tell you there's nothing you could have done . . ."

"Max." I gripped his shoulders. "Take a breath. Keppler and I haven't spoken since we argued on Wednesday. Maybe he left to prove some point about the pendant?"

"I don't know. I don't think so. We had a plan to talk to you about it tonight, but then you couldn't come, and now . . ." Max rubbed his face with one hand.

I glanced at the empty doorway and lowered my voice. "You think I should tell Audrie about the pendant too?"

Max nodded. "I think you have to do something. You've been telling Audrie and Molly for months that you don't have it, but neither of them seem to believe you."

"You're right. Keppler's right. I should have at least talked it out with him."

"You can still do that when he gets home." Max pulled his stocking cap over his head. "I'm going out to look for him. Last time he disappeared he was in my garage, so with any luck . . ."

"I'll come with you."

"No, Rochelle." Max slid a hand to the back of his neck and slipped the pendant over his head. "You stay here with this just in case." He closed it in my hand. "You'll be safe with Audrie, and I'll call you in an hour whether I find him or not."

"Okay, just be careful." I hugged Max, feeling unprepared for the dangers that may or may not be waiting.

He hugged me back, tighter than usual. "We'll find him. Don't worry."

We parted ways in the dining room, and I returned to the living room where Kat sat in my chair next to Todd. "Where are Kinley and Audrie?"

Kat sniffled and rubbed her cheek with her sleeve. "Audrie went upstairs to change, and Kinley went to call Alexander and find out if Charlie said anything to him that'll help us find him."

I sank into the chair with my sister and enfolded her in my arms. "It'll be okay."

"No, it won't. We were having so much fun. I should have known. Every time things are good, it all comes crashing down."

Any words to refute what she had said would be pointless. Instead, I held her tighter and looked at Todd, who sympathetically squeezed my sister's shoulder. I wanted to cry too, but I had so many people to take care of that I couldn't afford to break down.

"I have to check." Footsteps pounded overhead, and Kinley followed our aunt down the stairs. "If he's there, then we can all stop worrying. Please, Aunt Audrie. This time I need your help."

"Kinley, you're sick and it's freezing outside. You need to be in bed."

"What's going on now?" Kat lifted her head but remained huddled against me.

Kinley looked like she wanted to throw up, but forced a smile. "A few days ago, Charlie asked if he could stay at Alexander's this weekend, but I said no because Alexander would be out of town."

"You think he went there anyway?" As much as I wanted to believe it, I worried the solution couldn't be that simple.

"It's all I can come up with right now." Kinley took a side step toward Audrie. "I called Alexander's hotel, but he didn't answer the phone. I don't know what else to do."

"Fine." Our aunt dropped her hands to her sides. "But if he's not there, we're going to come home and wait for him to show up. He clearly chose to leave, and if you report him as a runaway, he'll be in more trouble. Find him or not, you'll come home and go straight to bed. Am I clear?" As much as I disagreed with my aunt's attitude toward Keppler's disappearance, I admired her ability to remain calm and logical. My emotions always interfered with my judgment.

"Yes." It was weird hearing my cousin pinned by the same phrases she usually used on me. "Thank you." Kinley turned to us, but her eyes locked with mine. "All of you stay right here. I mean it, Rochelle."

Max's words returned to me, and I wondered if we were in danger without Audrie, but someone had to drive Kinley. "I promise. We'll stay right here."

My eyes met Todd's, and I could see my own doubt reflected in his face. We both knew if Keppler hadn't told us where he was going, he didn't want to be found.

CHAPTER 15
CHARLIE

December 9, 2090

O rville, Kansas had been run-down when I was a kid, and it hadn't improved during the years I'd been away. Many businesses on Main Street had closed, and those that remained all had cracked display windows and peeling paint. Head down against the wind and hands in my pockets, I walked until my feet left the pavement and crunched over the gravel of the dead-end road I'd walked every day of my childhood.

In the dull moonlight, my house loomed, always dilapidated but now with broken windows and missing shingles. It didn't bother me to see the house falling apart, but sitting on the front steps, Griff, as big and intimidating as ever, stopped my feet.

"Hey, kid. I was worried you wouldn't come." Although I expected him to lunge at me, he simply stood and held his hands at his sides. "I'm sorry I let you down the last time I saw you. It only took a couple of months for Shane to come after the pendants again. Now I know he set you up, and I wish I would have believed you from the start."

I stared at Griff from ten feet away, trying to decide how to proceed. "You would have killed me if I hadn't gotten away."

"You know better than that, Charlie." Griff almost laughed. "You never would have gotten away if I didn't want you to. I had to set an example. Let the other guys know they wouldn't get by with undermining my authority. Shane? I could take care of that traitor, no problem. But you're my brother. I don't want you dead."

I shook my head. "We're not brothers." Any fear of meeting Griff evaporated. I wouldn't have to negotiate to save my life. Miraculously, he already believed exactly what I wanted him to, and we could argue without consequence.

"Why? Because you found yourself a new family?" He spat on the ground. "Because you believe they care about you? That you belong with them?"

"Because you and I are nothing alike. I don't want anything to do with your plans."

"You really think you're going to live happily ever after in that desolate little town." He turned and walked toward the house. "Maybe everything has gone well so far, but what happens when one of them disagrees with you and gets that temper going? Or they decide you're not worth keeping around?"

I jogged to catch up with Griff and fell into step beside him. "What's your point?"

"I invited you here for an intervention. To remind you of who you are." He walked around the house to the back. As always, it was a mess of junky cars in all stages of repair. Glass from shattered windows crunched under our feet. "You told me all about this place—it's where you learned to be a mechanic, to fight, to be your father's son. I know you have the same propensity for anger, the same lack of control."

Feeling Rochelle's arm gripped tight in my hand, I took a step back. "You don't know anything."

"I know you belong with The Defiance. We're the only kind of family you deserve." Griff leaned back on the hood of a rusty car. "It's time to come home, kid, before you do something you regret."

"What, do you have some kind of deal with my dad or

something?" I looked across the yard in all directions. "Is he going to come out and tell me I'm too worthless to deserve a family? Tell me I'm lucky you—"

"Your dad's dead."

I tried to feel relief, pity, something other than the empty numbness that gripped my entire body. "Alcohol poisoning, I suppose."

"Not exactly. I hate to deliver this news, but a few months after you . . . left, this was in the paper." He pulled a clipped article from his pocket and handed it to me. "I'm sorry. I know she was important to you."

Taking the article, I read the headline. *Family perishes in drunk driving accident.* My heart stopped as my eyes scanned the black-and-white clipping. My father, Harvey Keppler, had been driving drunk. His wife and daughter were in the car with him. He didn't slow down at the curve in the road and drove right through the guardrail and into the water. All three drowned before rescuers arrived. His son had been removed from the home years earlier and ran away from the home for children. He was presumed dead.

Tearing my eyes from the article, I lunged at Griff. "This is a trick. Tell me the truth." I only got two swings in before he shoved me away so hard I lost my footing. My hands caught me, and shards of glass sliced my palms. Pushing myself back to my feet, I went after him again until his fist caught my chin, splaying me face-first in the dirt.

My burst of anger faded and I couldn't move. It took every last ounce of strength not to cry as I thought about my sister, terrified in the back seat of a swerving car, alone as it filled with water. She was supposed to be safe. When I was eleven, I had returned home to find a goodbye note from her saying our mom had taken her to live with grandparents I had never met. I had been purposely left behind because, according to my mom, I was already on my way to becoming an abusive alcoholic like my dad. Why had my mom brought her back?

"I should have been with her." I slapped the ground, driving pieces of glass deeper into my bleeding hand. "I promised I'd get her out of here . . . I promised."

"Get up, kid." Griff gripped my upper arm and pulled me to my feet. "Take it easy. I don't want to hurt you."

Turning away from him, I picked up the article, shoved it into my pocket, and sat down on the hood of the nearest car.

"I thought it was only fair that you knew." His hand landed on my shoulder.

Sliding away from him, I rested my forehead on the mud-smeared sleeve of my coat. "What do you want?"

Griff leaned back on the car. "I want you to come home and help me finish what we started. Remember, we want to save kids like us. We want to give them an advantage so they don't end up like your sister."

That "we" crashed like cymbals in my head.

"All of your stuff is still in your room back in Kansas City. Even your notebooks. I read some of your stories and they're good. I should have told you, the no-reading-and-writing rule doesn't apply to us."

I bowed my head, thoughts churning. Griff deciding Shane was the culprit behind stealing his pendant was believable. Even Griff forgiving me and asking me to come back was within the realm of possibilities. But Griff tossing aside one of The Defiance's most important rules set off alarms in my head. I may not need to be scared of him hurting me, but he planned to use me to get what he always wanted. I just didn't know how. And that scared me.

"*What. Do. You. Want.*" I wiped my bleeding hand on my jeans and turned to him.

Griff sighed. "I want you to go back to Maibe for a few weeks, find the pendant, and then bring it to me when I tell you the time is right. I want Auggie Aumont's pendant."

"It's not there. Molly wanted it. Rochelle looked for it and I helped."

"Molly thinks this Rochelle knows a lot more than she's admitting." His brow furrowed. "If you're really as close to her as Molly says, you should be able to get that information out of her. We both know you're good at conning people. Almost as good as you are at writing."

"Why would I steal from the people who helped me?"

"If you really care about them, taking the pendant and running would be the best way to repay them. Before you pull something like your dad. Look at how well you controlled your anger against me a few minutes ago. And I'm not the one who hurt Isabelle."

"I would never . . ." I slid off the car and stumbled forward. "I'm not like him."

Griff laughed. "Go back to Maibe, Charlie. Find the pendant, say your goodbyes, make up whatever you want, and you'll come home to a hero's welcome in time for the new year."

I shook my head. "What about Molly? The pendant isn't enough for her. She wants Rochelle to join her in The Defiance."

"I keep telling her that's a waste of time." He shrugged. "If we're going to include a third partner, I want him to be you."

"What if I just stay here?" I didn't want to help Griff, and I didn't want to hurt Rochelle. Every instinct screamed at me to run away from all of it. "Maybe this is where I belong."

He stood. "Take your time to think about it. Stick around here for a while and enjoy the nasty winter weather coming in. You'll go back sooner or later." He reached in his pocket, pulled out a wad of bills, and peeled off two. "Take care of yourself, kid. I have to get back, but we'll have plenty of time to catch up soon. I know you'll do the right thing."

I nodded and took the money, voicing a thought I'd had since the moment Griff heard about the pendants. "If you had never found out about the pendants, everything would be better right now."

"The pendants are a good thing, Charlie, not the imminent doom you're imagining. You always trusted me before."

"Trust" wasn't the right word. I wanted to believe we could be brothers, that we were looking out for each other, that even when we hurt people, stole from them, blackmailed them, we were doing it for the greater good. All of those delusions had been shattered by the pendants, and I still didn't want Griff to leave me alone in Orville.

"See you soon, kid." He turned, shoved his hands into his pockets, and disappeared into the darkness.

I watched him until he vanished, then turned back to the crumbling house that had never been my home. My family was gone because I hadn't been there. I could never go back to Maibe and lie to the Aumonts just to take the pendant and run. But if I did, if I joined Griff and proved my loyalty with Auggie's pendant, I could protect Rochelle and everyone else in Maibe.

CHAPTER 16
ROCHELLE

December 10, 2090

I slowly pulled the door to Kinley's room shut so I wouldn't wake her and tiptoed down the stairs, still wearing the skirt and blouse I had worn to church. In the living room, Todd sat on the couch, and Max and Kat each sat in one of the armchairs.

Audrie had dropped us all off at home after church. She had continued to the train station to meet with her partner, who was passing through and had files she needed for a case they were working.

I fell back onto the couch next to Todd and rested my head on his shoulder. Between worrying about Kinley, who wasn't feeling any better, and Keppler, who hadn't shown up or called, I had only gotten a few hours of sleep.

"How's Kinley?" Kat asked.

"Still sound asleep. She probably doesn't even know we were gone for an hour."

Todd's arm enveloped me and his cheek rested against the top of my head. I closed my eyes and enjoyed his warmth around me. At least he was feeling better.

"If we could just figure out where Keppler would go." Max slumped in his chair. "I should have paid more attention to what he said. I knew he wasn't acting like himself."

"It's my fault." I opened my eyes so I wouldn't be lulled into sleep. "I should have talked to him after we argued."

"I was talking to him and it didn't help." Kat crossed one ankle over the other. "I think it's Audrie's fault, and Alexander's. If he wouldn't have had his stupid meetings, Charlie could have stayed with him instead of feeling uncomfortable with Audrie around."

"It's not Alexander's fault his meeting was the same weekend as Audrie's visit." Max stood. "When he gets home tomorrow, he'll know what to do."

Kinley had talked to Alexander on the phone several times. He couldn't get a train back until Monday morning because of weather delays, and he had no idea where Keppler could be.

"I bet he will." Kat rolled her eyes and crossed her arms in front of her. "More like he abandoned us when we needed him the most."

Before Kat and Max could break into a fight, a shrill *brrriiing* filled the house. All of our heads snapped to the phone sitting on an end table by the window. We all froze in place until it rang again, and I sprang to my feet, pulling it to my ear before it woke Kinley.

"Hello?"

"Is Rochelle Aumont there?" an unfamiliar male voice asked.

"This is Rochelle." The others looked at me curiously but I could only shrug.

"Hold on." A loud clattering and muffled voices echoed in my ear.

"Rochelle, it's Molly." The voice on the other end of the line didn't have to identify herself. "I'm glad you answered the phone. That makes this easier."

"What do you want, Molly?" I imagined if I ever talked to her again I would be angry, but my chest flooded with relief and my voice remained calm and steady.

Todd mouthed, *Hang up.* Kat's eyes went wide as she leaned

forward in her chair, and Max darted across the room and pressed his head to the phone next to mine.

"First of all, I want to apologize for the way things turned out at our last meeting. I hoped for a different outcome." When I didn't reply, she continued. "More urgently, I have information about Charlie. That is, if he isn't home yet."

"He's not." I gave Max a warning glance not to make a sound. "What do you know?"

"He had a meeting with Griff in his hometown of Orville, Kansas early on Saturday morning. Griff gave him the money to get home, but he was concerned Charlie felt conflicted about returning."

"Why are you telling me this?"

"Because I owe you." Molly sounded sincere. "If you want him back, you'll have to go get him. He was outside of the house he grew up in the last time Griff saw him."

Before I could say another word, a loud click snapped in my ear followed by the dead line buzz. I lowered the phone to its cradle. Max's eyes were wide with excitement.

"Rochelle, what's going on?" The hesitation in Todd's voice revealed worry and dread.

I paced back and forth as I recounted every word Molly had spoken.

"What does The Defiance want with Charlie?" Kat's eyes followed me, the color drained from her face. "I thought they just wanted the pendants."

"That's not important right now." I hoped my sister wouldn't ask any more questions. "We have to decide what to do."

"We'll go get him, of course." Max bounced from the window to the Christmas tree and out of the room.

"You can't trust her, Rochelle." Todd stood stiffly and stepped into my path to stop my pacing. "This is probably a trap, just like everything else."

"But what if it's not?" Thoughts raced through my head and I couldn't catch my breath.

"Right here." Max came in with a book of maps, and his finger pressed to an open page. "Orville, Kansas. It's a three-and-a-half to four-hour drive. If we leave after everyone goes to sleep, say midnight, we can get Keppler and be home in time for breakfast."

"Who's we?" Todd's eyes locked with Max's.

"Rochelle and me. Who else?" He tossed the book of maps onto the couch. "She's the only person who can talk any sense into Keppler, and I'm not letting her go alone."

"I don't want her going at all." Todd gripped my hand. "It's too dangerous for both of you. We have to tell Kinley or Emma. We need help with this."

"If Audrie finds out, none of us will be going anywhere." Kat stood. "We have to figure this one out ourselves."

"Agreed." Max pressed his hands to the top of his head. "Sorry, Todd, I know it's risky, but we'll be careful. I'll take care of Rochelle."

"That doesn't make me feel any better." Todd turned me toward him, face drawn tight with concern and eyes wide, pleading. "Rochelle, you know it isn't safe. You know what happened last time."

"What if he's hurt?" There was just as much of a possibility that he was afraid to come home, which only increased my determination. I looked down at my feet, toe-to-toe with Todd's. "I can't just leave him out there all alone."

"I'll go to the library and do some searches to get Keppler's old address and borrow some extra fuel to make the trip. I'll be in your garage by midnight. Can you get the keys to the truck?"

"Absolutely." I would find a way. "I'll sneak out as soon as Audrie and Kinley are asleep."

"Rochelle. Max." Todd's voice broke through our planning. "Think about this for a minute. You don't know where you're going. The weather is supposed to get really bad. And since Charlie isn't being held against his will, just let him come home when he's ready."

"You should all know I would come and find any of you if you went missing. Even if the last conversation we had was the worst argument." I focused my attention on Todd, who knew everything Keppler had said and hoped Kat wouldn't ask. "I have to fix this."

"I'm going with you," Kat broke in, hands on her hips.

"No, definitely not." I watched her eyes narrow.

"Why? Because only you get to do dangerous things?" Her voice was loud enough I worried it would wake Kinley. "Because I'm not brave like you and I'll mess everything up?"

"No." I gripped her shoulders to quiet her. "Because I'm the one who needs to apologize to Keppler, and someone has to stay here and take care of Kinley."

"What about me?" My cousin came down the stairs, rubbing her forehead.

"We're worried about you," Kat replied smoothly. "You still look awful."

"Thanks for that reminder." She trudged to the couch and sat down. "Did the phone ring earlier?"

"Wrong number," I lied.

"Oh." Her shoulders slumped in disappointment. "I was hoping it was Alexander or Charlie."

"What do you guys think about blueberry pancakes for brunch?" Audrie walked into the room and my heart skipped in my chest. I hadn't heard her come in. How much of our conversation had she overheard?

Kat sighed and sat down next to Kinley. "We don't have any blueberries."

"No problem." Audrie plastered an overly cheerful smile on her face. She'd been trying to help out around the house, but Kat and Kinley weren't cooperating and I'd been too distracted to give her the visit she deserved. "I'll stop at the store. Come on, Todd, Max. I'll drop you guys off at home while I'm out. The girls and I need to have some family time."

"They *are* family," Kat said, frowning.

Audrie and I turned to Kinley, both of us hoping for different outcomes. As much as I understood my aunt wanting to spend more time with us, I didn't see any reason for her to be rude to my friends.

Kinley sighed. "She's right, guys. Audrie came all this way to visit us and we've been terrible hosts. Todd and Max can come over any other time."

"It's okay." Todd nudged Max with his elbow. "We both have families waiting for us too." He hugged me and whispered, "Call me as soon as you can." Then out loud said, "I'll see you tomorrow."

Max gave me a one-arm hug. "Midnight," he whispered before pulling away and waving at Kinley and Kat.

"See you around." I waved as they left with Audrie, knowing Max's heart was set on rescuing Keppler, and my conversation with Todd wasn't finished.

"Sorry, guys." Kinley melted into the cushion so her head rested on the back of the couch. "I just don't have the energy to fight with her when she'll win anyway."

My cousin's easy surrender formed deep cracks in the once firm ground beneath my feet. "Maybe you should go back to the doctor." I sat down and touched the back of my hand to her warm forehead. "This is the third day you've had a fever."

"If I'm not feeling better by the time Alexander gets here

tomorrow, I promise I'll make him drive me to the doctor." Her eyelids hovered half closed. "For now, we just have to get through today with Audrie." So much for the weekend I planned to bring my family together.

"Kat and I have everything under control." I stood and fluffed the throw pillows for Kinley to rest her head. "We'll help Aunt Audrie with brunch, and then we'll spend the entire day with her." I wanted to get to know my aunt, to ease into a comfortable conversation about the pendant and gauge the TCI's plans for it. If only I had more time and less distractions.

"Thanks, guys." Kinley laid her head on the pillows and curled her knees toward her chest as Kat covered her with a blanket. "I'm never grounding either of you ever again."

My sister took my arm and pulled me through the dining room and into the kitchen. "I bet we'll both be grounded by this time tomorrow."

"Not both of us. Just me." I walked to the sink and looked out the window at the gray morning, the fog thick enough to blur Kinley's old house across the street. "I'll take the blame for everything."

PART 2

DOING THE RIGHT THING

CHAPTER 17
ROCHELLE

December 11, 2090

"That has to be the place." Max pointed to the last run-down house on a dead-end street. The truck crunched over the gravel road directly in front of the house, and I put it in park. We had left Maibe just after midnight, but thick fog and a missed turn had almost doubled the expected three-and-a-half-hour trip. Fortunately, Max's extra fuel had meant we didn't get stranded.

After turning off the engine, I leaned back in my seat and let my muscles relax. "Todd was right about the bad weather. Remind me to never drive in the fog again." I had spoken to Todd on the phone twice when I snuck away between playing board games and watching movies with my family. Both times he begged me to tell Kinley instead of looking for Keppler myself. I had insisted Max and I had everything under control. Our last conversation would have turned into a fight if Audrie hadn't yelled for me to come downstairs.

"I'll drive us home. It's only fair." Max leaned toward the windshield, observing the muddy yard scattered with trash. "And don't worry about Todd. He's never been able to stay mad at you before. He won't start now."

I handed the keys to him, exhaustion coursing through me. Max, on the other hand, could run on the promise of adventure and caffeine for days.

"Do you really think he's here?" Although the fog gave everything a fuzzy-around-the-edges appearance, I could see the broken windows and sagging porch—and the lack of Molly or her sidekicks—clearly enough. There were plenty of places they could hide, but I didn't expect a trick. The urgency in her voice when we spoke on the phone told me it was important to her overall plan that Keppler return to Maibe. I would have to deal with her, but I could figure that out after Keppler was safe.

"There's only one way to find out." Max pushed his door open and started toward the house.

Running my apology to Keppler through my head, I got out of the truck to follow, but a hand gripped my shoulder and yanked me toward the back bumper. "Max!" I struggled against the arms restraining me until cold metal pressed against my throat.

"This is my territory," a gruff voice growled next to my ear. "Why are you here?"

"We're just looking for our friend." Max approached slowly with his hands up in front of him. "We don't want any trouble."

"Those vehicles around back belong to me now." He clutched my elbow too tightly and kept his knife to my throat. "The family's dead. They don't need 'em."

I didn't dare say a word for fear any movement would irritate the sharp edge of the knife.

"We don't want anything that belongs to you." My friend took a deep breath. "Just let her go and we'll get out of here." I'd never heard Max's voice shake with uncertainty, and that scared me more than the unpredictable stranger.

"How about a trade." It wasn't a question. "Give me that truck and you can have the girl."

"Let go of her." Keppler's familiar voice rang out as running footsteps crunched on the gravel toward us.

The man lowered the knife but kept an iron grip on my arm. "I found her first."

"Then I'll fight you for her." Keppler's hands curled into fists as he skidded to a stop in front of me. Despite the cold, he wore only jeans and a short-sleeved T-shirt. He wasn't wearing his glasses and his lip was split.

"Fine." The man tossed his knife aside. "But if I win, I get the girl and the truck."

Before I could move, he shoved me away from him. I slammed into Max, who had been inching toward me, and we both landed on the muddy lawn.

By the time I sat up and got my bearings, Keppler and the man were on the ground in a flurry of kicking and punching. Max scrambled to his feet and dove into the fight.

Scanning dirty papers and discarded bottles, I glimpsed the knife in a shallow puddle behind me, crawled to it, and picked it up. When I turned back to my friends, Keppler sat on the ground, face contorted in pain, right hand clutching his left shoulder. Max gasped for air, struggling to escape the choke hold the stranger held him in. Finally getting a clear look at the man's face, I realized he was much younger than I expected, maybe in his twenties. He was thin but muscular, and clean shaven to reveal a face marred by scars.

"Let go of him." I stood shakily, gripping the knife in my hand.

"Or what?" The man's cold eyes met mine as he squeezed Max tighter.

"Or I'll call out my backup." Keppler lifted his sleeve to reveal the capital D branded on his arm.

The man shoved Max away from him and stumbled to his feet. "You're bluffing."

"We always travel in a pack, and this town is ours." With a

groan, Keppler forced himself to his feet. "If you get anywhere near this property again, you won't live to see the next sunrise."

The man staggered backwards when Keppler took a step toward him. He looked around as if he expected others to jump out from behind the house and materialize in the tree line.

"What do you guys think?" Keppler shouted into the mist slowly soaking us all. "Should we give him a head start?"

"I don't want any trouble." The man glanced over one shoulder and then the other as he backed away. "I'm outta here. It's all yours." He turned and ran down the road we had just driven up, vanishing into the fog.

"That was crazy." Max sat in the mud, coughing through his words. "That guy wasn't afraid of you, but when he saw your arm . . . Do you really have backup?"

"No. What are you doing here?" Keppler's face contorted in pain and he clutched his shoulder. "Do you know what could have happened?"

His eyes burned into mine and I let the knife fall to the soggy ground. "We've been worried about you all weekend." I helped Max to his feet.

"You could have told me you were taking off," Max said sullenly.

"I didn't tell you because I didn't want you here. How did you find me?"

I looked at Max and he cringed. "Molly called me."

"Aumont, how many times have I told you . . ." He took a sharp breath, squeezed his eyes shut, and then without another word, turned and limped toward the house.

I surveyed Max, nose bleeding and shadows of bruises already spreading along one side of his jaw. "You okay?"

"This is nothing." He looked down at his filthy clothes. "Good thing I had those puddles to break my fall." My friend shoved his shaking hands into his pockets. "Are you okay?"

I touched my throat, still feeling the cold metal of the knife. "I'm fine. Let's just get Keppler and get out of here."

"Just stay close." Max looped his arm through mine and we walked to the lopsided front porch where Keppler sat with his left arm bent oddly across his abdomen, face scrunched in agony.

"Get back in the truck and go home now." Keppler didn't look up. "I've told you over and over that the world is dangerous. Do you believe me now?"

"If you're trying to convince me Maibe is the only safe place on Earth, then no, I don't believe you." Max tilted his head at the collapsing porch. "Although being raised by wolves would have been better than growing up in this place."

I nudged him with my elbow and extended my hand to Keppler. "Come on, let's get out of here. We can talk on the way home."

He shook his head. "Maibe isn't my home. I'm back in The Defiance, and getting your pendant is my new mission."

"And you're actually going to do it?" Max let go of my arm and sank to his haunches, trying to see Keppler's downturned face.

"No. I'm staying here and you two are going home." His earlier irritation faded to pleading. "If I disobey Griff, I'm dead. Might as well get it over with."

I sank to the step beside him. "You can't stay here. It's freezing and you're hurt."

"I deserve worse." His breathing hitched then he continued. "They're all dead. I promised to protect her . . . to get her out of here . . ."

I took the newspaper clipping he pulled from his pocket, and Max sat next to me to read it.

"Isabelle wasn't supposed to be here." Keppler covered his face with his right hand. "I don't understand why they came back."

"There's no way we're leaving you here all alone." I wanted to hug him, but afraid I would hurt him, I patted his knee instead. "You helped us, now let us help you. Where's your coat?"

He lowered his hand and shivered. "Right inside the door. I was sleeping before you got here."

Max jumped up. "I'll get it."

To my surprise, Keppler took my hand and held it tight. "The whole place has been cleaned out. Everything's gone . . . I don't know what I'm supposed to do."

"I know it's hard, but we're here for you." My hand squeezed his, wrapped in dirty scraps of material I recognized as pieces of the hoodie he had been wearing Friday. "What happened to your hands?"

"Broken glass." His blue eyes dulled. "Aumont, you have to say, right now, you'll give the pendant to your aunt. You know I don't like her and I wouldn't ask you to do this unless I believed it was your best choice. You're putting yourself and the whole world in danger by holding onto that thing."

I wanted to do the right thing, not the least-wrong thing, but my choices were limited. "Okay. I'll give it to her." The fear in Keppler's eyes made me wish I had given it up the day I met Audrie. "I should have listened to you from the beginning."

Max returned with Keppler's coat and glasses.

"No, I'm sorry. The things I said . . ." He looked down at his muddy shoes and shook his head. "I don't want to hurt you."

"I know that." I took the coat from Max and held it open so Keppler could slide his right arm inside, then draped the other side over his left shoulder.

"You don't know me like Griff does. I'm just like my dad." He turned away from me. "And look what he did."

"We know better than that, *hermano*." Max descended the steps to stand in front of us. "Would your dad have taken on that guy to protect his family like you did a few minutes ago?"

Keppler just shook his head, eyes locked on the ground.

"You know Griff isn't right. He's just trying to get his way." Isn't that the same game Molly always played? Say just the right thing to get the emotional response she wanted. "Once you're warm and have something to eat, you'll be able to think more clearly. Let's go home."

Keppler didn't move. "I can't keep lying to everyone and I can't tell them the truth. It's better for me to stay here."

I leaned back against the step behind me and tucked my hands in my pockets to warm them. "Then I'll stay with you. There's no way I'm leaving you here alone."

"I'll stay too." Max sat down with his back against the wobbly railing and stretched his legs across the bottom step. "You know, right about now, Kat is making breakfast. Probably pancakes, or that ham and egg casserole. Or both."

"And if we were home, Kinley would be able to check out your shoulder." I disentangled a leaf from Keppler's hair. "You could take a hot shower and sleep in your warm bed."

"If we go . . ." He lifted his head and turned to me. "I have to tell Kinley and Alexander that I'm in The Defiance. They deserve to know who I am—"

"It won't change their minds," Max interrupted. "You know Kinley isn't going to throw you out, especially when you're injured, and Alexander will know a way to hide you from Griff. If anything, you can give him intel on The Defiance."

Keppler shook his head and squeezed his eyes shut. "You both have to let me tell them. No interrupting and no sugar coating."

"Okay." I raised my eyebrows at Max. "We won't say a word, but we'll be right there with you when you tell them."

Keppler nodded and let us help him to his feet. "Then I'm ready to go home."

CHAPTER 18

CHARLIE

December 11, 2090

"We're here." Rochelle's icy hand brushed my face. "We're home."

I opened my eyes but didn't lift my head from her shoulder as Max guided the truck into the ice-coated driveway and parked next to Alexander's vehicle. The last sixty miles of our trip had taken three hours due to the slippery roads. The gas indicator had been on empty for the last hour.

"I've never been so happy to park in my life." Max cut the engine, one hand still gripping the steering wheel so tightly his knuckles were white.

Rochelle nodded and looked longingly at the house where warm light glowed in every window against the dreary gray of the winter afternoon. We all shivered. The heater in the truck barely worked well enough to keep the windshield defrosted, and our clothes were still damp from being out in the rain.

"I can't go inside until I talk to Kinley and Alexander." Maybe it would be less humiliating to be thrown out if I was already outside. Maybe it would be easier to leave if I didn't walk back into the warmth and comfort of the home I couldn't keep.

"Remember when we thought we'd be home before breakfast?" Max cupped his hands and breathed into them. "Do you think they noticed you're missing?"

I forced myself to sit up, groaning as the jolt of pain shot across my chest and down my left arm.

"They noticed." Rochelle nodded toward the house.

Alexander half ran, half slid toward us on the icy sidewalk with Kinley right behind, pulling on her coat.

I remained in the truck as Max and Rochelle slipped out through the driver's side door. Watching through the windshield, I couldn't help but hear them through the open door.

"Todd told us where you went. He said you should have been back hours ago. How could you pull something like that?" Kinley's hoarse voice conveyed more exhaustion than anger, and her grip on Alexander's arm reminded me she hadn't been feeling well the night I left. "What happened to you guys?" Her eyes scrutinized their muddy clothes and Max's injuries before landing on me, slumped in the truck.

"It's too cold out here, Kinley." Alexander helped her into the second sleeve of her coat. "You take these two and I'll get Charlie. We can figure everything out inside."

Kinley nodded, wrapped one arm around Rochelle and the other around Max, then steered them toward the house.

Alexander shuffled his feet to my side of the truck and opened the door. "You have no idea how worried we've been." By the concern on his face, I knew I looked pretty bad. "Let's get inside where it's warm and let Kinley take a look at you."

"I can't go in there until I tell you the truth." Blinking hard, I swallowed the lump in my throat. "You won't want me inside. You'll hate me."

"You could never do anything to make us hate you." He reached his arm toward my elbow. "I don't know what's going on, but we'll figure it out inside. Come on."

Too cold and tired to argue, I let Alexander help me limp into the house, let Kinley wrap a blanket around my shoulders, and accepted the steaming mug Kat placed in front of me, though I couldn't look at her. Then, sitting at the kitchen table between Max and Rochelle, more calm and composed than I imagined possible, I explained how I joined The Defiance, why I ran, and everything that had happened since I left on Friday night. Rochelle held my hand the entire time, and although Max looked like he wanted to interrupt, he sat supportively and silently beside me with an ice pack pressed to his jaw. Alexander sat across the table with his arm around Kinley, who dabbed at her nose with a tissue. Kat leaned against the counter with an unreadable expression on her face. Audrie stood in the doorway, arms folded.

"I know I messed up." My voice started to shake now that the story was over. "You should report me to the authorities like it says in the paper."

"We can't do that." Kat broke the silence. "Not after everything he's been through."

"We'll find another way." Kinley stood and put her hand on Kat's shoulder.

"You'll report him now or I'll do it for you." Audrie stepped into the room. Her eyes locked with mine. "He should have never been here in the first place. He put Rochelle in danger—"

"No, he didn't." Rochelle interrupted her aunt with the same tone Kat usually used to challenge Kinley. "I put all of us in danger because of the choices I made..." For a second I thought she would keep her promise and reveal the truth about the pendant, but her voice trailed off.

"Enough, Rochelle." The anger in Audrie's voice only made her niece's hand grip mine tighter. "You're in plenty of trouble as it is, and this boy is a criminal."

"He's a kid and he made a mistake." Alexander stood. "He shouldn't be punished for trying to survive."

"We won't abandon him now." Rochelle's voice was soft but resolute. "He's part of our family."

"You have a lot to learn about family." Audrie took another step toward us. "Rochelle, go to your room."

"Hey." Kinley closed the space between them in a second. "You are not in charge here. If you aren't going to be helpful then go and figure out how to keep The Defiance from getting near this house. And know if you even hint to anyone that Charlie has that symbol on his arm, you will never be invited into this house again."

"How long do you really think you can hide it?" Audrie's voice rose in frustration. "When it all gets out, you'll be in just as much trouble for harboring him."

"We can talk about that later." Kinley's voice held the confidence and authority I was used to. "Right now, Charlie needs a doctor, and Rochelle and Max need some dry clothes."

Shaking her head, Audrie turned on her heel and strode out of the room.

"I can't go to the doctor." The pain was so excruciating with every movement, I tried to stifle my shivering and remain as still as possible. "I just want to take a shower and go to bed."

"I know." Kinley disappeared into the bathroom, still talking. "But from the way you're holding your arm, I'm ninety percent sure you have a fractured collarbone, and I don't like those dirty rags wrapped around your hands. Do you remember the last time you had a tetanus shot?"

"I've had worse scrapes and I'm still alive." She had asked me about my vaccination records in the past, but I'd always managed to evade her questions or imply that the home for children had taken care of my medical needs without actually lying to her. The truth was, my dad didn't believe in doctors, the home for children didn't care about my health, and I was terrified to have a needle stabbed into my arm.

Kinley reappeared with a palm-sized bandage. "Well, this should cover that ridiculous symbol, and I'll be with you every second to make sure we can keep it secret."

"Maybe you can let him rest for a few hours." Max's hand lightly squeezed my good shoulder. "He's had some rough days and not much sleep."

"Max, you need to get home to your family and get some rest." Kinley's voice was gentle. "Alexander, can you drive him? And when you get back, I'll have Charlie ready."

"But Kinley." Max's chair slid back and he stood beside me. "He hates doctors and hospitals."

"It's okay, Max." Rochelle still held my hand. "We don't have to protect him from Kinley."

"You did good today, getting everyone home safe." Kinley put her hands on Max's shoulders. "I'll take care of them for now. You go home, keep ice on your jaw, and you can come back tomorrow."

Max sighed and nodded. "Hang in there, Keppler. I'll visit first thing in the morning." He followed Alexander out the door.

"Rochelle, you've done enough too. Go upstairs, get cleaned up, and get some rest. We'll talk more when I get home."

Rochelle looked like she was about to protest, but then her head dropped forward. "Okay." She leaned toward me and whispered, "Listen to Kinley. Everything will be okay." Standing, she faced her cousin. "I'm sorry I made you worry." She trudged away, not waiting to hear her cousin's disappointment.

Kat approached us from the other side of the room. "I'll take care of Rochelle and Audrie. Don't worry." She looked at me. "And I'll have dinner ready by the time you guys get home." She hugged Kinley and then she was gone.

"Charlie, look at me." Kinley lowered herself to the chair beside me. "You've never had a tetanus shot before. Have you?"

I shook my head.

"Have you ever had any vaccines before?"

"Not that I can remember." I swallowed, trying to relieve my dry throat. "I've heard they can be dangerous." Griff warned against any doctors or medicine because the world wanted to eliminate street kids, and the whole system was against us. He could be paranoid at times, but I didn't want to take any unnecessary risks.

"We'll get your first one today. It's nothing to worry about. I promise you'll barely feel it." She cupped my face with her hand. "And if anyone asks questions, we'll tell them you went looking for your family, but you were attacked and robbed along the way. It's plenty reasonable and close enough to the truth."

I nodded. "I never should have lied to you. I never should have let you sign the guardianship paper without knowing what you were getting yourself into."

"You're right. You should have told me. And I still would have signed it." She unwrapped the bandage and carefully pressed it over the symbol on my arm until it was hidden from view. "You're part of this family and we all love you. None of that has changed."

"Everything has changed." Exhausted and overwhelmed, I blinked up at her. I didn't want to think about Griff, or deal with Audrie, or go to the doctor, but those were small problems. "Isabelle is gone and Griff knows where I am."

"One thing at a time." Kinley took both of my hands, cringing at the dirty pieces of sweatshirt acting as bandages. "I'm on your side. I know a lot of people have broken your trust, but I won't do that to you." She stood and disappeared into the bathroom.

"If I could go back, I never would have joined The Defiance." Cupboards clicked open and water sloshed into the sink. "Then I would have been there for Isabelle. I should have gone back right away." My chest ached with regret.

"You had no reason to believe she would end up back there." Kinley returned, washcloth in hand. "And you were taken to a home for children because your house wasn't safe in the first place." Her hand slid under my chin and lifted my face as the warm cloth dabbed at my cheek. "We all do the best we can, but we can't know the future and we can't change the past."

"It's still my fault." I didn't pull my face from her hand, but I couldn't meet her eyes either. "Audrie is right . . . none of you are safe as long as I'm here."

"Even if Rochelle never met you, Molly would have been here to drag her into this mess. It's a good thing she had you to warn her what she was getting into." Kinley's hand moved the washcloth across my forehead to the other side of my face. "I'm so sorry about Isabelle. I can't even imagine how hard that must be."

"Thank you. For everything." Once again, I was reminded that Kinley and I were a lot alike. She had lost most of her family, and she knew how it felt to carry all of the responsibility on her shoulders. If anyone could begin to imagine how I felt losing Isabelle, it would be her.

"I wish I could have done more, but I promise I'm going to find a way to hide you from Griff." Scooting forward, she wrapped me in a gentle hug. "Everything is going to be okay. You're not alone anymore."

Too tired to argue, I decided to let Kinley take care of me for a few days, but I would never let her take the fall for my mistakes. Griff and The Defiance were my problem to deal with, and I had to do that alone. After everything she and the others had done for me, I couldn't let them take on any more risk than they already had.

CHAPTER 19

ROCHELLE

December 11, 2090

Sitting on the couch, wrapped in a blanket, I watched the wind-driven snow gust past the bay window. Even after taking my time to shower and get dressed, Kinley and Keppler still hadn't returned from the doctor.

"I just got off the phone with Emma." Kat slipped into the room with a mug in her hand. She'd been splitting her time between making dinner and reassuring me Kinley was more worried than mad. "She's relieved you're safe, and she said she would tell Todd you're home."

"You should have told me. I would have talked to him."

"Here, drink this. You're still shaking." Kat handed me the warm mug and sat down beside me. "You can't talk to Todd right now. He's grounded for knowing about your plan and not telling anyone. It was pretty impressive when he talked to Kinley and Audrie. He was practically under interrogation, but he was so calm. He didn't even tell them I was involved."

I squeezed my eyes shut against the dull ache in my head. I'd gone too many hours without sleep but had too many unresolved problems to rest. "He tried to stop me."

"I know. He was really worried about you too." She looked down at her hands. "Rochelle, from now on, if you're going to do something dangerous, you have to talk to Kinley first. I don't like watching everyone worry that something terrible happened to you, and I don't like being afraid that they're right."

"Don't worry." I took a sip of the steaming tea. "I'm done doing dangerous things."

My sister looked at me, eyebrows raised, and I knew she didn't believe me.

"I don't want to interrupt." Audrie stood in the doorway with her hands at her sides. She had a way of keeping her footsteps silent when she wanted to make a surprise appearance. "But I need to talk to Rochelle for a minute. Can I sit with her, Kat, while you finish dinner? I'm sure everyone will be home and ready for a warm meal any minute."

My sister nodded but didn't move to get up.

"It's okay." I dreaded the conversation I was about to have with Audrie, but I had made a promise to Keppler, and it couldn't wait any longer.

Kat hugged me. "I'll be right in the kitchen if you need anything."

When she left the room, Audrie closed the French doors and sat down on the other end of the couch.

"I know the past few weeks have been difficult for you, and I want to help." She gripped one of her hands inside of the other, perhaps the closest my aunt had to a nervous tell. "I also know this isn't what you want to hear, but I think it would be best for you to move to New York with me. At least for a little while."

Only days earlier, I had promised Kinley I would never leave her. I had also encouraged my family to hear Audrie out. I decided to do just that. "That sounds like a lot of fun," I started cautiously, "but I've never been that far away from Kinley and Kat, and all of my friends."

"You would be able to call them and write to them." She

scooted a cushion closer to me. "We would even come and visit once I determined it would be safe for you."

From the moment I met her, I had questioned my aunt's intentions. Keppler said she only cared about the pendant. Kinley thought she had come for me because I reminded her of her favorite brother. "Aunt Audrie, why do you want me to move to New York?"

Her eyes brightened and she smiled. "Most importantly, so we can spend more time together. But also because it's dangerous for you to stay here right now, and I don't want you to get hurt."

"Wouldn't I be in your way though? Like when you have to travel for work. Then you'd be worried."

My aunt nodded. "I suppose I haven't explained very well. The school that you'll attend, the Advanced Education Institute, is operated by the TCI. We recruit smart, brave, innovative kids, like you, and provide them a top-notch education. You would live in the dormitories there, but any time I'm home on the weekends, you could come and stay with me."

Flattered by my aunt's belief that I qualified for an advanced education, and intrigued by the opportunity to attend something like college, I locked eyes with my aunt. "If I went there, would I become a TCI agent like you?"

"You could, but you wouldn't have to." Audrie laughed. "Most of the kids don't become agents, but some of them help us develop new technology or go on to work civilian jobs that protect our country's security." My aunt glanced at the closed door then whispered, "But all of that aside, you could help me save the world. I know you don't think you remember anything to do with your dad and the pendant, but if we had more time to talk about what we both remember, I'll bet we could figure it out together."

My heart pounded in my ears. Moving to New York with Audrie

would be an opportunity, an adventure. I would be letting my family down, but I could finish my dad's mission to save the world.

"Rochelle, are you okay?"

I nodded. She knew exactly what to say, exactly how to convince me to do what she wanted because we were so much alike. "I wish I could go with you, but I have all of my responsibilities here, and if I left . . ."

"Rochelle, about what you did today . . ." She sighed and crossed one leg over the other. "Why didn't you tell me what you were planning?"

"Because I thought you would stop me." I huddled deeper into my blanket. "Because I know you don't like Keppler."

"You're right. I don't like him. But I would have helped you if you felt it was that important."

"So you aren't going to turn him in?"

Audrie frowned. "I don't have many options there. He's not really safe here, and more importantly, none of you are safe with him here."

"But there are other options?" Forgetting about the lure of New York and a real school, I shrugged off my blanket and stood to feel more in control. "Options that don't involve Keppler getting in trouble for making a mistake."

Audrie sighed. "Each of them carry an increasing risk for everyone involved."

"If I tell you what I know about Dad's pendant"—I swallowed hard and took a breath—"will you promise to do everything you can to help him?"

Audrie's fierce green eyes burned into mine. "If you keep up these games, you're going to get Kinley and Kat hurt along with yourself. Is that what you want?"

Diverting my eyes from hers, I shook my head. "Promise you'll treat Keppler like family, like he's your nephew, and I'll tell you everything."

Audrie stood, eyes angry but expression calm. "I'll do my best."

Ignoring the iciness of her words, I held out my hand. "Then it's a deal?"

Her hand gripped mine. "Deal."

Feeling along the neckline of my T-shirt, I found the chain and slid the pendant into view. I'd hidden it in my dresser after Max returned it to me and put it back on after my shower. "Keppler found it in the seat of Dad's truck. I never knew it was there, but Keppler told me it was dangerous. He told me to give it to you." I raised my face, holding the pendant out to my aunt. "But I didn't know what my dad would want me to do."

"He wouldn't want you to get mixed up in all of this like he did." Audrie snatched it from my hand. "How long have you known about this?"

"Since the summer." I stared down at my socks. "I wanted your help, but I felt like it was my responsibility to do the right thing."

"The right thing?" Audrie's hand flashed out and gripped my wrist so tightly it hurt. "You have so much potential but so much to learn. You're just like your dad. Trusting all the wrong people and not the ones who want what's best for you."

"He wasn't wrong. He saw good in everyone." I forced myself to meet her eyes. "It's always there if you look hard enough."

"As is the darkness." She let go of my arm and dropped her hand to her side.

"I'm sorry I lied to you. It doesn't mean I don't love you." I watched for a softening in her expression, but her face remained rigid.

"I'm disappointed in you." She took a deep breath to control her voice. "But I suppose you're in enough trouble with Kinley already." So much for my aunt's earlier compliments. Both she and Kinley would forever believe I was reckless and irresponsible.

I nodded and turned away. I wanted to cry for falling short of my aunt's expectations, for causing Kinley more stress when she didn't deserve any, and for being incapable of helping Keppler with everything he was going through, but I kept my eyes dry long enough to escape.

The tears came as I rushed upstairs and intensified to sobbing by the time I crawled under the blankets on my bed. For miserable minutes, I cried into my pillow, overwhelmed by everything I had lost in my life, everything Keppler had lost in his, and the hopelessness of his situation.

"Rochelle?" A cold hand touched my face. "Rochelle?"

Blinking my way out of sleep, I looked up at Kinley, who sat on the edge of my bed. "What happened? Where's Keppler?" Wide awake with the returning memory of the past day, I sat up.

"He's downstairs, resting. He'll be in a sling for a while, but he's going to be okay."

I nodded and slid away from my pillow to sit next to her. "Good. I was really worried."

Kinley's arm wrapped around me. "Is that why you were crying?"

"Sort of." I rubbed a hand over my cheek, but the tears had dried. "Every time I try to do the right thing and help people, I just make everything worse."

"Even doing the right thing comes with consequences. That doesn't mean you shouldn't do it." It was a much gentler answer than the lecture I expected.

"Are you mad at me?" I doubted Audrie had told her about the pendant, and I wasn't ready to tell Kinley I had also lied to her for months.

"No." I watched in the mirror as her fingers parted my hair and twisted it into the same kind of braid she always wore. "We have some things to talk about after I deal with the Audrie situation. For now, I'm just relieved you're safe."

"I really thought we'd be home sooner. You weren't supposed to have time to worry."

"I know. Life is full of difficult decisions, and sometimes it's hard to know whether we're making the right ones." She finished with my hair and twisted the rubber band from her wrist around the bottom of my braid. "Don't worry. We're going to get through this."

I smiled at our reflections, almost identical sitting side by side. For months I had wanted to be just like Audrie and nothing like Kinley. I still admired my aunt for her poise, professionalism, and control over her emotions, but I didn't like the way she treated Kinley or Keppler, or that she couldn't see things from my point of view. My cousin, on the other hand, could be controlling and overprotective, but she had always been there for me. I looked up to both of them for different reasons, but any choice about the future I made would let one of them down.

CHAPTER 20

CHARLIE

December 11, 2090

I sat on the couch, leg propped up on a pillow, arm in a sling, white bandages wrapped around both of my hands. The broken glass, remnants of my dad's car projects, had slashed deep gashes into both of my palms. It felt like he was continuing to hurt me even after his death.

Kat perched on the edge of a chair pulled up close to the couch, gently holding one of my bandaged hands in hers. I had been worried she would be angry with me for leaving her at the festival, but she had told me she understood why I had to leave, she was proud of me for telling the truth, and I had made the right decision to come home for help. She believed, now that I had nothing to hide, I wouldn't leave again and I let her believe it. We'd been sitting there for half an hour and neither of us had said another word, but there was comfort in her presence and the warmth of her hand.

"I never said Rochelle was a bad kid." Audrie's voice drifted in from the kitchen. "I think she has some friends who are really bad influences. It would be best to get her away from this place and back on the right track."

If Kinley or Alexander replied, I couldn't hear over the gust of wind slamming against the bay window. They had been in the kitchen with Audrie since our awkward dinner, and the entire conversation had focused on Audrie taking Rochelle back to New

York with her. I felt bad for Kinley—still sick, a day of panic until Rochelle returned home, hours in the hospital with me, and now arguing with her aunt.

I glanced over at the chair where Rochelle slept, legs curled under her. It was for the best that she didn't have to hear the conversation in the next room. She had been quiet at dinner, sliding food around her plate while Audrie tried to convince Kinley to sign papers allowing me to work with the TCI as an informant. I was so hungry, I focused most of my attention on eating the food in front of me and avoiding Audrie's stern expression.

Kat's hand pressed mine lightly. "Can I get you anything? A glass of water or another blanket?"

"No, I'm okay." I didn't want her to let go of my hand. It was the only thing keeping me calm. She nodded and we sat in silence, listening to the roaring storm outside.

"Hey guys." Kinley entered the room, so abruptly we both jumped. "How are you feeling, Charlie?"

"I'm okay as long as I don't move." I forced a smile, hoping to take a little of the worry off her shoulders. The doctor had verified Kinley's suspicion of a broken collarbone with x-rays. He provided a sling to keep it immobilized for the next six to eight weeks, cleaned and bandaged the wounds on my hands, and injected the tetanus shot Kinley wouldn't let me talk my way out of. There wasn't much more he could do but recommend over-the-counter painkillers and ice packs to help with pain management.

"We're taking a break from the ice," Kat explained. "He's more comfortable without it on his shoulder for right now."

"Kinley, I thought you were going to bed." Alexander crossed the room toward us. "You really need to get some sleep."

"I know . . . I just have so much to do." Her eyes jumped from Kat to me to Rochelle.

"Ice packs are in the freezer, and he can have more ibuprofen in three hours. If he spikes a slight fever, it's a harmless reaction from the tetanus shot. See, I know what I'm doing, plus I have plenty of letters to write, so I'll be up if Charlie needs anything." He noticed Rochelle and smiled. "At least someone is getting some sleep."

"Don't wake her up," Kat whispered. "Then again, she won't be able to feel her legs in the morning if she sleeps like that all night."

"I can help with that." Alexander scooped Rochelle into his arms and her eyelids fluttered before her head rested against his chest. "Lead the way, Kinley."

She stood and kissed the top of my head. "Sleep tight. If you need me, send Alexander to wake me up." She squeezed Kat's shoulder. "Time for bed for you too."

Alexander followed Kinley out of the room as Kat yawned then kissed my forehead and stood. "Promise you won't disappear before morning?"

I nodded. As much as I wanted to tell her how much I cared about her, I knew it would be cruel. Not in that moment, but the day Griff came for me. If I had never met the Aumonts, I would have already been on my way across the country. Staying ahead of trouble. But Griff had provided me an opportunity to protect my family, and it would be selfish to pass it up. If I could keep the Aumonts safe from inside The Defiance, then Rochelle wouldn't have to move away.

After Kat followed the others upstairs, I heard familiar footsteps in the other room and my chest clenched. Despite the dread like cold water rising all around me, I knew what I had to do.

"Audrie?" I sat up so I could see her step into the room. "Can I talk to you for a minute, please?"

She glided toward me and sat down in the chair where Rochelle had been sleeping. "I have a minute."

"At dinner, you said if Kinley signed some paperwork, it would keep her out of trouble in case anyone finds out about the brand on my arm." I glanced at my arm, now safely concealed by the sleeve of my shirt. "What would happen to me if she signed it?"

Audrie leaned forward with her elbows on her knees. "You would stay here while your injuries heal. Then you would take up your old friend's offer to rejoin The Defiance and keep the TCI updated on his plans. We'd do everything possible to keep you safe and get you out as soon as we had the information we needed." She shook her head. "But Kinley isn't going to give anyone, especially me, even temporary guardianship of you or Rochelle."

I swallowed hard to clear the lump from my throat. "I can't help you with Rochelle, but Alexander is also my guardian. I can convince him to sign the papers if it'll protect Kinley. Would his signature be enough?"

"Yes." Audrie sat up and cocked her head to the side. "But why would you do that?"

"I don't want them to get in trouble." Fighting the pain, I sat up straighter. "They're the only family I have."

She studied me before smiling. "I may have been wrong about you after all. Let's talk it over with Alexander."

"Talk what over?" He appeared in the doorway, shoulders stiff, hands in his pockets.

Audrie leaned back in her chair. "Charlie is interested in working with the TCI as an informant, like we talked about at dinner. It's the best solution for everyone, and all we need is your signature. I have the paperwork in my bag."

Alexander looked at me and pressed his hand to the back of his neck. "And what exactly does my signature mean for Charlie?"

"It means I would have custody of him during the time he works for the TCI. Which may happen, or may not, depending on how things play out in the coming weeks." She leaned back in her chair. "It would mean Kinley faces no charges for harboring a member of The Defiance, because if he gets caught, I can say I placed him here. And it would mean Charlie has a chance to turn his mistake into a solution for this country."

"And you can guarantee he'll be safe?"

"This isn't without risk for him. While he's in Defiance territory, I won't have much control over what happens. But I'll do everything in my power to provide him with the resources he needs to remain safe and get him out as soon as we have the information we need."

"And when you're done with him, he comes back here?" The usual certainty in Alexander's voice wavered.

Audrie shrugged. "If he's still under eighteen, you and Kinley resume your role as his guardians. Just remember, if you sign the papers, I can help all of you. If you don't, you're all on your own."

I shifted to face Alexander. "I don't want to be another problem for Kinley. What's going to happen to Rochelle and Kat if she gets in trouble?"

Ignoring me, he rubbed the bridge of his nose. "When would you take him?"

"Not until he's out of that sling. A lot depends on when his old buddies reach out. If that happens before I step in, I need Charlie to contact me immediately."

"You're sure this is what you want?" Alexander sat down on the coffee table, blocking Audrie from my view. "I can look for other options. Maybe find a place for you to lay low for a while—"

"No." The word came out forcefully. "This is what I have to do. Please, help me do the right thing this one time."

Alexander sighed and nodded. It took fifteen minutes for Audrie to explain the papers and collect the necessary signatures. The three of us agreed it would be best not to tell Kinley until we knew exactly when I was leaving. Audrie gave me her card and advised me to memorize her phone number so we could remain in touch, and then she headed upstairs to get some sleep before her departure the next day.

"I don't like this, Charlie." Alexander rubbed both hands over his face. "You shouldn't be mixed up in any of this."

"It's too late for that." The realization of how long I could be away from home hit me like a punch in the stomach. "I'll come back as soon as I can. Even if I'm eighteen by then."

"It won't be that long. You heard Audrie—if things change, you might not even have to go at all." We both knew nothing would change. The Defiance wouldn't collapse during the few weeks my arm was in a sling, and they wouldn't stop terrorizing the country. "For now, you need to get some sleep."

Nodding, I propped the right side of my body in the corner of the couch to keep my left shoulder off the pillow—the only comfortable position I'd found.

He covered me with another blanket, then rested his hand on the top of my head. "I wish I could go in your place and teach that Griff to pick on guys his own size."

I kept a serious face although I wanted to laugh. "You have the wrong haircut to impersonate me. Plus, you'd have to convince him I started lifting a lot of weights."

Alexander laughed. "I suppose he'd notice the difference. Although it might be easier to pull off than trying to explain all of this to Kinley."

"She'll understand, eventually. We shouldn't worry about it yet. We have a few weeks." Six weeks before Audrie came for me, and less than a month before Griff expected me back. I closed my eyes, feeling at peace with my decision. For the moment, I was far from Griff and comfortable at home. It couldn't last forever, but if I could have a few more days, a few more weeks with my family, maybe it would be enough to get me through everything to come.

CHAPTER 21
ROCHELLE

December 12, 2090

I woke up slowly, at first aware only of the warmth and comfort of being tucked into my bed. Then the events of the past few days flooded in. I had to check on Keppler, talk to Audrie before she left, and tell Kinley the truth. Shoving the covers aside, I jumped out of bed and rushed to the guest bedroom at the end of the hall.

The bed was made and Audrie's suitcase was gone. Outside, large snowflakes poured down in front of the window. The murmur of Kinley's voice drew me back down the hall, and the phone cord led into her room. I pushed the door forward to reveal my cousin sitting on her bed, phone to her ear, writing in a notebook as she listened.

She looked up and smiled, holding up one finger to indicate she needed another minute. "That's perfect," she said into the phone. "I'll get the forms filled out as soon as I receive them and we'll see you for orientation in January. Okay. Thank you. Bye." She hung up the phone and slid it onto her nightstand.

"Good morning, sleepyhead. I'm sorry we didn't get to talk more last night." She slid to the edge of her bed so her feet rested on the floor. "My conversation with Audrie seemed to never end and then I didn't want to wake you up."

I nodded, feet frozen in the doorway, remembering my own

conversation with our aunt. "She left already?" My voice broke and tears welled in my eyes.

"Rochelle, come here." Kinley held her arms open and I rushed into them. "Audrie wanted to talk to you, but you were sleeping so tight, I wouldn't let her wake you up. She planned to stay all day, but then she got a call from work."

Unsure whether Kinley was telling the truth or just trying to make me feel better, I rubbed my eyes, trying to stop the tears.

"I don't know what's going on between you and Audrie, but I bet you would feel better if we talk about it."

Nodding, I lifted my head from her shoulder. I needed Kinley to know everything and make it better. That's what I had wanted since I found out about the pendants, but I couldn't stand to have both Audrie and Kinley disappointed in me.

As if sensing my hesitancy, she released me from her embrace and took both of my hands. "It's okay. You can tell me anything."

I cleared my throat and blinked away the tears. "Keppler found the pendant during the summer in Dad's truck. I didn't tell you because I didn't want you to have another thing to worry about. I didn't tell Audrie because I didn't know what she planned to do with it." I met her eyes, gentle with understanding. "When I told Audrie last night, she said I was putting everyone in danger. That's the first time she's ever been disappointed in me."

Kinley reached for the box of tissues on her nightstand and held them out to me. "It must not be too bad. This morning, she still wanted to take you to New York. She thinks Max and Todd are bad influences." My cousin's forehead wrinkled. "I can see where she's coming from with Max. But Todd?"

"Kat told me he's grounded." I dabbed at my eyes. If Audrie spent enough time in Maibe she would see that I was a bad influence on Todd. "He's the one who tried to convince me not to go."

"That's what I figured." She scrunched her nose. "I'll talk to Emma and see if I can get his grounding reduced."

"What about me?"

"You are too brave for your own good and the best friend anyone could ever ask for, but you're not in trouble this time."

"Are you sure you shouldn't see a doctor?" I was only half joking.

My cousin smiled, but it faded quickly. "Remember what I told you about making decisions last night?"

I nodded.

"We have some hard ones to make in the coming weeks. I couldn't sleep last night until I decided to take charge instead of waiting for the next bad thing to happen."

"Is that what you were talking about on the phone?"

She nodded. "I have a friend in Omaha who has a sister Kat's age. Her parents will let you and Kat stay with them and you'll both be able to go to a really nice school. I was just on the phone with the guidance counselor, setting up your schedules."

"How are you going to tell Kat?"

"I think we'll wait a bit." Kinley's wide eyes pleaded for my cooperation. "I've been debating this since Molly kidnapped you. Rochelle, I don't think any of you are safe here anymore." She cringed and rubbed her forehead. "Don't tell Charlie yet, but I'm going to contact an older couple my parents knew. They live an hour north of here on a farm where no one would ever think to look for him."

I took another tissue and blew my nose. "What about you? I can't leave you here alone."

"At least if you're in Omaha I can still visit you on the weekend." She wrapped one arm around me and rested her head against mine. "I know you don't want to go with Audrie, so if we stick together on what we want, I'm hoping she'll agree to let you go to

Omaha with Kat. Molly won't know where to find you, so you'll be just as safe there."

"It's not that I don't want to go with Audrie." I took a deep breath before my cousin's deluge of information pulled me under. "I just don't want to leave here."

"I don't want you to leave either. But I'll do whatever it takes to protect you." She forced a smile. "Try not to worry though. No one is leaving until after the holidays, and maybe our whole situation will be better by then."

After everything I had witnessed over the past weeks, I didn't expect the world to improve before Christmas, but I wasn't ready to shatter our hope. "Is your head okay?"

"Just a lingering side effect of my illness." She dropped her hand to her lap. "My fever is gone and I'm feeling much better compared to the weekend." My cousin smiled and nudged my shoulder with hers. "But I'm thankful for an excuse to take a few days off and stay home with you and Kat and Charlie."

I laughed with her and folded my legs under me. "Is Keppler doing okay?"

"Asleep last I checked." Kinley picked up the notebook she had been writing in earlier, closed it, and slid it under her pillow. "A broken collarbone is pretty painful, so he'll need a lot of rest and patience from us."

"He didn't even care about his shoulder when we were at his house." I closed my eyes, remembering our conversation in the cold rain. "He was so heartbroken about what happened to his sister. I didn't know what to say."

"I know. I can't even imagine." She shook her head slowly. "He told me once about how he took care of her from the time they were little kids. He's having a hard time with not being there to comfort her in those last scary moments." Looking at me, she shivered. "Rochelle, from now on, you have to promise me that we'll talk about everything. Just like we used to. Whether you're here or somewhere else."

I nodded. "Okay."

"I mean it." She gripped my shoulders so I had no choice but to look at her. "I'm not Audrie. You don't have to question my motives. I want what's best for you. That's it. I want you safe. I want you to have normal worries. I want you to have better than what I had."

My hands found Kinley's. "I know that. I've never questioned your motives, I just don't want you to have so many worries. It's not fair."

"I don't want it to be fair." My cousin blinked back tears. "I'd rather live my life under a five-hundred-pound weight of worries than ever lose any of you. I couldn't live with that." She shook her head but didn't attempt to dry her eyes.

"You won't lose us." I pulled a tissue from the box and wiped her tears. "I promise we'll talk about everything. No secrets. Just like when we were kids."

Kinley sniffled and nodded.

"And even if I have to leave, I promise I'll still call you all the time." I lay back on her bed and stared up at the ceiling. "And no matter where I am, I'll still follow your rules, so you'll know I'm safe."

"Thank you. That makes me feel better." She lay back next to me. "Remember snowy days like this when we were kids? We would make popcorn and watch movies all afternoon."

"Life was so easy back then." I turned my face to the wall of white outside Kinley's window. "We could watch movies today and pretend we don't have anything to worry about."

"I'm in. Maybe we can talk Alexander into joining us if he ever comes back from his office. He's been acting weird today, and he looks like he didn't sleep all night. I'm starting to worry about him."

"We'll let him rest during the movie." I sat up, pushing the possibility of leaving Maibe out of my mind. Nothing would change until after Christmas. I took my cousin's hand and pulled her to her feet. "There's no time to worry today."

CHAPTER 22
ROCHELLE

December 15, 2090

"Max. The prompt said our character was wrong about the time of the party." Lareina held the notebook close to her face, trying to distinguish Max's handwriting.

Kat rolled her eyes and leaned back against the couch to be closer to Keppler. "What did he write this time?"

Aaron and Lareina had visited earlier that afternoon, and we had spent an hour playing a writing game. Each of us had to add the next sentence as we passed a notebook around the circle, but Max had trouble staying on topic.

"Something about taking a left turn at the piano?" Aaron squinted over Lareina's shoulder from where he sat in the armchair with an open textbook on his lap. He was the first person I'd met who studied more than Kinley.

"It makes sense." Max knelt at the coffee table between Lareina and me. "Because wrong is the opposite of right, which is the opposite of left."

I laughed. "Wait. What?"

"Just pass it to Keppler." Max reached for the notebook. "I'll bet twenty dollars he can make it work in the story."

Keppler's face twitched into an almost smile. "Not even I can fix that."

"Plus, you only have three dollars." Lareina handed Max his wallet and passed the notebook to Aaron.

"How did you . . ." Max patted his back pockets, then took the wallet and studied it. Keppler laughed and Kat raised one eyebrow.

Lareina's cheeks turned pink. "Sorry, I couldn't help myself. I'm experimenting with ways to use my skills for good." She turned to Aaron. "Just don't tell Nick until I can prove it's actually working."

"Can you teach me?" Ever since my close call in Orville, I couldn't stop thinking about how defenseless I was. If I had to leave Maibe, it only made sense to be prepared.

"How to pick pockets? You don't need to know that."

"Or maybe I do. What if I end up in this weird situation and the one thing I need to save my life is in a stranger's pocket?" I ignored Keppler, who was shaking his head at me. "Remember how picking that lock got us away from Molly and back home? That could come in handy."

Kat's shoulders stiffened. "You don't need to know any of that, Rochelle, because you're going to stop doing dangerous things."

"It won't hurt her, Kat." Max stood, stuffed his wallet back into his pocket, and sat down on the edge of the couch cushion. "Maybe we should all learn a few things. Just in case."

"I said no," Kat snapped.

"Come on, Kat." Max continued in a joking tone. "I bet—"

"All you ever do is get Rochelle in trouble." Kat pinched Max's upper arm. "If you want to be reckless, fine. But leave her out of it."

Max let out a yelp as he stood and took two clumsy steps away from my sister. "Geez. I'm sorry."

"Whatever." Kat stood, still glaring at him. "I have to start dinner. Lareina, Aaron, do you want to eat with us?"

Lareina forced a smile. "Thanks, but Aaron and I should get

back. Nick will be home from his shift soon, and he's planning to cook for us. I'm equally curious and worried."

Since Aaron was released from the hospital, Lareina had been staying with him during the day while Nick checked groceries at his new job. Then she returned to the home for children in time to help with dinner, bedtime, and her overnight duties.

"That's okay. Maybe next time." Kat walked around the coffee table. "I have a few things to send with you, so you'll have something to eat just in case dinner doesn't turn out." She glanced at Max standing apart from our little group, shook her head, and left the room.

"She doesn't usually . . ." Keppler looked from Max to the French doors my sister had disappeared through. "She's just a little on edge."

"No need to explain." Aaron closed his book and reached for his crutches. Lareina pushed them within reach. "You guys have had a lot to deal with." No one had questioned Kinley's cover story about Keppler running away to find his family and getting robbed along the way.

Lareina stood and helped Aaron up. "If it would make you feel better to know some of the things I learned out there, I can show you sometime."

"Maybe it's not a great idea," Aaron hedged.

"I'm teaching her for survival purposes, not setting her on the path to a life of crime." She straightened the collar of his polo with one hand. "Everyone should be prepared for the worst. That's how you prevent it from happening."

"Don't we know it." Aaron sighed but his smile returned. He extended his arm to Keppler, still half sitting on the couch, and shook his hand. "Get plenty of rest and you'll be healed up in no time." Despite his own injuries, Aaron was more concerned with healing everyone around him.

"I will. Good luck with your physical therapy."

"Thanks. I have a good feeling about it." He grinned at me. "I'm registered to start studying in the medical training program in the spring. I'm already getting a head start with the books Kinley gave me."

"You'll be Doctor Aaron Swanson in no time." I hugged him, then Lareina.

Max joined the conversation to say his goodbyes, but his usual goofy grin and unremitting energy were absent. By the time I turned back from walking Lareina and Aaron to the door, he stood near the couch with his hands in his pockets.

"Are you okay, Delgado?" Keppler leaned back into the cushion and then forward again in his impossible quest to get comfortable.

Max rubbed his arm where Kat had pinched him. "Not really."

"Come over here." I sat down on the coffee table and held my hand out to him.

"Are you sure?" He started toward me anyway. "Every time I'm near you, something bad happens. Kat says so, Todd says so, even Alexander implied it."

"That's not true." I took his hand and he sank down next to me. "I choose to go on adventures with you."

Max raised his eyebrows at Keppler. "Do you want to weigh in on this?"

Keppler adjusted his glasses. "You're both just as reckless on your own as you are together. You've probably survived this long because you were together."

"See?" I wrapped my arm around Max. "Todd is overprotective, Alexander has to be an adult, and Kat is a little grumpy today."

"A little?" A sliver of a smile flitted across his face and then we were both laughing.

"Before we get too offtrack, I do have to talk to you guys about something serious." Keppler frowned down at the sling holding his arm in place. "I appreciate you guys always being there for me, and I'm thankful you brought me home. But if Griff contacts me again, I have to go and neither of you can come looking for me."

"I'm not supposed to tell you this, but Kinley has a plan." The conversation drifting in from the kitchen assured me my sister wouldn't overhear. "She knows a place where you might be able to hide out for a while."

Keppler looked interested, eyebrows quirking, then shook his head. "I'm not saying that won't work, but we always get caught off guard, and we have to be prepared for the worst-case scenario."

"But we don't have the pendant anymore," Max said.

"That doesn't matter." He wouldn't meet our eyes. "If Griff comes, I only have one choice. I belong with The Defiance and you two belong here."

"We've talked about this before." Max's shoulders stiffened beneath my arm. "Just because you haven't always lived here doesn't mean you can't belong here. You're like us, how could you think you belong with them?"

"Because nothing happens by chance." His use of that phrase twisted my stomach. "The only reason I ended up here was to make sure The Defiance never fulfilled their pendant plans. Joining Griff is the only way I can finish that job and the only way you guys can go back to normal life."

"What if I don't want to go back to normal life? Maybe you ended up here because we're supposed to help you." Max stood. "No way you're going to have all of the adventures without us. Rochelle, say something. Tell him he's wrong."

I looked at Max helplessly and my heart tore in half. If Keppler left he'd be on his own with The Defiance, but fighting with the squatter in Orville had been a reality check for me. We would be in way over our heads against The Defiance. I could never find the research that came with the pendants on my own. The only choice

I had was to work with Audrie and help her do the right thing, if she ever forgave me for lying to her in the first place.

"I think." My eyes slid to Keppler and then to the floor. "I don't want him to go, but he's right. We should be prepared for the worst, and we're no match for The Defiance."

"Fine. Take his side." Max's face crumpled back to an unfamiliar expression of despair. "I have to go."

I wanted to say something to make Max feel better, to fix everything for everyone, but no words could do that. "We should trust Kinley. She has a plan."

"A plan to separate all of us." He walked to the door then turned back. "How can we save the world then?"

He didn't wait for an answer before walking out, and I sank to the couch.

"We should have talked about this a long time ago, but I knew he wouldn't like it."

"I don't like it either, Keppler." My eyes burned, but crying wouldn't solve anything. "Max and I . . . we're both tired of saying goodbye to people we love. You have to give Kinley's plan a chance."

Keppler nodded. "Like I said before, this is only in the worst-case scenario. You let Todd leave when he wanted to find his mom. You have to understand why I'm asking you to let me go."

"Letting Todd go was the biggest mistake of my life."

Sighing, Keppler rubbed his face with one hand. "And joining The Defiance was mine. Or maybe it was letting myself believe Isabelle was safe and better off without me. I can't decide between the two."

Knowing nothing I said would make him feel any better, I took his hand instead and sat next to him for several silent minutes.

"Aumont, when you said you didn't want to disappoint your dad, you sounded so sure." He cleared his throat. "How do you know he's not gone?"

I looked at the snow-covered trees outside the window as I considered my answer. "Because I believe in heaven, and I pray all the time that he's there."

"Instead of being stuck in the waiting room?" Keppler turned to me, face twisted in uncertainty. "Kat said that can happen if your soul isn't ready for heaven."

If Keppler didn't look so serious, I would have laughed. "Kat described purgatory as a waiting room?"

"Not exactly. She said it was a miserable place where you're stuck waiting and I pictured it as the waiting room at the hospital." He turned away from me but didn't let go of my hand. "How am I supposed to figure out where Isabelle is and whether she can hear me? I don't want her to think I abandoned her."

"All you need to know is that she's watching over you. You can talk to her anytime you want, but I'm sure she already knows you didn't leave her behind."

"That's it?" He turned back to me, eyes narrowed in frustration. "I'm just supposed to talk to the air without any evidence my sister is out there?"

I gently pressed his hand to calm him. "You know how sometimes you're so busy writing, you don't look up when I walk in the room?"

He nodded.

"I could be Kinley or Kat, but something tells you it's me instead, right?"

His eyebrows furrowed in confusion. "I guess so."

"It's like that for me with my dad and my grandma. I can't see them anymore, but sometimes I just feel them in the room with me. Sometimes I dream about them and it feels so real."

Keppler's shoulders slumped a little. "I haven't had anything like that with Isabelle."

"You will." My head slid to the side so it lightly rested against his. "Just because you don't feel her now doesn't mean she isn't with you."

Minutes ticked by as we sat together quietly. Then Keppler stood, keeping his face turned from me. "I should check on Kat. She was really upset."

Even though he never looked back, I waited for him to leave before wiping a tear from my cheek.

CHAPTER 23

CHARLIE

December 18, 2090

"Every glittering moment carried them farther away from murdering pendant thieves, infected cities, and cities under siege. The train picked up speed once again, racing through darkness toward hope for a better future and the only place that had ever felt like home." I let my binder fall to the desk and looked up at Lareina, who was sitting in the armchair across from me. We had spent the past three days going over her story, and when everyone in the house thought I was sleeping, I transformed it into the narrative she wanted.

"That's perfect." She smiled and I felt relieved at the possibility I wouldn't have to rewrite the last chapters for a third time. "I couldn't have described it better."

Miserable after Griff's revelations about Isabelle and running on barely any sleep due to my shoulder, I had avoided small talk. Writing her story was a distraction from my own problems and a chance to learn the truth. I reached for the notebook and pen on the edge of my desk, ready to take my next set of extensive notes. "Let's continue with the next chapter then?"

"There isn't another chapter. That's the end." Lareina stood and flopped the stack of loose-leaf pages to the front of the binder. "Now it just needs a title." She took my pen and wrote "Hope For The Best" across the top. "Do you think that captures it?"

"It's fine. But you never explained what happened to the

pendants." She had taken her time building up to the fact that Nick also had a pendant, and waited for my shock to fade before continuing. After that, I had tracked the pendants through a fight with Nick, to Dallas despite Aaron's injury, into Nick's pocket despite his betrayal, and onto a train bound for Nebraska.

She closed the binder and sat down with it on her lap. "Nothing happened to the pendants. You know the rest of the story. We were briefly captured by Molly's useless recruits, we found Rochelle, and we came here."

"You mean you still have them?" I stood so quickly I almost toppled my chair. From the beginning, I had been certain either the detective or the TCI confiscated them along her journey.

"Before I answer that question . . ." She looked at me, eyebrows raised and lips in a tight line. "Why are they so important to you? You told me you want to protect Rochelle, but I get the impression you have a deeper connection to all of this." Since her first visit after my return to Maibe, she had been asking me a similar question that I had declined to answer.

I took a minute to adjust my sling and decide how much to reveal. Through her narrative, I had watched Lareina manipulate and deceive person after person. How much could I hold back without her knowing I wasn't being completely honest?

"Charlie." She leaned forward with her hands on the desk. "I can't be honest with you unless I know what you're hiding from me."

"Just give me a minute." I had to know whether she brought the pendants to Maibe. I had to know she wouldn't do something stupid with them that would put my family in danger. But the truth was the price I had to pay to find out. "When I was on the streets, a guy named Griff offered me a place to belong, a family. I was desperate, so I joined The Defiance before most people even knew what it was."

"You're one of them?" She scraped her chair back and stood, clutching the binder like a shield. "Does Rochelle know?"

"She's known for months." Ignoring Lareina's reaction, I took a deep breath in preparation to reveal the rest. "The story about why I left is mostly true. We just cut out the part about Griff meeting with me and asking me to bring him Rochelle's pendant and come back to The Defiance."

"Come back?" She stood poised to run, never taking her eyes off me. "I thought you could never leave The Defiance in the first place."

"You can't." Slumped in my chair, I told her about the friendship I'd formed with Griff and the way he'd changed after finding out about his dad's pendant. I described his obsession with using the research to make The Defiance the most powerful organization in the country and my pathetic attempt to stop him. "I ran away, and I planned to keep running. But if going back protects Rochelle from Molly, then I have to do it."

"Does Rochelle know you plan to give him her pendant?"

"Rochelle gave her pendant to Audrie." With each day, I regretted urging her to do that a little more. When I returned to The Defiance, I had to be on the best possible terms with Griff, and Audrie wasn't going to loan me a pendant to give me that advantage. "Until now, I feared it would complete Griff's collection. If you would have told me about your pendants from the beginning, I could have made a better decision."

"Great, so now the TCI has it." Lareina pressed the binder to her forehead so I couldn't see her face. "I told you we needed to do research to make an informed decision."

"Research?" I gripped the edge of my chair to fight back the pain and annoyance. "I just told you I was in The Defiance. What else could I possibly need to know?"

"Remember at the festival, I told you that Nick and I were

going to talk to Ava Welch's uncle?" She lowered the binder, voice calm and steady. "From conversations he had with his brother, he was under the impression the TCI had something to do with the project."

"How does that change anything?"

"I don't know yet. But what if the plan was to create a way to enhance viruses and the vaccine was an accidental by-product? That makes the TCI the villains. Maybe they planned to use it as a weapon all along, and now you just handed them one of the keys to it."

"First of all, you have no evidence to support your theory. You can hate the TCI and everything they stand for, but what you said about The Defiance in your story barely scratched the surface of what they're capable of." I pressed a hand to my forehead and took a deep breath. "If you really have the pendants, you have to give them to me. If anyone else finds out you have them, Maibe will be back on The Defiance radar and Rochelle will never be safe."

She sighed and sat on the edge of the chair, still pushed far away from the desk. "Is this really about Rochelle? Or is this about Griff expecting a pendant and you not having one?"

"Of course it's about Rochelle." I never wanted to see one of those pendants again. I didn't want to rejoin The Defiance. "A pendant means Griff will trust me, he'll believe Rochelle is useless to The Defiance, and I'll be able to fulfill my mission."

"What mission?" Lareina slid her chair forward. I had said too much and she knew it.

"Do you promise not to tell Rochelle?" When she nodded, I explained my agreement with Audrie to work undercover for the TCI. My second chance to stop The Defiance.

Lareina shook her head. "Rochelle knows you're part of The Defiance and she doesn't care, but you're afraid to tell her you're working for her aunt?"

"Not because I think she'll be mad." I stumbled through an explanation of trying to protect Rochelle by keeping her out of the loop and therefore clear of the danger. "The truth is, I never would have taken Rochelle's pendant for Griff because giving it to Audrie was the only way to get her out of the Aumonts' lives. Now that she got what she wanted, she hasn't called. Now Rochelle, Kat, and Kinley can all stay together like they're supposed to."

Lareina nodded. "Your intentions are in the right place, but it's a mistake to lie to Rochelle about this."

"You're going to give me advice about lying to people?" I coughed and a searing pain tore through my shoulder. "Maybe you knew Rochelle a long time ago, but I've been here for the past year. You can't just show up and—"

"Okay, okay. You don't have to take my advice, but I intend to keep investigating." She sighed. "And then I'll decide the right thing to do with the pendants."

"So you still have them?" I could barely breathe.

Taking two steps back, she reached into her pocket and pulled out the two pendants she'd described in her narrative. "I'll be sure to hide them where no one will look for them until I've reached that conclusion."

I looked at the pendants, feeling the usual dread and knowing I had made a mistake by pushing Lareina away when she possessed something that I needed to help everyone I cared about. Maybe I could start over and convince her to let me protect the people she considered her family as much as I considered them mine.

"Why?" The question burst out of me. "When the pendant brought you nothing but trouble, why did you try so hard to hold onto it? Now that there's no one after you, why are you still investigating?"

"Because it feels important." She fidgeted with the homemade bracelet given to her by a child at the home for children. "For my whole life I always felt unimportant, invisible, so I guess I just wanted to do something good. One meaningful thing before my time is up."

"This isn't your battle." I nodded toward the bracelet. "I think what you're doing at the home for children is far more meaningful than anything involving the pendants."

Lareina smiled. "Time will tell."

"I mean it. They're lucky to have you." The three months I'd stayed at a home for children were more miserable than all of my time on the street. The only way the next generation would have a better future would be for us to face the people and places that hurt us and fix what we knew was broken. Exactly why I had to help stop The Defiance.

"Thank you." Lareina tucked the binder under her arm and slid the pendants back into her pocket. "But I'm not giving you either of the pendants."

"Because you don't trust me?"

"Don't take it personally. I don't trust anyone. But I won't tell Rochelle anything she doesn't already know. Give me some time to think about this and then we can talk more."

Knowing I'd lost for now, I walked Lareina to the door, then returned to the library and sank into an armchair. For half an hour I stared out the window, trying to decide what to do. If I could get Lareina on my side, I could have the upper hand in every scenario. Audrie didn't have a reason to suspect more pendants in Maibe. Griff expected a pendant but not a specific one. The second one could be hidden forever so neither the TCI nor The Defiance could win. But could I convince Lareina to hand one over? Was it right to give even one more pendant to Griff? Was it wrong to hide the other and deprive the world of a promising vaccine?

Footsteps approached the doorway, and Rochelle trudged in and flopped down on the couch.

"Rough day?" I asked.

She lifted her head, face rosy from the cold and hair tangled from the wind. "More like a roller coaster. I talked Max into visiting Todd and now we're all friends again. Then I took Max to see Alexander, and he assured him he doesn't think he's a danger to the rest of us, but then he lectured us about asking for help when we're in over our heads."

I was surprised Rochelle hadn't brought Max home with her to mend our friendship. He hadn't visited since our argument and hadn't even called to ask my advice on the time machine. Maybe I had underestimated how mad he was about my possible departure from Maibe. When I didn't say anything, she sat up and pulled her knees under her chin. "I tried to call Audrie twice this morning, but she wouldn't answer."

"The pendant is gone." I walked to the couch and sank down next to her. "Maybe you just don't need her in your life anymore. Nothing happens by chance, right?"

"But I kind of do need her right now. Kinley is worried about where I'll be the safest, and even though she doesn't want me to go, I think that's with Audrie. The school she wants me to go to sounds really neat, and she said I can help her figure out what my dad knew about the pendants. I just need to know there's a plan so I can prepare and say goodbye to everyone . . ." She choked on her words and closed her eyes. "I can't handle it if Molly shows up and hurts my family."

"You leaving won't stop Molly." I rested the right side of my body against the back cushion, keeping my left shoulder slightly forward. "And I don't think you should go with Audrie."

"The only way to stop Molly is with Audrie's help. Leaving Kinley and Kat is going to be the hardest thing I've ever done, but it's only temporary."

"If you're going to leave at all, don't you think it would be better for you to go to Omaha with Kat? So she won't be alone?" Kinley had pulled me aside over the weekend and told me about her plan. The older couple she knew lived on a farm and could easily keep me hidden. She also told me Kat would be going to Omaha, and she wanted to send Rochelle there too, but Audrie would likely complicate that. Then she hugged me and told me not to worry because nothing would change until after Christmas.

"If Molly found me, then Kat would be right there." Rochelle turned to me. "I'm scared for them, Keppler. I got us into this, and I have to do whatever it takes to fix all of it."

I nodded, understanding exactly how she felt going somewhere she didn't want to go for the good of her family. I would miss her, my life in Maibe, and the family I had for the best year of my life. But part of the reason I had to leave was so the rest of my family could stay together. "Aumont, promise me you won't go with Audrie unless you absolutely have to, and if you do, that you'll come home as soon as you can. Don't let her guilt you into staying, or bribe you to finish school in New York."

"Nothing will keep me away from Maibe. We'll both be right back here in a few months. We're a family and Audrie can't change that."

But Griff could. Despite everyone's reassurances, I knew if I left Maibe—especially without a pendant—I wouldn't be back. Sooner or later, Griff would catch on to why I had really returned, and I wouldn't be lucky enough to escape a second time.

"Don't look so worried." Rochelle stood and stretched. "For now, everything is okay. Just don't tell Kat about any of this so we don't ruin the holidays. We'll make every minute count. But you should talk to Max soon. He's worried about you and what will happen to you in your worst-case-scenario plan."

I nodded, but I didn't know what I would say to Max or how I could prevent him from worrying about me when I couldn't stop worrying myself.

CHAPTER 24

ROCHELLE

December 19, 2090

I woke up tucked under a warm blanket on the couch, unable to remember how I got there. Sitting up, I rubbed my eyes and stared at my math book and literature notes scattered across the coffee table. Disoriented, I turned to the bay window where snowflakes fell from a still light sky. I had been working on homework with Todd and Max but couldn't remember them leaving or when I had fallen asleep.

Still groggy, I slid my blanket aside, and as I sat up, felt the folded note in the back pocket of my jeans. Earlier in the afternoon, I had been across the street with Lareina. Over the past week, she had been teaching me how to open padlocks with paper clips, slide objects out of pockets without being noticed, and generally escape dangerous situations. I met her at Kinley's old house, and we worked in the kitchen while Aaron slept on the couch in the next room. We wrapped up the lesson before Nick came home.

Today as I left, she had handed me a note and said, "Read this when you have a minute. If you agree, call me." I was already running late to study with Todd and Max, so I had shoved the note into my pocket and rushed back to my house. Now, I unfolded the note and held it close to my face in the dim light.

Rochelle—

I've been thinking about everything you told me about Molly, her dad, and the pendant. I'm sure she left out plenty of information. As you know, I've been looking into the connection between the research group and the TCI. I don't have any solid information, but Molly's house could contain the lead I'm looking for. She couldn't take everything with her, and everyone leaves something behind whether they mean to or not.

I'm planning to do a little looking around the day after tomorrow. You know Molly better than anyone, so I would love to take you along and get your insight into where we should search and whether anything seems out of place. You don't have to do this, but you're my friend and I didn't want to keep it from you. Call me at the home for children. I'll be awake all night.

—Lareina

Refolding the note, I stood and slid it back into my pocket. It felt wrong to break into Molly's house, but if I could find something there that would help me stop her or indicate what I should do next, then it would be worth it. Resolved to call her later, I stumbled toward the kitchen.

"My dad has some pretty demanding construction jobs lined up for this summer." Todd's voice drifted on the air with the aroma of bread baking and vanilla. "So I'll have to be healed up by then. Hopefully sooner."

"Just keep getting plenty of rest." I imagined my sister stirring something on the stove as she spoke. "That's the good thing about being hurt during the winter. There's nothing better to do than lie on the couch with a warm blanket."

For a minute I lingered in the dining room, enjoying the comfortable normalcy of Kat and Todd having a conversation in the warm kitchen. Although I tried to push it away, the anxiety crept in of Kat living far away in Omaha, Keppler hidden on a farm I'd never visited, and me at a boarding school a thousand miles away from everyone I loved.

Taking a deep breath to clear my head, I continued into the kitchen.

"Hey, Shelley. How was your nap?" Todd pulled out a chair next to his.

"Good, I think." I slid in next to him. "How long was I asleep?"

"Almost two hours. You kept telling me you weren't tired, but you fell asleep halfway through the math assignment."

Kat laughed and turned from what she was mixing at the counter. "Imagine Rochelle sleeping through a math lesson. Just don't do that while Kinley's teaching."

Grinning, I let my head slide onto Todd's shoulder. It was such a relief to have him home and see him healed enough to get back to his less strenuous activities. "I guess I need to drink more coffee."

"You need to get more sleep." Todd's cheek pressed against the top of my head.

"I second that." Kat wiped her flour-covered hands on a towel. "You're up when I go to bed and you're already awake when I get up in the morning. Do you even sleep anymore?"

I had been putting in time studying, finishing the gifts I had been sewing for my family, and doing extra chores so Kinley had less to worry about. Deep down, I knew I was distracting myself from thinking about saying goodbye to the only life I had ever known.

"I get all the sleep I need. Where's Max?" I sat up. "And Keppler?" They hadn't spoken in days, and I had hoped to get them in the same room while Max was over, but Keppler had been resting downstairs and Max hadn't even asked where he was.

"Max had to go babysit his cousins." Kat picked up a steaming pot, and poured water and noodles into the strainer in the sink. "Alexander came to get Charlie for his follow-up doctor appointment after Max left. So no, they didn't talk to each other."

"Let's get back to the original subject though." Todd's voice was gentle but his eyes studied me intensely. "Rochelle, I'm worried about you. For the past week, you've barely been able to keep your eyes open, and I never see you eat anything."

"That's an exaggeration." I laughed, trying to brush the conversation aside. "You know Kinley would never let me get by with that." The truth was, Kinley was so distracted she was barely taking care of herself, let alone noticing what I was doing.

"I mean it, Rochelle." Todd's voice dropped to the most scolding tone he was capable of. "You need to take care of yourself or you'll get sick."

"I need to take care of myself?" The wave of frustration couldn't be stopped. "You're the one who disappeared for six months. You almost died. Which one of us doesn't know how to take care of ourselves?"

Todd's shoulders slumped but he didn't take his eyes off me. "At least I've learned my lesson. You make the same mistakes over and over."

"Hey. Hey. Guys." Kat crossed the kitchen and stood across the table from us. "Don't do that. You're best friends. Plus, I hear enough fighting from Kinley and Alexander."

"The last thing I want is to fight with Rochelle." Todd spoke to Kat instead of me. "I'm just worried she's pushing herself too hard. I don't want anything bad to happen to her."

Kat nodded and looked at me. "I know how you feel. But we both know she can be pretty stubborn."

Todd shook his head. "She just gets so busy taking care of everyone else, she forgets to take care of herself." After saying such rotten things to him, he still wouldn't fight back.

"I'm sorry, Todd. I didn't mean any of that. I'm just really tired."

"It's okay." He brushed tears from my face before I even realized they were there. "You'll get some rest tonight, and tomorrow will be better."

I forced a smile and nodded, wishing I could believe that promise the way I had as a child, and wishing Todd didn't look so hurt. "You're right. I'll be rested, and I'll help you with your literature paper. I promise." Any thought of telling him about my plans with Lareina vanished; it would only make him worry.

Todd smiled, dimples and all. "Good. Because I'm really struggling."

"There. That's more like it." Kat hugged me with one arm and tousled Todd's hair with her free hand.

Todd pulled away from her and patted his hand over his hair, but it still stuck up like he'd been the one sleeping. "I really need a haircut."

"Or a comb and some gel." Kat parted it to one side and held it down. "We could make that work. Start a new trend."

"Very funny." He ducked away from her hand and shook his head. "I'll ask Emma to cut it. Then I'll be back to normal." He grimaced at his cast. "Well, almost."

"You look great either way." I wanted to say something to make him feel better, to shatter the wedge I felt myself driving between us, but before I could, the door creaked open and voices entered the laundry room.

"Finally." Kat rushed over to the door and pushed it open for Keppler, Alexander, and Kinley. "What took so long? Did something go wrong?"

"Everything is fine." Kinley placed her hands on Kat's shoulders and guided her deeper into the room. "We had a lot of last-minute appointments, so Charlie was in the waiting room for a while."

Alexander pulled the door shut, sealing in the kitchen's

warmth. "We were in the waiting room all but the twenty minutes it took Dr. Brooks to tell us Charlie is healing right on schedule." He pressed a hand to the back of his neck as he often did when worried. "He'll be good as new in no time."

"Not that fast." Keppler looked at Alexander and shrugged. "I'll still be in the sling for another four to five weeks." He sounded relieved, unlike Todd, who wanted to be back to loading lumber and shingling roofs.

"I'm glad we have everyone on the road to recovery." Kinley walked around the table and tousled Todd's hair just like Kat had done. "How's my other favorite patient doing?"

"A lot better." Todd blushed from all of the attention. "My ribs still hurt a little."

"That'll fade in time." Kinley offered her hands and helped Todd to his feet. "Why don't you go and lie down for a little while. I want some time to catch up with Emma when she stops by to pick you up." She nodded toward Keppler. "Charlie, you should go in and sit down too. I know doctor appointments can be exhausting."

The boys obediently went to the next room, and Kinley's hands rested comfortingly on my shoulders. "Alexander, does Charlie have a reason for wanting to stay in his sling? You both seemed a little disappointed with the news."

"Of course not." He looked everywhere but at my cousin's eyes. "We just decided to be realistic. You know, so we wouldn't set him up for disappointment."

"Are you sure that's all? Because the way you two were talking—"

"I'm sure, Kinley." He sighed, recognizing his abrupt tone. "Sorry. It's just been a long day."

"Okay." Kinley nodded. "Maybe you should take a break and stay for dinner."

"Are you sure?" He looked down at his socks.

"We have plenty. Right, Kat?"

"I'm always ready for company." Kat returned to the stove. "Dinner will be ready in less than thirty minutes."

Alexander nodded. "I'll check in on Charlie and Todd." He smiled and left the room. He'd been checking in on Keppler at least twice a day since we'd come home from Kansas. He always seemed relieved to see him, as if he expected to find that he'd vanished.

Kat shook her head. "Boys are weird. All of them."

Kinley laughed and sat down next to me. "Just keep thinking that, and my life will be so much easier." She wrapped her arm around me. "Speaking of dinner, I haven't seen you clear your plate all week. Is everything okay?"

I had been trying to keep my word and talk to Kinley about everything on my mind. She knew I was worried about Kat's reaction to her plan, I'd told her about Lareina teaching me to defend myself and pick locks, and I'd even confessed how upset I was that Audrie wouldn't take my calls. The note in my pocket was something I would have to hold back. My cousin was making a real attempt to see things from my point of view, but breaking into the house Molly's sister owned would be something I couldn't make her understand.

"I think I hurt Todd's feelings just now, and I feel bad."

Kinley's hand gently rested on my back. "I'm sure it's nothing you two can't work out. We're all under a lot of pressure right now, dealing with some tough stuff, but everything will be okay." I felt like she was talking to herself more than me. "I'll go change, and then the three of us can finish getting dinner ready. We don't spend nearly enough time together."

Kat looked at me, and then at Kinley's retreating back, with her hands on her hips. "What's with everyone today? Is there something I don't know?"

I wanted to tell her every minute we spent together was

precious. I wanted to spill all of my secrets, but I knew it would spoil the time we had left. Instead, I shrugged and lowered my head to the table.

CHAPTER 25

CHARLIE

December 20, 2090

"The middle school is set to open for seventh and eighth graders in January." Rochelle sat at the conference room table between Todd and me, delivering her report to the council so smoothly I couldn't believe she had missed a month of meetings. "The building is ready, we have teachers hired, and there are sixty students registered in total. Going forward, we'll add a ninth grade in August and a tenth grade the following August until we have a fully functioning high school."

I jotted down the details, adding Rochelle's report to my notes from the information Trevor and Neil had already provided.

"Excellent." Alexander wrote something in his binder and looked up. "Does anyone have questions or problems we need to address on education?"

"I'm pretty sure Rochelle covered everything." Neil leaned back in his chair with his hands behind his head. "Very impressive, by the way. I motion we continue."

"I second that." Trevor sat across the table from us between Neil and Kiara, who had both made notes in their own binders. As chaotic as the early meetings had been, it always astonished me how civil and organized they had become.

In my peripheral vision, I watched Emma a few chairs down from me. Todd had wanted to resume his council duties, Emma thought he wasn't ready, and their compromise had been her attending with him.

Kiara flipped forward a page in her binder. "None of you will be surprised to hear that the winter festival was an absolute success. Currently, I'm working on a spring event in March or April. Details to come in January."

Despite missing several meetings myself, I had continued to write my reports with help from the notes Kiara had taken during my absence. My stomach twisted every time I thought about the notes under my pen as the last ones I would take for a council article. It was the final meeting until the new year, and I would be far away from Maibe by the time they reconvened.

"Todd, I know you've been putting together a report on security." Alexander turned to the back of his binder. "What do you have for us?"

"Well, thanks to Max and Charlie, we have a functioning surveillance system at the train station." He cleared his throat. "There are four cameras currently up and running, and Max and I will install two more as soon as I can climb a ladder." He looked down at the single sheet of paper in front of him. "That's all I have for now, but I'll put together a real report for the next meeting."

"That was fine." Trevor shrugged. "Much more detailed than Neil's famous five-second report."

Neil laughed. "When everything's working, there's nothing to report. It's good to have you back, Todd."

"It's good to have everyone back." Kiara closed her binder. "I'm glad we could end the year on a happy note."

No one had mentioned Molly or her empty seat. There had been plenty of rumors circulating around town since Rochelle's brief disappearance, and I was sure the others knew about Rochelle's kidnapping, Todd's homecoming, and Molly's criminal activities. Alexander had probably cleared up any discrepancies and directed them to avoid questions or comments about our experiences.

"That takes care of our council business for this year. I look forward to working with all of you in the new year." As Alexander gave his closing, I wondered if he had talked to Rochelle about her possible absence from the council if she moved away with Audrie. Everyone in the Aumont house acted as if the week we had left in December would stretch on forever. I felt the end rushing toward us like a fist I couldn't dodge. "Meeting adjourned. Everyone have a great holiday break."

The attentive hush broke into the usual end-of-meeting chatter, with everyone gathering around Todd and Rochelle. I ignored the conversations, adding a few clarifications to my notes as I reread them.

"Hey, Charlie." The empty chair next to me pulled away from the table, and Kiara sat down. "After filling in for you, I've realized you have a tough job. We all appreciate everything you do to keep the community up to date with our meetings and events."

"No problem. I actually look forward to these meetings." It was the truth. At first, I thought Alexander had made a big mistake by recruiting a bunch of teenagers to the town council, but that risk had paid off.

Kiara nodded toward my sling. "I heard about what happened." Kinley's cover story about me running away to find my family had made its rounds through Maibe too. "Don't ever feel like you have to leave. We all want to keep you here."

"Thanks. I'd like nothing more than to stay."

"Good." Kiara squeezed my arm and stood. "Merry Christmas, Charlie."

"Merry Christmas." I closed my notebook and watched Kiara leave with Trevor. To my left, Rochelle and Todd talked together, and Emma had wandered over to join them.

"Charlie, Rochelle, get your coats." Alexander stood at the head of the table, stacking his binders and notes. "I have a broken washing machine that I have to take to Max before I drop you two off at home. He thinks it holds the key to time travel."

"I'll go with you." Todd turned to face his sister. "Please? If you hadn't come to the meeting, I would have been riding with Alexander anyway."

"Not this time, Todd." She pulled her coat over her arms. "It's been a long day; you should get some rest."

"All I ever do is rest." Todd slid his chair back and stood, chin set in defiance. "I'm tired of you deciding when I'm well enough to do something. I know when I'm tired, and I'm not."

Emma took a step back. "I'm just trying to help you."

"I don't need your help." Todd shoved his chair under the table and left the room.

Leaving her coat behind, Rochelle hurried after him.

"I'll talk to him, Emma." Alexander walked around the table and gave her a one-armed hug. "He can come with me. I won't let him lift anything and I'll bring him right home. Is that okay?"

She nodded and rested her forehead against Alexander's shoulder. "He's been struggling since he got home. He gets frustrated so easily, and he's been more withdrawn this week. I don't know how to help him."

"I'll see what I can find out." Alexander collected Todd's and Rochelle's coats from the back of their chairs. "Charlie, are you ready?"

"Can I wait for you here? I'm having a disagreement with Max." He hadn't stopped by since I'd revealed my worst-case-scenario plan, and I had told myself I was too busy writing Lareina's story and too tired from my injury to defuse the situation.

"I can take Charlie home." Emma sank into the chair beside me.

Alexander studied me, eyebrows raised, then shook his head. "Okay. You guys can leave the lights on; I'll be coming back." He met my eyes and tipped his head toward Emma.

I nodded, understanding he wanted me to take care of her.

"Todd isn't upset with you," I said when the jingle of the bell on the front door indicated the others had left. "He's just trying to adjust to all of the changes. It's hard feeling like everything's out of your control."

She turned to me, hazel eyes dull with worry. "That's very perceptive. Are you feeling that way too?" In addition to those who had been there the day I arrived home from Orville, Emma and Todd knew the truth about me.

"A little, I guess. I deserve worse though." The walls I put up to hide my feelings always crumbled around Emma.

She tilted her head to the side. "Why do you think that?"

"Because I failed to protect my own sister. When I ran away from the home for children, I could have gone back. I could have tried to find her, but I took the easy way out and joined The Defiance. That was selfish." I had been considering what would be the selfless thing to do since Lareina revealed her pendants. Would it be selfish to give Griff a pendant if it gave me the leverage I needed to protect my family and maybe even the world? Was it wrong to help The Defiance hurt people if I sabotaged their ability to take control of the country? Was it even worth wasting the energy to think about when Lareina hadn't contacted me?

"I'm so sorry about what happened to your sister, but that's not your fault." She slid her chair over so we sat shoulder to shoulder. "I'm so proud of you for stepping up and taking care of her when you were too young to even be taking care of yourself. But you're not the one who left her behind, and you didn't know where to find her."

"I should have at least tried." She knew about Kinley's plan to hide me, and as much as I wanted to ask her what I should do about Lareina and the pendants, I refrained from spilling any more secrets. "Have you ever had to make a decision and neither choice was a good one?"

Emma thought for a minute. "When my mom left, I was eleven, and at first we thought she would come back, so I was trying to fill in with laundry, cleaning, cooking, and taking care of Todd and Lily." She closed her eyes and shook her head. "After she had been away for a month, my dad saw that I was overwhelmed. He told me I was doing a good job, but if it was too much, he could send Todd and Lily to live with his parents in Oregon. They had agreed to raise them."

It was impossible to imagine Emma considering that for even a second. "I already know you decided to keep them."

"Not at first. I almost gave them up." She took a sharp breath. "Alexander and Kinley wouldn't tell me what to do, but they helped me make a pros and cons list, and when I looked at the situation on paper, my life was a lot easier without them, and their lives were better with the stability I figured they would have with Dad's parents, although I had never met them."

I nodded along with her, remembering having similar feelings concerning Isabelle. "What changed your mind?"

Emma smiled. "I loved them too much, and I couldn't imagine my life without them. Once I realized that, a few more responsibilities and chores didn't seem like such a big sacrifice."

"And it was the right decision?"

"Absolutely. It's been a bumpy ride, but I've never regretted it." She patted my arm. "I know you're feeling like things are out of your control right now, but everything will work out. Someday, you're going to be the greatest journalist of our time and report the stories that change lives and make the world a better place."

Imagining myself in her future made me smile. "I wish that could be real."

"You're the one who gets to decide. I'm going to help Todd find some introductory college classes in construction or drawing. I'll find a journalism class for you."

I blinked my burning eyes. It was the closest I'd come to crying in front of someone since the day I'd come home. Isabelle had been the one with a future, not me. "I don't want to leave Maibe."

"And none of us want you to go." Emma gently squeezed my hand.

She didn't know about the deal I'd made with Audrie, and I couldn't explain the responsibility I felt to prevent Griff from hurting the people I cared about. Running and hiding were no longer options. Even though I felt sick every time I thought about it, rejoining The Defiance was my only choice.

"This is the kind of day that calls for ice cream." Emma stood and picked up my coat. "We'll stop at the diner on the way home. Ice cream makes everything better."

I laughed because she said it with such conviction. "It can't hurt." Trying to forget about my problems, I slid one arm into my coat and she draped the other side over my injured shoulder. "Todd is going to be okay. He just needs some time."

Emma handed me my notebook and wrapped her arm around me. "You'll be okay too. I'm glad we got to talk."

I was glad too. Maybe I couldn't tell Emma everything, but she had given me the insight into decision-making I had been looking for. First, I would enjoy my ice cream, and then I would call Max and set up a meeting. If I told him everything I had to hide from everyone else and pitched it as an undercover secret mission, he would keep it to himself. I needed someone to help me evaluate my situation, figure out what to do about the information Lareina had revealed, and make the right choice for my family.

CHAPTER 26
ROCHELLE

December 21, 2090

jiggled the paper clip in my hand and slowly twisted it until I felt the familiar click Lareina had taught me to wait for. "Got it!" My free hand flew to the knob, and the back door of Molly's house creaked open.

"Perfect." Lareina helped me to my feet. "You're getting really good at that." She blinked away the giant snowflakes that coated her eyelashes.

"All thanks to you." My attention was drawn to the doorway I'd so often run through with Molly on our way inside for a snack after playing in the backyard.

"We'd better get inside." Lareina glanced around the snow-covered yard, then took a backward step toward the door. She'd insisted we inch along the side of the house to leave as few footprints as possible. "Nick gets off work in forty-five minutes, and it's better if he doesn't know about this." She had told me how much Nick disapproved of her breaking into houses and stealing even though it had been essential to their survival. Without Aaron to mediate, she didn't think her friendship with Nick would have lasted.

I nodded. I had promised Todd I would be at his house that afternoon, and the sooner we found what we were looking for, the less late I would be. Taking a deep breath of cold air to fight off any more memories, I followed Lareina inside.

"No lights." She stopped my hand before it reached the light switch. "We don't want anyone to get suspicious."

"Right." The house didn't feel much warmer than outside, and I wondered if Molly's sister had had the utilities turned off. I wasn't sure how much she knew about Molly's latest antics, but she hadn't returned to Maibe to deal with it in person.

A gust of wind slammed the door and Lareina jumped. Gripping my arm, she spun around, hand to her chest.

"It's okay. Just the wind." I twisted away from her iron grip on my arm. "Where should we start?" I thought I would feel uneasy breaking into a house, but Molly's house had been my second home for most of my childhood, and I felt surprisingly comfortable there.

"We're looking for any kind of documentation connected to the research, the pendants, or the TCI."

"Molly's dad would probably have kept that stuff in his office." I led Lareina through the kitchen and dining room and took a right into the last room before the front staircase. It was as I remembered it, complete with bookcases, file cabinets, and a desk.

A shelf of framed pictures caught my eye, and I walked closer to examine them in the dull light from the window. Photos of Eric Bennett and his family stretched back through the years. The one on the end featured my dad and Eric, grinning, in caps and gowns at their high school graduation. They had been best friends, inseparable for their entire lives until the power that came with the pendants corrupted Molly's dad as it had done to her.

After my dad's funeral, he had sat with me for fifteen minutes. He'd offered his condolences, told me my dad was a great guy, and promised—despite never being able to fill my dad's shoes—to stand in for him in any way he could. I had been so overwhelmed by my loss, I never thought to question his sincerity.

"Rochelle. Are you okay?" Lareina stood next to me, although I hadn't heard her approach.

"There are just a lot of memories here." I took a step back and turned away from the framed photographs. "How about you look around down here, and I'll check upstairs."

"Are you sure?" She whispered as if we weren't alone. "I can come with you."

"We don't have much time." I wanted to find the lead she believed existed and get to Todd. "It'll be faster if we split up."

Before I could change my mind, I left the room and took the front staircase, two steps at a time, until I stood in the shadowy hallway upstairs. I wandered through bedrooms, opening closets and drawers to find them empty or filled with clothes as expected. By the time I reached Molly's room, I had convinced myself that the girl who had once been my best friend was too smart, organized, and meticulous to leave anything behind she didn't want to be found.

Molly's room was as I remembered it, down to the pastel-purple color scheme. The trunk of dress-up clothes that had once been at the foot of her bed was gone, as was the dollhouse that had sat in the corner. Ignoring the wave of memories, I focused all of my attention on searching the closet, dresser drawers, and under the bed. After finding only clothes, socks, and extra blankets, I sat down on the bed and tried to identify anything I had missed.

A photo album on the nightstand caught my attention. I picked it up and flipped through pictures of Molly and me in our soccer uniforms, on the swings at the park, and eating pizza at my kitchen table. Pages and pages of a life that felt like a hundred years ago.

Could everything have been different if we hadn't drifted apart? If Molly and I had remained friends, would I have been successful at talking her out of joining The Defiance? Chest aching with guilt for letting my oldest friend make all of the wrong choices, I closed the album and a folded piece of paper slid onto the comforter. Curious, I picked it up and smoothed it open.

Rochelle—

You're the last person in this world I would ever want to hurt, but you're making everything so hard. Remember when you used to trust me over everyone else? Now I can't even get you to consider my perspective. I miss all of the years when we were best friends. Back then, neither of us would have believed I'd consider joining a group like The Defiance. But the world has changed so much from what we thought it would be, and The Defiance is my only chance to have a future.

I'm sorry about the mistakes my dad made. I'm sorry if I've been too forceful about your pendant. I'm sorry I pushed you away when we were kids. You were the only real friend I ever had, and more like my sister than the one I have. I don't want to do this alone. I need your help.

I read the letter over and over until tears blurred my vision. The last time I had spoken to Molly, before she left Maibe, I'd felt uneasy about her feelings toward The Defiance, but I thought she was going to visit her sister. I'd left her to walk home alone while I went to dinner with Max and Keppler. She needed me and I had abandoned her.

Had she written this letter that night? Had she intended to give it to me?

"Rochelle." Lareina's voice shattered the silence around me and I jumped. "What's wrong?"

I held out the note. She sat down next to me and read it.

"She says you're the last person she'd want to hurt," she scoffed. "I saw what she did to you."

"That's because I let her down." I rubbed drying tears off my face. "I'm letting everyone down. It's my fault that Kat and Kinley are so stressed and Audrie won't take my calls." I sniffled. "And Keppler…" Remembering who I was talking to, I stopped abruptly.

"It's okay." She folded the letter. "He told me about being in The Defiance and knowing about the pendants."

"He did?" After the months he'd spent hiding his past from Max and me, and hiding the truth from everyone else for almost a year, it seemed out of character that he'd tell Lareina.

"He's helping me write my story. When we got to the part about Ava, it all just came up."

She had told me about Nick's friend, Ava Welch, and I recognized the last name from Eric Bennett's research team. I had a vague impression that she and Nick were sure the TCI had been responsible for murdering the whole family. But, as with every conversation I had with Lareina, I felt she was holding something back.

"Did he tell you the part about me having my dad's pendant and giving it up to my aunt who won't talk to me anymore?" It wasn't a confession I'd planned to make to Lareina, but in the dim light of that lonely room where shadows of the past threatened to swallow me, she felt like the only tether I had to the present.

Lareina nodded. "And you're sure your aunt isn't the one who got your dad involved in all of this?"

"She told me she had asked him to keep his eyes open for anything suspicious surrounding Eric Bennett and his research, but Dad kept insisting his best friend wasn't involved in anything shady. It wasn't until a month before he died that he brought up the pendant, and he had been sick for a while, so she thought he was confused." I shook my head and looked down at my hands.

"And you believe her?" Lareina twisted her hair and dropped it behind her shoulder. "How do you know she isn't lying to you? That she didn't hurt your dad to get the pendant?"

It was a valid question, but one I had evidence to disprove. "Because Eric Bennett was a pharmacist and visited my dad all the time, the TCI didn't show up to search until Dad was gone, and before she left, Molly put something in my tea that caused the same symptoms my dad experienced."

"I'm sorry." She scooted closer and wrapped one arm around me. "I was so sure the TCI were the villains. I wanted it to be simple. Case closed. But this whole thing is a lot more complicated than that. Isn't it?"

I nodded but my eyes drifted back to the closed photo album. "There aren't exactly villains in this story. Just a bunch of people trying to get to the pendants before someone else does. They all want to shape the world into their own vision of better. I'm not sure who's right or wrong, but I've chosen to believe Audrie has the right intentions."

Lareina sighed. "You made the best choice you could with the information you had. If I've learned anything from my investigation, it's that people who hold on to those pendants get hurt."

"When I first found out about all of this, I wanted to find the vaccine and save the world." I cleared my throat. "But now that The Defiance could show up for Keppler any day, I wish I had made him take it."

"You would let him give it to The Defiance?" She gripped my shoulders and turned me toward her. "Why would you do that?"

"Because, whatever choices my dad made, he intended to do the right thing. To do something good." Sniffling, I thought about the mess of pendants—some with The Defiance, mine with the

TCI, some of them still unfound. "No one will ever put them all together to get at any of the research. The only good thing I could have done with it was use it to save my friend from the worst life I promised he'd never have to go back to." I took a deep breath. "Now it'll just sit in some TCI vault."

We sat in silence for a minute before Lareina spoke. "There's nothing in this house about the TCI, pendants, or secret research. Let's get out of here." A soft creaking from the bottom of the stairs made her jump. Her eyes went wide.

I put a hand on her arm and was about to reassure her when she clamped her own hand over my mouth.

Before we could move, another creak, an unmistakable footstep halfway up the stairs, snapped our attention to the door.

"Someone's here." Lareina released me and stood in a half crouch facing the door. "Get behind the dresser and get ready to run. Don't argue."

She picked up the lamp from the nightstand, and I squatted beside the dresser on the same wall as the door. Peeking around the side, I watched her inch toward the door with the lamp hoisted over her head as the floorboards groaned out in the hallway.

"Is anyone up here?" The voice registered as familiar, but I didn't have time to place it before Lareina swung the lamp, just missing Nick, who ducked in time to avoid the improvised weapon.

"Whoa, it's me." He stumbled backward and sat on the floor with his hands shielding his face. "It's Nick."

"Nick?" Lowering the lamp, she observed her friend with wild eyes. "What are you doing here?"

"Aaron heard you talking about coming here. He was worried because you hadn't come back yet." He pushed himself to his feet and folded his arms in front of him.

"We've only been gone for twenty minutes." I stepped out from behind the dresser.

Nick glanced at me, then turned his attention back to Lareina, eyes narrow. "I thought you were done with breaking into houses. And now you're dragging Rochelle into this."

"We're trying to find answers." Her voice rose in frustration. "You want answers too, remember? You want to know what happened to Ava and why." I didn't know how much Nick knew about my family's connection to the pendant, so I let Lareina do the talking.

He dropped his arms to his sides. "I know enough. She's gone, and I don't want the same thing to happen to you."

"We have a responsibility." Lareina looked down at her shoes. "I can't just do nothing."

"This is something that you, Aaron, and I need to decide together." He sighed and his expression softened. "Can you go into work a little late tonight so we can figure this out once and for all?"

"Wait. What time is it?" We had been at Molly's longer than I realized.

"Four thirty." Nick turned to me. "Todd was walking to your house when I was on my way here."

"He was walking?" Todd got exhausted just moving from room to room. He wasn't supposed to walk a block in the snow. "I have to go."

"We'll walk with you." Lareina caught my arm as I rushed to the door. "Remember, it's not safe for you to be out there alone."

On Nick's insistence, we returned the lamp and album to the nightstand. I shoved Molly's letter into my pocket.

"There. Everything is just as we left it," Lareina assured Nick as he stepped aside so we could pass into the hall.

"Good." He followed us down the stairs. "Now we just have to lock the door and hope the snow covers the tracks I followed around the house. Then we can put all of this behind us."

I hoped Lareina would listen to him and drop her investigation. She could put her experience with the pendants, whatever it was, behind her, but I was stuck right in the middle.

CHAPTER 27
CHARLIE

December 21, 2090

"**G**ive me just a minute to make sure I have all of this straight." Max sat in the armchair across the coffee table from me. "Audrie wants to make you a spy, which Alexander knows about but Kinley doesn't. Lareina has two more pendants. And you think you should rejoin The Defiance so you can sabotage Griff's plans and keep Molly away from here?"

I nodded. Max had rushed over after I called him and listened attentively to all I had to say without interrupting.

"Keppler, all of this is insane." He spoke in a hushed voice and glanced back at the closed French doors. We were both aware that Kat was just a room away. "You're really not going to tell Rochelle?"

"That's what I want to talk to you about. I'm worried Rochelle would do something dangerous, which is why I want to keep her out of it. She always wants to do the right thing even if it gets her kidnapped or killed." I shifted my weight to relieve the pressure on my shoulder. "Is it selfish for me to lie to her if I'm trying to protect her?"

"Usually I'd say yes, but considering everything that's happened, I think it's the right thing to do." Max stood. "The real question is, what are you going to do about the two pendants?"

"Griff is expecting me to bring him Auggie Aumont's pendant. I could tell him the TCI has it, but he would probably kill me for letting that happen. I could tell him we never found it, but then he might come here looking for it. If I gave him a pendant, it would prove my loyalty. But I can't do that without Lareina's help, and she hasn't returned my calls."

"Maybe you should just let Kinley hide you, and then you wouldn't have to deal with any of it."

"Where does that leave the Aumonts though? If I hide, I don't help anyone but myself. If I cooperate with Griff, I can keep him away from Maibe, and Molly away from Rochelle."

Max walked to the window and looked out at the heavy snowflakes. "If you're going to rejoin The Defiance, you have to take a pendant. That way Griff won't be suspicious of your motives, you'll be back in as his right-hand guy, and I'll know you're safe."

It was the same logical conclusion I had come to over and over, but how could I convince Lareina that putting another pendant into the wrong hands was the only way to protect the world from the dangerous research it could unlock? "I might be safe, but every pendant Griff gets brings him closer to unleashing a virus worse than the fever."

"No it doesn't." Max turned and crossed the room. "You can give him every pendant out there as long as you always have one hidden away. He needs all of them, not most of them."

"You don't think it's selfish? If I turn over one pendant, I'm not putting everyone at risk in exchange for my own security?"

"Audrie already has at least one, and Lareina will still have one. So, there's two he'll never touch." Max slid onto the coffee table in front of me. "And if you don't give him a pendant, he's going to see it as a betrayal. Remember what happened the last time he decided you betrayed him? You can't protect Rochelle, or anyone, if you end up dead."

"So far we're on the same page. What do I do about Audrie?"

Max shrugged. "Don't tell her about the extra pendants. But work for her like you planned when Alexander signed the paper."

"I never planned to work for her." My voice came out too loud and I glanced at the door. "That was just insurance to keep Kinley and Alexander out of trouble in case anyone found out they were harboring a criminal."

"You'd make a terrible criminal." Max laughed. "Think about it this way: Working for the TCI is added insurance that you'll have the resources and backup you need to save the world and still get out alive."

I shook my head. "Playing both sides while I work my own agenda triples my chances of getting killed by both sides."

Max's usual grin drooped to a frown. "Joining The Defiance for a second time gives you a good chance of getting killed, but you're willing to do that."

"Because it's time for me to stop running from my problems and do the right thing. If I've learned anything here, it's that nothing happens by chance. That's why the pendants keep finding me like I'm some kind of magnet. I'm supposed to protect the world from them. What else can I believe?"

"Now you're starting to sound like Rochelle. But Rochelle would take my ideas into consideration."

"She would never let either of us give a pendant to Griff. Remember why she didn't want to turn hers over to Audrie?" I didn't give him time to answer. "Because they're also the key to a lifesaving vaccine."

Max scratched his head. "I'm pretty optimistic, but even I know it's highly unlikely we would be able to collect all of the pendants, find the research, and get it to someone trustworthy who could develop a vaccine. Even if we did, there's no guarantee the vaccine would actually work."

"When you put it that way, it sounds crazy." I sank back into my chair. "But it's what Rochelle would do, and I'm willing to do it in her place as long as she isn't involved."

Max sighed. "Let's just weigh this out." He held his hands in front of him, palms up. "You can go on a world-saving mission, but if one thing goes wrong and all of the pendants end up with Griff ... Game over." He dropped one hand. "But if you convince Lareina to give you one and hide the other, you save the world from a new, deadlier outbreak and we can pursue the vaccine at a later time."

"That sounds reasonable." I nodded. "No, that sounds like the most responsible thing to do. But how do I convince Lareina?"

He frowned. "Tell her what we just talked about. She seems rational."

"But she doesn't trust me and she wants to make an informed decision." I sank back into the cushions. "She's like Rochelle but less naïve about the dangers of the world."

"Rochelle could probably convince her. But we can't tell Rochelle or she'll want to use the pendants to find the vaccine." He dropped his arms to his sides. "This is like being in a maze and every turn just leads to a wall."

"I'll keep calling Lareina. If I'm really lucky, she'll find some information that convinces her to trust my plan."

"While you're working on that, we should discuss how I can help you with all of this. I'll create a code so we can stay in touch and be double agents together. I swear I'll never tell Rochelle about any of it." Max spoke so quickly his words jumbled together.

How could I explain to him that in order to accomplish my mission, I had to make the impossible sacrifice of giving up everyone I cared about? Once I left Maibe behind, I wouldn't be able to stay in touch, but now that we were talking again, I didn't want to ruin the short time we had left. "You're the best brother anyone could ask for. I'll talk to Griff and when I figure out what the next step is, I'll contact you."

Max shifted to the couch, usual grin returning to his face. "And when this is all over and you get back, we'll have stories to tell. We can be the two old guys sitting in the hardware store, telling all the kids about how we saved the world."

Not wanting to consider the very real possibility I would never be an old man, I was thankful for a soft knock on the door.

Kat peeked her head in. "Do you guys know where Rochelle is?" She pushed the door open farther to reveal Todd standing next to her.

Max looked at me. "Visiting Lareina, probably. She's been spending a lot of time over there."

Kat sighed and patted Todd's arm. "You go sit down. You shouldn't have walked all the way over here in the snow. I'll make some calls and see if I can track her down."

Todd obediently shuffled into the room, face pinched in pain as he sat down next to Max. "I only walked a block and a half, but it feels like I walked three miles."

"You've only been out of the hospital for a couple of weeks." Max squeezed his friend's shoulder. "You have to take it easy a little while longer."

"I know, but yesterday, Rochelle said she would be at my house a half hour ago, so I thought she could have slipped on the sidewalk, but I didn't see her on my way over. What if something terrible happened to her?"

"I'm sure she's just running a little late." It surprised me Rochelle would miss plans with Todd, but she was busy.

"I can't keep up with her." Todd leaned back until his head sank into the cushions. "I'm well enough that I don't need her to take care of me, but not well enough to do much but help her study. I don't blame her for skipping out on our plans. I'm pretty boring."

"No one thinks you're boring. Especially not Rochelle." Max rested his elbows on his knees. "And even Rochelle can't keep up with Rochelle."

Todd groaned and sat up. "I never should have left. I feel like I'm losing her."

Max snorted. "That will never happen. The world will explode before Todd and Rochelle aren't synonymous with peanut butter and jelly, macaroni and cheese, chocolate chip cookies and . . . lemonade." Before either of us could protest, Max continued. "You two can read each other's minds, remember?"

"We can't really read each other's minds, Max." Todd smiled. "We were just joking around."

"You had me convinced. Although I was only eight." Max laughed. "I suppose you're going to tell me broccoli can't really make me run faster than the rest of the football team."

"Sorry, buddy. I didn't want you to find out this way, but Neil bet me five bucks I couldn't make you eat broccoli." Todd grinned and shrugged. "But those were some impressive touchdowns."

I laughed. "Kinley would call that the placebo effect."

"Very funny, *hermano*." Max sprang to his feet. "Now I'm getting hungry. I'm going to find out if Kat has any cookies and maybe some lemonade." He backed toward the door, expression serious. "I'll bring you guys some too. You'll love it."

Todd's smile vanished with Max. "Rochelle isn't taking any of this seriously enough. We don't know where Molly is. How do I know she isn't tied up in the trunk of a car right now?"

"I'm sure she's with Lareina." I tried not to let Todd's panic trigger my own tendency to overreact. "She's been over there every day."

"I don't know what's wrong with me." He rubbed his hands over his face. "I thought once I got home everything would be okay, but I have nightmares like I'm still *there*. Emma thinks it'll help if I talk about it, but I can't make her understand. It won't change anything. It won't go away."

"I used to think that too, but it does help to tell someone your story." I remembered my own fears of letting Rochelle and Max in on the darkness of my past, but the more I revealed, the freer I felt. Even Lareina seemed to float out of the house after I'd finished writing her narrative. "I don't think it'll ever go away, but it does get better."

Todd nodded in the same understanding way as Emma. "How did you deal with it all alone? Before you got here . . ." His voice trailed off.

"I didn't *deal* with it. Before I came here, I thought the whole world was rotten."

Todd rubbed the side of his face. "What do you think now?"

"I think there are plenty of rotten people, but I also believe there's hope, and as long as we have that, there's a future."

"Charlie, how safe are we here? From The Defiance?" Todd looked at me, eyes wide with fear like my little sister's during a thunderstorm.

"They were always interested in taking over more populated areas first, so I think Maibe will escape the worst of it for now, but there are things we don't know, so it's reasonable to be cautious." I wished I could tell him my plan to reassure him the wheels were in motion to keep The Defiance away from Rochelle. "In the unlikely situation that they show up, I'll do everything I can to stand in their way."

"Thank you for being here when I wasn't. I should have been here to look out for Rochelle." He looked down at the coffee table. "Maybe then I wouldn't have this problem."

Before I could think of a response, footsteps approached from the next room and the door opened all the way.

"Look who just got back from across the street." Max stood in the doorway with his arm around Rochelle, snowflakes melting in her hair.

She squirmed away from him, rushed across the room, and

wrapped her arms around Todd. "I'm so sorry. I promise I didn't forget about you. I just lost track of time."

Todd hugged her back and cleared his throat. "I was afraid something happened to you on your way to my house. You're freezing. How long have you been outside?"

"Just a few minutes. I'm fine." She leaned back so she could see his face. "You can't panic every time I'm running late."

"After everything that's happened, what else am I supposed to do?"

I stood and followed Max into the next room, closing the door softly behind us. "You think they'll be okay?"

"This is Rochelle and Todd we're talking about." Max offered me a cookie. "I think Kat feels bad about what she said to me last week because she's making us lemonade."

"You know cookies go with milk, right?" I couldn't pull my attention away from the closed doors behind me.

"That's what I thought until last week." He put a hand on my back and steered me toward the kitchen. "Enough problems for today. Let's save some for tomorrow."

CHAPTER 28

ROCHELLE

December 23, 2090

I stopped writing and stretched my hand, glancing across the table at Keppler, who continued writing without looking up. Emma sat at the end of the table, pen in hand as she graded essays. Everyone else had finished the literature final a half hour earlier, but Keppler and I had continued our tight race to write the best and most detailed essays to finish the semester.

Flipping through the four pages in front of me, I decided I couldn't analyze another word from the two poems we'd been provided. Rereading my last paragraph, I added a closing sentence, stood without scraping my chair on the floor, and tiptoed to the end of the table.

Emma looked up from the paper she was grading and smiled. I handed her my four pages, and she tipped her head in the direction of the living room. Voices drifted in from the kitchen where Alexander, Kinley, and Max talked while Kat taught Lily how to make potato soup.

I nodded and slipped into the living room. Todd and I hadn't spoken since our fight on Thursday. When I'd told him the truth about where I'd been and showed him Molly's undelivered letter, he'd gotten up and called Emma for a ride home. He had said he didn't want to put her through what he'd just gone through with me.

The blue and silver ornaments on the Christmas tree glittered against the strings of lights. No one sat on the couch, the love seat, or in either of the chairs. Deciding Todd must have slipped past us to join the others in the kitchen, I turned to leave and noticed two white socks sticking out between a stack of wrapped presents and the side of the love seat.

"Todd?" I glanced around the bushy evergreen branches to the pocket of space behind the Christmas tree. "What are you doing?"

He sat with his back against the wall under the window, hands behind his head. "I needed a quiet place to recover from that test, and I kind of hoped you'd come looking for me."

I squeezed into the space between my friend and the love seat. "Remember when your dad dragged you out by your feet when we used to hide here?"

He laughed and nodded. "Maybe if we just stay back here, you won't have to go with Audrie."

"Is that what's bothering you?" My throat tightened with dread. "You're worried I'll have to leave?"

"I'm worried you'll have to leave. I'm afraid it's dangerous for you to stay. I've seen what the world can be like, and I don't want you to get hurt, but I don't want to lose you either."

"I know all of the uncertainty is really overwhelming." Taking a deep breath, I leaned back against the wall. "But the one thing I'm sure of is that we're going to figure it out together. Just like we always do."

He rubbed one hand over his face. "I'm kind of a disaster right now. Are you sure you want my help to figure things out?"

"Absolutely." I squeezed his hand. "I've been a little bit of a disaster lately too. I'm sorry for snapping at you. You didn't deserve that. And for being so late the other day. I don't want you to ever feel like I'm not here for you because I always will be."

"I know. And Molly should have known that too. Don't beat

yourself up over that letter. You were always nice to her even when she didn't deserve it."

"It wasn't enough. I just wish I could have done more." I turned to Todd, his face creased with concern. "I know I can't be responsible for everyone. And now I'm distracted again. I'm sorry."

"It's okay. I love you anyway." He scooted over an inch so our shoulders touched. "While we're apologizing, I'm sorry I left you for so long . . . that I left you in the first place."

"I love you anyway." My chest ached with the memory of fear I would never see him again. "But I did miss you a lot. I would have done anything to bring you home."

Todd turned to me, hazel eyes gentle but serious. "The trade you made with Molly . . . I never want you to do anything like that again. If there's a next time, just leave me there and run."

I focused so intently on the string of lights in front of me they blurred together into glittering globes. "That's exactly what I felt last year when I had the fever. When I told you to stay away so you wouldn't get sick."

We sat in silence for a minute before Todd spoke. "Rochelle, if the worst happens and you have to go live with Audrie, promise you'll come back. Even if you like it better there, at least come home and visit sometimes."

"I won't like it better there, and I'll be home the minute it's safe." As much as I didn't want to leave Maibe, it was the only way I could help the TCI stop Molly and make sure the pendants were used for good. It was my chance to do the right thing, but I also knew it would be temporary. The life I wanted was already right in front of me. "And while I'm away, I'll write to you every day. But try not to worry for now. Audrie won't even answer her phone."

"Okay." Todd let out the breath he had been holding through

my rushed assurances. "We'll deal with all of that when the time comes. For now . . ." He reached into his pocket and pulled out a folded square of paper. "I promise by next year I'll be able to afford a real present."

"This is a real present." I smiled and carefully unfolded the sketching paper, eager to see Todd's latest drawing. The familiar scene appeared square by square—Maibe's Main Street buildings with full display windows. The light poles and building fronts were decorated with wreaths and garland. People, bundled against the cold, walked along the sidewalks, some of them talking, others looking into the windows. "This is so detailed. It had to have taken you forever."

"I've had a lot of time to focus on my drawing." He smiled so big his dimples appeared. "And I wanted it to be perfect for you."

"I love it." Flattening the drawing across my knees so I could continue to admire it, I reached across Todd for a rectangular box, wrapped in red paper, under the tree. "Your turn."

He accepted the gift and his eyes sparkled with anticipation as he shook it. "Hmm." His fingers slipped beneath the folds of paper, pulled the box free, and lifted off the lid to reveal the new stocking hat and gloves I had made for him. Todd turned the hat inside out, changing it from black to green. "Two hats in one. That's clever."

I grinned as he pulled it over his head and slipped his hands into the gloves I'd started making while he was still missing. "Your old ones looked pretty worn, and I know you'll be right back to helping your dad when the doctor okays it."

"Now I just have to get rid of this cast." Todd wrapped his arms around me and kissed my temple. "Your gloves are the only ones that keep my hands warm and actually make it through the whole winter without falling apart. How long does it take you to make these?"

"Not long now that I have the pattern figured out." I

straightened his new hat so it covered both of his ears. "If I keep practicing, maybe I can make enough to sell."

"Someday, you're going to have the most successful sewing business in the area." Todd relaxed, his shoulder slumped against mine. For the first time since he'd come home, he looked like himself with his usual haircut and face finally filling out. "And, in a few years, I'll be a partner with my dad at the hardware store. We'll have life figured out and nothing to tear us apart. I just wish I knew how we get there from here."

"One day at a time." I looped my arm through his and laid my head on his shoulder.

"One day at a time." His head rested against mine and for peaceful minutes we sat together in the quiet warmth of the room until a set of legs became visible through the branches.

"Hey guys. Come out here." Max's arm reached into the space between the love seat and the Christmas tree. "I have a serious matter to discuss."

"Max? Serious?" Todd whispered in my ear.

I shrugged and took Max's hand. He gripped mine and pulled me to my feet.

Keppler stood behind him, eyes wide with disbelief. "How did you know they were back there?"

"Some things never change." Max reached his arm around the tree again. "One time when we were kids, they hid from me back here for two hours."

Todd rose into view with Max's help. "We were playing hide-and-seek, Max. That's how the game works."

Max shook his head. "I'm pretty sure everyone is supposed to find their own hiding spot. Keppler, you want to weigh in on this?"

"Not really." Keppler took three steps backward and sat down on the couch. "My head hurts and I want this *serious meeting* to be over with." He had been in a bad mood since the day before. From what I understood, he was trying to get a hold of Lareina, but she never called him back. I knew how he felt since I was going through the same thing with Audrie, but I hadn't heard from Lareina since our failed search of Molly's house, so I couldn't help.

"Fine. We'll save that debate for another time." Max nudged me toward the couch. "Everyone sit down."

Todd and I joined Keppler on the couch. Max shrugged off his book bag, pulled out three small boxes of different shapes, and distributed them to us, instructing us to open them at the same time.

I removed the lid to reveal a round, silver locket on a chain. The smooth back was tarnished and several of the stones making up the design on the front were missing. "It's pretty . . . in a vintage way."

Keppler pulled out a tarnished watch and held it up to his ear. "Mine doesn't work."

"Mine works a little too well." Todd held his watch in front of me so Keppler and I could both see the minute hand zipping around the face. "It would be good in a time travel movie."

"That's neat." I laughed and looked at Max. "How'd you make it do that?"

"I didn't make it do that. You're missing the point." Max plopped down in the nearest armchair.

"You got us a bunch of Christmas presents that don't work, yet you're worried about a game of hide-and-seek from ten years ago?" Todd gave up on his clumsy attempt to fasten his watch with a cast and held his arm out to me.

"They do work." Max leaned back smugly in his chair. "Just not in the way you're expecting."

"I'm too tired for riddles, Delgado. I just wrote a six-page essay in an hour."

"Impressive. You win." I slid Todd's watch band through the holding loop. "There."

Todd leaned back into the couch. "What does my watch do besides tell time at warp speed?"

"It's a tracker. If any of you go missing again, I'll know where you are."

I slipped the locket over my head. "You mean that's what you want them to do? Like you want old washing machines to travel back in time?"

"No, I mean, time travel is hard. It's never been done before. Making trackers turns out to be incredibly easy." He pulled one of his old cell phones out of his pocket and slid his finger around the screen before turning it toward us. "See, the green dot is Rochelle, the blue dot is Keppler, and the red dot is Todd. Right now, you're all right here at 808 Monarch Street." He put two fingers on the screen and pulled them apart until it showed a map of Maibe with our three dots all in one spot.

"So, if I walked to the grocery store right now?" I looked down at the old locket.

"As long as you had that with you, the green dot would move over here." Max pointed at the map.

"If you don't quit playing around with this old stuff, you're going to get in trouble." Keppler shook his head at the watch laying across his open palm. "Kat said her classmate used his dad's Wi-Fi code and got sent to reform school."

"He has a point." I squeezed Keppler's arm to remind him to keep his voice down. Using unauthorized codes and devices carried serious legal consequences. "Remember what Alexander and Kinley said about storm tracking?"

"They didn't say anything about tracking my friends." Max sighed when no one laughed. "The truth is, I'm tired of you guys disappearing, and sitting here helpless while you're being tortured. It's worth the risk of a little legal trouble."

"We've been through this . . ." Keppler looked at Todd and stopped.

"He knows everything Rochelle knows." Something about Max's phrasing piqued my interest.

"Then you all know you're not supposed to follow me when I have to leave. No one is supposed to know where I am." Keppler spoke in a hushed voice, keeping his eyes on the doorway.

"I won't follow you." Max's shoulders slumped forward, disappointed at our lack of enthusiasm for his trackers. "But at least if your dot is moving around, I'll know you're still alive."

"And he'll know it's you, because no one is going to steal that watch." I loved Todd for trying to lighten the mood. "Maybe mine, but not Charlie's."

"I appreciate the thought." Keppler slid his watch onto the end table. "But when I leave, it'll be dangerous for any of you to know where I am."

"Come on, Keppler." Max sat on the front edge of his cushion, still clutching the phone in his hand. "I already said I wouldn't follow you. This is just extra insurance for the worst-case scenario."

"That scenario makes this even more dangerous." Keppler glanced at Todd and me before turning back to Max. "It's dangerous for me, and it's even more dangerous for you."

"Hey, guys. What's going on?"

Our heads swiveled in the direction of my sister's voice. She stood in the doorway, hands on her hips, watching us through narrowed eyes.

"Nothing," Keppler answered as my sister approached. "Just talking."

Max slipped the phone discreetly back into his pocket, and Todd covered his watch with the sleeve of his shirt.

"It sounded more like arguing." My sister perched on the arm of the couch next to him and picked up the watch on the end table. "What's this?"

"A broken watch." Keppler gave Max a look. "I was just explaining to Delgado that fixing cars doesn't qualify me to fix that."

Kat looked at me with one eyebrow raised. "Whatever you guys are up to, knock it off before you ruin the holidays." She took Keppler's hand and pulled him to his feet. "Dinner is almost ready. Charlie, I need your help with something. The rest of you, go wash your hands and set the table or something." She took one more look at the watch before tossing it onto the love seat behind her and leaving the room hand in hand with Keppler.

Max stared at the doorway they had disappeared through. "For a guy who flinches at human contact, he sure holds Kat's hand a lot lately."

Todd looked up at me. "There's nothing wrong with holding hands."

"I didn't say there was." Max stood. "But it is the first step to *Sorry, Max, I can't help with the time machine because I have plans with Kat.*"

Todd laughed. "Remember that, Rochelle. If we want to get out of helping Max with his projects, we just have to tell him I have plans with you."

Max turned to me, eyebrows raised. It was as close as Todd had come to admitting our relationship was more than just a friendship. Max had been losing bets that Todd would officially ask me out since we were twelve, and Kat had been advising me to ask him out myself since our cancelled homecoming dance. I didn't see any reason to push him into something he wasn't ready for.

I smacked Max's shoulder with the back of my hand. "You know, you could go tease Keppler and Kat. He's the one who won't wear your watch."

"Good point." Max picked up his bag and clapped Todd's shoulder. "Don't worry, buddy. I know you'll figure it out one day."

"Figure what out?" Todd stood as Max darted out of the room. "What am I doing wrong now?"

"Nothing." I slipped off the hat he still wore. "Unless we're late for dinner. Kinley is under a lot of stress, and Kat is in a mood."

"In that case." He offered me his arm. "Do you want to help me set the table?"

I took his arm, and we made our way to the kitchen to face whatever came next.

CHAPTER 29

CHARLIE

December 24, 2090

"**A**umont, this is a bad idea." I paced from the basement stairs to the living room couch just outside my bedroom.

"It's Christmas and she's family." Rochelle sat on the couch, already wearing the velvety green dress and shiny black shoes she'd chosen for Christmas mass. She took a deep breath and picked up the phone on the end table, finger poised to dial her aunt's number.

"But every time you get her involved in your life, she causes problems." I couldn't decide if my worry was about Audrie coming to take Rochelle away or deciding I was healed enough to join the TCI before I had a pendant. My mind had been far from those concerns all day. Alexander had come over to help us eat Kat's amazing five-course meal, then we watched Christmas movies and opened presents. But as usual, Rochelle couldn't leave well enough alone. "You gave her the pendant and that was your only obligation."

"But she said I can help her figure out what else my dad knew about the pendants. And I need her help to stop Molly before she does something she can't take back." Rochelle dialed the number Audrie had ordered me to memorize and lifted the phone to her ear.

"Molly is far past that point." I pressed the palm of my hand to the back of my head and returned to pacing. Everyone else was upstairs, getting dressed to go to midnight mass. I had planned to go with them, but I'd decided I didn't belong there, dressed in a shirt and tie in a church pew. The loud ringing on the other end came through the phone. It rang once, twice, then three times. I held my breath, willing Audrie not to answer like every other time Rochelle called.

"Hi, Aunt Audrie. This is Rochelle. Merry Christmas."

Muscles rigid, I sat down on the couch.

"Hey, kiddo. Merry Christmas." Audrie's voice came through the phone loud and clear. "It's so good to hear your voice. I wanted to call you a long time ago, but I've been traveling for work the past few weeks."

I shook my head at Rochelle, not believing Audrie's excuse.

Rochelle smiled and patted my hand. "I called a few times since we never really got to say goodbye."

"Oh, Rochelle. I owe you an apology." Audrie's voice picked up that sickly sweet tone. "I overreacted when I was visiting. You did the right thing by helping your friend and giving me the pendant. It just really scared me to think about what could have happened to you."

I nudged Rochelle's arm and mouthed, *That's all you wanted to hear.* I pointed at the end table, indicating she should hang up the phone.

Rochelle shook her head at me. "I know I need to get better at asking for help. That's the other reason I called."

I flopped back onto the couch and covered my face with my hand. There was no stopping Rochelle once she had her mind made up.

"Nothing bad has happened in the past two weeks, but I've heard all of the news about The Defiance taking over Texas and

I'm worried. I want to help you stop Molly and The Defiance from using the pendants."

From the other side of the couch, I couldn't hear how Audrie responded.

"I've been thinking about that too. Do you think if I stayed with you for a few months, we could solve everything? Then I could come back home."

Letting my hand slide to the side, I watched Rochelle nod with the phone to her ear.

"Okay. You're right. It's something we should all talk about so we can decide what's best." Rochelle listened for a minute and smiled. "I love you too. I'll see you soon." She hung up the phone and turned to me. "Audrie is going to visit in a few days. She'll call as soon as she knows when she'll arrive."

"Aumont, why would you say that stuff?" I didn't lift my head from the pillow under me. "You don't want to leave here."

"I don't want to . . . But I think I have to. I've been talking with Kinley, and she's so worried about Kat and me."

"There's no way Kinley would send you to live with Audrie." I sat up.

"She will once she understands it's what's best for all of us. Now that Audrie is speaking to me again, everything will be okay." Rochelle forced a smile. "That reminds me, I saw Lareina this morning when I helped Kat deliver cookies to the home for children. She sent a note for you."

"And you're just telling me now?" I slid to the edge of my cushion. "I've been trying to contact her for days."

"She's been really busy at the home for children, and I think she's fighting with Nick." Rochelle looked down at her shoes. "You were at Max's when I got home, so I left it in the library on the desk. Sorry, I forgot about it until now."

"It's okay." I was annoyed that Lareina had avoided me all week and then sent me a note after I had left several messages, both with Nick and the director at the home for children. But none of that was Rochelle's fault.

"Rochelle?" Kinley's voice yelled from upstairs. "Rochelle, where are you?"

"Don't tell her about Audrie yet. I'll take care of that tomorrow." She hurried toward the stairs.

The serenity I'd felt all day faded as I considered the possibility that Audrie was using both of us for her own agenda. The only adults I trusted were Kinley, Alexander, and Emma, but they barely counted as adults and they were powerless against The Defiance and Audrie. Taking the stairs two at a time, I returned to the same conclusion I always circled back to: even if I didn't trust Audrie completely, I had no other choice than to work with her.

"We could have curled your hair or something." In the dining room, Kinley brushed Rochelle's hair over her shoulders. "And what is this?" She lifted the locket.

"That's my present from Max." Rochelle smiled. "It's pretty, right?"

Kinley wrinkled her nose at the tarnished necklace. "Maybe if you were eight." She tucked the locket under the neckline of Rochelle's dress. "Come on. I have a few minutes to fix your hair before we go."

Rochelle made a face at me, but she let her cousin take her hand and pull her upstairs.

Just as they vanished, Alexander came in from the kitchen, looking down at his tie as he looped it around itself. "Where did Kinley go?"

"Upstairs, with Rochelle."

Alexander cringed at the tangled mess of his tie and undid it, letting it dangle around his neck. "Are you sure you don't want to come with us? I don't like leaving you here all alone on Christmas Eve."

"It's okay." I wanted to run into the next room and read Lareina's note. "I'll probably just go to bed."

Alexander gripped my shoulder and glanced around the room. "Just don't disappear on me. You haven't heard from Griff or Audrie since the last time we talked?"

He asked the same question every time we were alone. For a minute, I considered telling him about Audrie's call with Rochelle, but that wasn't my business to share. "No. Nothing."

"All right. Keep me posted." He rubbed the side of his face, and I noticed the shadows beneath his eyes. Between his work with the Nebraska leaders, his duties as Maibe's mayor, and keeping his family business running, I didn't know how he could get much sleep.

"You'll be the first to know." I didn't intend to follow through with that promise, but I didn't want to give him more to worry about either.

He nodded and looked like he wanted to say more, but footsteps overhead ended our conversation. We turned to the doorway in time for the girls to enter in their dresses. Rochelle's hair was smooth and free of frizz as it only was on special occasions. Kinley and Kat both wore their long hair in spirals down to their waists.

"Here, let me see you." Kinley looped Alexander's tie over and under, then folded his collar carefully over it. "There. Much better."

He smiled. "I'd be so lost without you."

"I agree." She stood on her tiptoes and kissed his cheek.

A knot formed in my stomach when I imagined her reaction to Alexander signing Audrie's papers. For his sake, I hoped she would never find out about it.

Kinley gave me a one-armed hug. "Are you sure you don't want to come with us? There's still time for you to change."

I shook my head and looked down at my socks. "I'm pretty tired." I had done plenty of questionable things in my life and brushed them off, but lying to Kinley made me feel like a rotten person.

"Maybe next time. Get some sleep and we'll see you in the morning." She rushed Alexander and Rochelle to the door.

"I'm starting Christmas breakfast at seven if you want to help." Kat hugged me tight. She smelled like vanilla. I was beginning to enjoy helping her cook even more than writing. "Merry Christmas, Charlie." She kissed my cheek and followed her family into the next room.

"Merry Christmas." I remained frozen even after she had vanished from sight. After witnessing my parents' marriage, I had decided I would never pursue a relationship. It had never occurred to me that falling for someone was less of a choice and more of something that just happened. But with Kat . . . If my life were normal and I could stay in Maibe . . . I shook the thought from my head as the screen door slammed. Instead of dwelling on the impossible, I hurried into the library and ripped open the envelope with my name on it.

Charlie—

I'm sorry it took me so long to get back to you. After a long discussion with Nick and Aaron, we decided to pack the pendants away and put the past behind us. No more searching for answers or looking for trouble. I'm sorry I couldn't help.

—Lareina

Pack them away? Put the past behind them? What did any of

that mean? She wouldn't help me. Because she didn't want to, or because her friends wouldn't let her?

Letter in hand, I wandered into the living room and sank to the floor among scraps of paper and discarded ribbons. Alexander and Kinley had bought me two of the tools I needed to work on the truck. Kat had given me a thick notebook with a bright yellow cover. On the inside she had written, *This should last you a few weeks.* Rochelle had made me a seat cover for the truck so I wouldn't have to listen to Max laughing about all of the holes I'd patched with duct tape. And I wouldn't be there to use any of them.

I hadn't bought any of them a gift, but I'd written each of them a personalized short story. It was my way of saying thank you and goodbye, but I kept my meaning cryptic so they wouldn't understand the real message until I had vanished and they analyzed my last writing for answers.

The phone rang and I jumped. Who would call after midnight? Maybe Lareina had changed her mind. I pulled myself to my feet and rushed to the kitchen where I picked up on the third ring.

"Hello."

"Hey, kid. Hope I didn't wake you up." Griff's unmistakable voice came through the phone. I hated having it in my house. "Molly guaranteed me your new family would be at church. I didn't figure you'd be with them. You haven't changed one bit."

In that moment, I wished I had put on a tie and gone with them. Anything to prove Griff wrong and avoid his phone call. But I had a part to play. "What's up?"

"I'm just about ready for you to come and join us. I have to do a little business traveling, but it'll be a short trip. How does New Year's Day sound for your welcome home?"

Stalling would only make him suspicious. Swallowing a lump in my throat, I sank to the floor. "I can probably make that work."

"Really?" He laughed. "Did you get tired of fighting your destiny, or have you finally come to your senses?"

"A little of both, I guess."

"Do you have the pendant?"

"Not exactly." I gripped the phone so tightly my hand hurt. "But I'm working on it."

"I know you'll come through for me." Griff's voice indicated there would be painful consequences if I didn't. "If there's anyone in this world I can count on, it's my brother."

I pulled my knees up to my chin as I felt my comfortable life crumbling into one of deception, danger, and death.

"Hey, kid, are you still there?"

"I'm here." My brain scrambled for words. "I'll take care of everything, and I'll see you on the first of January."

"That's what I thought. I'll have your room ready." Griff paused for a minute. "Do you need money to get here? I can send you a ticket."

"No, I have that covered." I had set aside enough money for a train ticket as soon as I had received my first paycheck for my paper route. Back then I thought it would be to run from Griff. Now I was glad it would prevent him and the rest of his gang from getting any closer to Maibe. "I'll leave early that morning when it's easy to slip away."

"Great. Then you can help me convince Molly to forget about that dead-end little town. Once you get the pendant, we'll have all we need from there." The relief that he didn't want anything to do with Rochelle or Maibe swept through me, then evaporated as I realized it was all dependent on the delivery of a pendant I didn't have. "Just a minute." I heard a murmur of conversation on his end of the phone. "Sorry, kid, I have to deal with a problem. See you in a week."

"See you then." I lowered the phone after the click and rested my head back against the cupboard door. There had to be a way to get through to Lareina. If I could just talk to her in person I could make her understand. After breakfast I would slip away and visit her. I still had a week to get the pendant.

Forcing myself to my feet, I returned to the living room, surveying the gifts I would never get to use. I picked up Max's tracker watch from where it had been on the love seat since the day before and put it on my wrist. For the moment it brought me a sense of comfort. I could always take it off.

One more week of Kat's home-cooked meals, Rochelle's hugs, and Kinley's fussing over my health. One more week of having a real family, a house that felt like home, and a real future. Scooping up the notebook Kat had given me, I made my way to the basement to start packing.

CHAPTER 30

ROCHELLE

December 26, 2090

"Kinley, I don't want to go to school in Omaha." Kat's anger was all that kept her from crying. "I don't want to live with people I don't know. People I've never met."

"It'll be okay, Kat." I wanted to hug her, but she was across the table, so I remained glued to my chair next to Kinley. Emma, who sat next to my sister, put a hand on her shoulder. "We'll both go with you and help you get settled. It'll only be for a semester."

"No." Kat ducked her shoulder away from Emma's hand and stood. "I'm tired of you two deciding my life for me."

Emma caught my sister's hand before she could rush out of the room. "Wait a minute. Let's give Kinley a chance to explain why she decided this is the best option. Try to see this from her perspective." We had asked Emma to come to our family meeting because she was good at keeping everyone calm and acting as the neutral voice of reason.

"Fine." Kat plopped back in her chair and folded her arms over her chest. "I'm listening."

Kinley sighed and clasped her hands on the tabletop. "I'm worried about your safety. If Molly or The Defiance show up looking for the pendant, or Rochelle, or Charlie, I won't be able to protect any of you." My cousin rubbed her forehead. "I'm not giving you up. I would never do that. This is only temporary."

Kat's eyes locked with mine. "What about Rochelle? She's the one who started all of this trouble, and she just gets to stay here and live her normal life?"

"No. I'm going to stay with Aunt Audrie for a while." I kept talking despite my sister's shaking head. "She's coming in a couple of days, and we're going to make a plan for me to leave with her right after I get you settled in Omaha."

"That's not what I want. I don't want to leave and I don't want you staying with Audrie. I want everything back the way it was before." She stood and stepped out of Emma's reach. "I'm not a little kid. We could have made these decisions together. Maybe I had ideas too. But what could I possibly know?"

"Kat, that's not—"

"Forget it, Kinley," my sister interrupted. "Don't talk to me unless you change your mind."

Before Emma could stop her, Kat rushed out of the room. The three of us listened to my sister stomp up the stairs and slam her door above us. I knew she would lock us out, curl up on her bed, and cry. After a few hours she would let me in to talk about it. For the ten years I'd had a sister, it was the two of us against Dad, or Grandma, or Kinley, but this time I was on the other side.

"I knew she'd be upset." My cousin pressed one hand to her forehead. "I don't blame her."

"Maybe if I just describe it to her the way you described it to me." I stood. "If she can picture the nice house where she'll be staying, and the school, and all of the opportunities—"

"Rochelle, stop." Kinley gripped my elbow and pulled me back into my seat. "What would have helped was for you to go to Omaha with Kat so she wouldn't be all alone. You never should have called Audrie without me."

I swallowed the lump forming in my throat. "I'm sorry I didn't involve you, but going with her feels right. Everything that's happening is my fault and it's only going to get worse. Unless I go with Audrie and help her figure out what else Dad knew about the pendants. I need her help to fix this and then everything can go back to normal."

My cousin squeezed her eyes shut for a second and when she opened them, they glistened with tears. "How am I supposed to know Audrie is taking care of you? How will I know you're safe when you're a thousand miles away? I don't trust her. She's going to have to say something pretty incredible to get me to sign anything." My cousin stood and turned her back to Emma and me. "I need some air. I'm going for a walk." She strode to the door and it closed hard behind her.

I wanted to run after Kinley and apologize for leaving her when I had promised over and over I never would. I wanted to knock on Kat's door and assure her she would have amazing opportunities at her new school, and the months we had to be apart would fly by. But I was the enemy; the one who had broken the fragile normalcy we'd worked so hard to piece together. My head sank to my arms on the tabletop.

"It'll be okay, sweetie." Emma's arms enveloped me as I cried.

"I don't want to leave them, but I don't have another choice."

"I know. But everything will be okay. You'll have an adventure for a few months while Audrie finds a way for you to be safe here, and then you'll be home and all of this will be over."

If only I could believe that were true. I had been bombarded by the images on the news and in the papers of The Defiance taking whatever they wanted in Texas, driving people out of their homes, and killing anyone who stood in their way. What would stop their slow-moving war, their absolute takeover, from pushing north and rolling right through Maibe?

"Kinley is just worried about you." Emma dried my tears with a napkin from the holder on the table. "And Kat needs a little time to process all of this. Once she sees her school and where she'll live, she'll understand this is for the best."

I didn't reply, but rested my head on Emma's shoulder and fought back new tears when I realized that, soon, I wouldn't have her to comfort me either. Every time I tried to imagine the excitement of living in New York with Audrie, my mind snapped to the loneliness of missing Maibe and everyone I loved.

The screen door slammed shut and I sat up, hoping Kinley had returned, but Alexander and Keppler walked in with a gust of winter air. Their clothes were smudged with dirt, faces flushed from working in Alexander's greenhouse.

"That bad?" Alexander looked at me, eyes gentle. Of course Kinley had spoken to him about our plan for Kat, and probably my foolishness of contacting Audrie when she had been leaving us alone.

Emma kept one arm around me. "Kat stormed off to her room and Kinley went for a walk."

"To where?" Alexander looked to the window as if he expected to see Kinley walking down the sidewalk.

"I don't know." Emma sighed. "Would you rather go find her or talk to Kat?"

Alexander pressed his hand to the back of his neck. "I'll go after Kinley."

"I'll talk to Kat." Emma squeezed my shoulder as she stood. "I'm sure I can get her to come help me with dinner."

Alexander helped me to my feet as Emma headed upstairs. "I can stay if you want me to. Kinley will come back on her own."

"I'll be okay." I hugged him, but I didn't feel the instant security I was used to when he was near. Even Alexander wasn't strong enough to protect us from the threat that was approaching silently and unpredictably. "I don't want her to stay out in the cold."

"I won't be gone for long." He gave me one last squeeze and disappeared through the door.

"I told you Kat wouldn't like any of this." Keppler walked to the sink and splashed water over his face the best he could with one arm in a sling. "But I thought you were all ready to go with Audrie. What's with the tears?"

"My dad used to tell me I was good at being the glue that held this family together." I handed him a towel from the counter. "I know going with Audrie is the right thing to do, but if none of us are speaking by the time this is over, then what's the point of anything?"

Keppler dried his face. "Just when I think Kat and Kinley will never speak again, they start hugging." He wiped his hands before hanging it over the back of a chair. "You guys are weird enough that not even this can tear you apart."

Normally, I would laugh when Keppler described what he believed to be the bizarre behavior of my family, but I was too despondent. "Will you come and sit with me? I don't want to be alone."

"Me neither." He looked down at his filthy clothes and shrugged. "I'll shower later."

I nodded and wiped away lingering tears. Together we walked to the next room and sat side by side on the window seat. When I closed my eyes, I saw Kat stomp out of the kitchen and Kinley rush outside. "I'm scared, I think."

"That much I can understand. I'm scared too." He scratched at a patch of dried mud on his sleeve. "I've been trying to find Lareina. To talk about the story we're writing. It's a good distraction. But they won't let me into the home for children because they have a flu outbreak, and she won't call me back."

"I'm sure she's really busy. Don't worry, she'll get back to you."

Lareina hadn't called or visited me either, but I had no reason to think she was purposely avoiding us.

Keppler sighed and his shoulders slumped. "I'm running out of time to finish the story." He didn't look at me, and I didn't like the certainty of his statement.

"You haven't heard from Griff yet?" I turned to him, fearing his answer.

Keppler paused then shook his head. "But I know it'll come. What is Kinley going to do if she sends me away and then he shows up to find me?"

It was another question I didn't have an answer to. A hole in our plan. I closed my eyes and felt as if I were plummeting toward the ground. It wasn't the quick panic of missing the next monkey bar or the rush of jumping off the highest diving board, but the helplessness of falling through the open air toward the unforgiving ground. It just kept moving farther and farther away to prolong the torture of fearing the pain to come.

"You're right. I can't leave her here all alone." My hand fumbled with my sweater, pulling it away from my throat so I could breathe.

"I think you're all better off together." Keppler looked past me to the wall of books. "But there's a risk, a consequence to every choice we make. Sometimes we have to give up what we love the most so we won't lose it forever."

I rubbed my forehead, trying to determine whether he was talking about me or himself. "It's not fair when other people have to deal with the consequences of my choices. I don't know what I'm supposed to do."

"Ask Audrie to find a way to protect you here. Maybe she can give you a TCI body guard or something." Keppler turned to me, eyes downcast and expression mournful. "Molly will figure out you don't know anything and she won't bother you anymore."

"What makes you so sure?"

"She's with The Defiance now. She has bigger things to do than torment you." He shrugged. "We're supposed to hope for the best. Right?"

"When we're not preparing for the worst." I sighed and folded my legs under me. "Wherever we have to go, and however long we have to stay away, this will always be home for both of us. Agree?"

"It's the only home I've ever had." He smiled but it only lasted for a second. "Aumont, promise me that you'll take care of yourself. From now on, forget about the pendants and focus on school, sewing, reading, anything else. Leave saving the world to people who are trained for it. Please, promise you'll avoid trouble."

I nodded, coerced by the fear in Keppler's eyes. "I'll be more careful."

We sat together, under the weight of misery, in the dreary shadows of late afternoon as the minutes ticked by. Neither of us said another word, neither of us stood to turn on the light, and neither of us moved when the back door opened and closed.

Kinley peeked around the half-open French door. "Rochelle and Charlie are in here." She approached us, followed by Alexander.

He glanced around the room. "Emma's still upstairs with Kat?"

I nodded. I hadn't heard them come downstairs.

"Rochelle, I'm sorry I raised my voice at you." Kinley sank down next to me. "I know this is hard for you too. I will try my best not to panic until we've met with Audrie and talked over all of the details. Okay?"

"Okay." I slid forward to hug Kinley. "We'll get through this."

My cousin kept one arm around me and nudged Keppler's shoulder with her hand. "The plans are in place for you to move up north the day after New Year's Day. That loser Griff will never figure out where you disappeared to."

"Thanks, Kinley." Keppler exchanged a look with Alexander, but my cousin didn't seem to notice. "I appreciate everything you've done for me."

"I promised to take care of you." Kinley pulled me to my feet as she stood and extended her hand to Keppler. "Go get cleaned up while we get dinner started. I have a feeling Kat won't be cooking for us tonight."

Keppler took her hand and stood. "When are you meeting with Audrie exactly?"

"The day after tomorrow." Kinley sighed. "We're meeting her in Omaha. I'm hoping we can resolve everything over lunch so she won't have to come back here."

His face faded to a sickly, pale shade. "But she might come here?"

"It's okay." Alexander patted Keppler's shoulder. "I'll be right here with you. Maybe I should go along to Omaha with you guys to make sure you get there safely."

"Sure, if you want to." Kinley smiled, pleased that he offered to accompany her. "We'll get everything planned out over dinner. Come on, Rochelle. Let's go see what we have in the refrigerator."

I knew Keppler didn't like my aunt, but I didn't understand why he looked like he would throw up at the mention of her visit. Even Alexander's volunteering to accompany us without Kinley's prompting was out of character. I could have asked my cousin what she thought, but we had bigger problems, so I let her steer me toward the kitchen.

CHAPTER 31
CHARLIE

December 28, 2090

"We'll be home as soon as we can," Kinley said as she pulled her boots on. "Just stay inside and keep the doors locked."

I sat at the kitchen table, trying to focus on her words. It was mid-morning and I was already exhausted. Ever since Griff's phone call, I hadn't been able to sleep. My inability to reach Lareina, and Kat's refusal to speak to Rochelle or Kinley only added to my pile of distractions.

"Charlie?" Kinley waved her hand in front of me. "Are you with me?"

Nodding, I rubbed a hand over my face. "Lock the doors and stay inside."

She studied me with her hands on her hips as the back door slammed and Alexander opened the door to the kitchen.

"Hey guys." He looked from Kinley to me. "Is everything okay?"

"That's what I'm trying to figure out." She raised her eyebrows.

"I'm just a little tired. It's hard to sleep." Hard to sleep, hard to breathe, and hard to concentrate. I hadn't written anything since my literature final, and although I feared losing my family, I was spending all of my time alone.

Alexander nodded. He knew more than Kinley, but not enough to understand the full extent of my anxiety.

Kinley reached across the table and patted my hand. "Try to get a little sleep while we're gone. Emma will check in at lunch time. She has a key to let herself in."

Footsteps padded toward us and Rochelle entered the room, clutching a piece of paper in her hand. "I told Kat we were leaving and spent five minutes trying to talk her into coming along, but she just slid this under the door." She dropped the note on the table.

Go away. I'm not speaking to you or Kinley.

"She can't hide from us forever." Kinley stood and slid Rochelle's coat from the back of the chair. "I'm sure she'll forgive you when we get home."

"I hope so." Rochelle slid her arms into the coat Kinley held for her, then turned her attention to me. "I'm sorry we have to leave you here. I told Kat she has no reason to be mad at you."

"I'll be all right." I didn't want them to go, but I understood Kinley's decision to meet on neutral ground and her hope that Audrie wouldn't return to Maibe with them.

"We'll be back soon." Rochelle hugged me, pinning my arms to my sides.

Instead of squirming away, I whispered, "Don't let Audrie tell you what to do. Tell her you want to stay here." Her head nodded next to my face before she let me go. I wished them all a safe trip and then I was alone in the kitchen.

The sky outside was a solid sheet of dark clouds threatening snow. My time in Maibe was ticking away too fast. A bag packed with two changes of clothes and the notebook Kat had given me was waiting at the foot of my bed.

I had stashed all of my writing in my dresser and stacked the rest of my clothes in the remaining drawers. Those were the easy things to put in order. Getting Griff his pendant while keeping my family together was an impossible challenge.

I was worried Kinley would find out about the papers Alexander and I had signed, but Alexander promised he would keep the lunch conversation steered away from me, and I trusted him.

Kinley would find out eventually. Alexander wanted to break the news in the gentlest way possible, and although I didn't tell him, I wanted that to be after I was gone. I couldn't bring myself to confess that Griff had contacted me. It would be easier on everyone if I just disappeared. No goodbyes and no explanations outside of what Alexander and Audrie could provide.

Heavy with worry and dread, I stood and trudged to the library. To my surprise, I spotted Kat sitting on the window seat. I froze halfway into the room.

"You can come in." Kat's voice was barely audible. "I was just trying to hear what they said about me."

"They're worried and they miss you." I closed the space between us, happy to see her, then lingered awkwardly in front of her. "Is it okay if I sit with you?"

Kat nodded so I lowered myself to the cushion.

"Are you mad at me too?" She had barely acknowledged any of us for a day and a half, so I didn't know what else to think.

She sat up and smacked my arm hard with the back of her hand.

"Ow." I scooted away from her. "What did I do?"

"You tell me. Were you a part of the committee that decided my whole future without consulting me?"

"No." I flinched, expecting her to hit me again. "Kinley barely consulted me about *my* future."

"Then I guess we're allies. Charlie, what are we going to do?"

"Take it one day at a time, I guess. It's okay if you're scared."

"I'm not scared." She looked straight at me. "I'm tired of being treated like a kid, and mad at Kinley for not understanding, and disappointed in Rochelle for not taking my side."

"Kinley is trying to keep us safe, and Rochelle feels responsible for everything that's happening. You can't stay mad at them."

"I know." Kat turned and rested her back against the window. "But I like my life the way it is. I don't want to move away. I don't want to live with strangers."

"You should talk to Kinley about all of this." I slid back so we sat shoulder to shoulder. I couldn't leave knowing Kat was miserable or that my family had been separated. "I bet she'll change her mind if you give her a chance to see things from your perspective."

"Maybe I should just go and see how long it takes for her to miss my cooking and cleaning. I could take a culinary arts class every week and run my own restaurant in a few years."

"She misses you already." If I had to give up my dreams for Kat to have hers, it was worth it. "You don't have to leave here to have your own restaurant someday. And I know when that happens, Rochelle and Kinley will be there on opening night waiting to be your first customers."

Her hand squeezed mine. "And you'll be there with them, taking notes to report on the event."

I nodded despite the lump in my throat. "It'll be my ground-breaking story."

The phone rang and we both jumped. It rang twice more before I could pull myself away.

"I'll get it." Hurrying to the kitchen, I picked up the phone and held it to my ear. "Hello."

"Charlie. I'm so glad you answered." Lareina's tired voice spoke on the other end of the line. "I really need to talk to you, but most of the kids are sick and I can't be away for long. Can you meet me behind the home for children, on the playground, in ten minutes?"

Kinley said not to leave the house. Now that Kat was speaking to me, I really didn't want to leave her alone, but this was my only chance to talk to Lareina and get the pendant. "I'll be right there."

"Where are you going?" Kat asked as I hung up the phone. "We're not supposed to go anywhere alone."

"Max really needs my help with something." I hoped she would believe me. "It'll only take a few minutes and then I'll be right back."

Kat sighed and nodded. "Okay. As long as you're back in time for lunch. I'm going to make us something way better than Kinley and Rochelle are eating at that restaurant with Audrie."

"That sounds great." I took a backward step toward the laundry room. "Just make sure to lock the door behind me."

CHAPTER 32

CHARLIE

December 28, 2090

When I reached the playground, I spotted Lareina sitting on one of the swings and ran over to her.

"Don't get too close." She held her hands up. "Hopefully I'm just tired, but I could be coming down with the flu like everyone else."

Nodding, I sat down on a swing a few feet away from her. "Maybe you should take a day off."

"I can't. Most of the other caregivers are already out." She wrapped her arms around herself even though she was already bundled in a heavy coat and hat. "I remember what it's like to be sick and afraid and all alone. I won't let them go through that."

Remembering the feeling she described, I couldn't argue. "What do we need to talk about?"

Lareina took a sharp breath. "I got all of your messages, but I didn't call you back because I didn't know what to do." She squeezed her eyes shut. "Nick decided we're safer if we just put all of this pendant stuff behind us and when he, Aaron, and I talked it over, we all agreed to hide them and forget about them. That way the world would be safe and we could move on with our lives."

Disappointed, I kicked my foot through the gravel under the swing set. "But you still know where they are? You could get to them in an emergency?"

"Aaron hid them since he was the neutral one in the argument." She sneezed twice into her sleeve. "But I figured out where he put them."

"You can still help me?" It was wrong to ask her to lie to her friends, but I was desperate and running out of time. "Please, Lareina. I only need one of the pendants. It's the only way I can keep Rochelle and all of Maibe safe. It's the only way I can get into a position to stop The Defiance."

"I don't want to lie to Nick and Aaron again." She cleared her throat. "But I don't want to sit around and do nothing either. What they don't know won't hurt them, right?"

"After everything you went through to protect the pendants, you can't just pretend they don't exist." I leaned toward her. "The story isn't over yet. But I can finish it and make sure we get the conclusion we want."

"It's not enough." For a second I thought she had called me there to deny me the pendant again. "It's not enough for me to play it safe and wait for something bad to happen to you and the Aumonts." Her wide brown eyes held me in place. "I know what it's like to be in over my head with no one to pull me out. I want to help you, but I want to be in this with you."

"What do you mean?"

"You said you were going to work for Audrie and keep her informed." She reached into her pocket and pulled out her closed hand. "I want to be in the loop too. I want to know what you find out, help you decide if the TCI is trustworthy, help you do the right thing."

Having an ally like Lareina could keep me from being sucked back into the treachery of The Defiance, but the dangers had prevented me from making similar arrangements with Max. "That's risky for both of us. I can't make any promises."

"I'm willing to take the risk." She opened her gloved hand to reveal one pendant resting against the blue material. "And you'll have to promise if you want to take this with you."

I stared at the shiny black surface, *SPERO* written across in white letters.

"It means hope." She smiled. "Exactly what we both need."

The key to saving my family and stopping The Defiance was right there in front of me. All I had to do was make a promise she could never hold me to.

"Okay. I promise." I crossed my fingers on the hand attached to my arm in the sling, hidden under my coat and stretched my other hand toward her. "I'll call you when I can."

"I'm trusting you." She dumped the pendant into my hand. "And that's really hard for me."

My breath hitched. How could I break her trust the way my own family and Griff had broken mine? "You can count on me."

"Take care of yourself. You have to make it home to write the rest of the story." She stood and smiled. "And I have to get back inside."

For a minute, I sat alone with Lareina's pendant, the third one I'd held in my hand in a year. There was no escaping them or what I had to do. But I had everything I needed to protect my family and three precious days before I had to leave. Lightened by the unexpected gift of the pendant, I shoved it into my pocket and ran back toward home.

It wasn't until I reached the back door that the concrete block on my chest returned. The door stood wide open.

Fingers frozen, I fumbled with the handle on the screen door and pulled it open.

"*Charlie.*" Kat's scream pulled me inside. "Char—" It wasn't a shout of pain or anger, but absolute terror.

Without thinking, I scrambled into the kitchen and right into a barrel-chested guy my age.

"Hey, Charlie." He gripped my shoulders before I lost my footing. "Long time no see." I recognized him from my time in The Defiance—Tommy, one of Griff's errand boys.

Behind him, Molly stood next to a guy I recognized from the gravel road where I traded Rochelle for Todd. He held Kat so her arms were pinned to her sides and his hand covered her mouth, accentuating her wide, frightened eyes. The kitchen table had been shoved halfway across the room and dishes lay scattered across the floor.

I wrenched out of his hold, grunting as my collarbone tweaked, and took a step back, trying to get my bearings. "What's going on?" All three of the intruders wore heavy coats, so I couldn't tell if they carried weapons, but experience assured me they wouldn't go on a mission without them.

"Griff told us all about your undercover work. You're a hero back home." Tommy scowled as he observed the room around us. "We came to get you out of this place."

Still trying to rationalize the scene around me, my tongue tripped over itself. "That wasn't the plan."

"Shut up, Charlie." Molly stepped in front of Kat. "Where's Rochelle?"

She had no right to be there. Anger seared inside my chest. "Not here. Let Kat go or I'll—"

"Drop the tough act." Molly took my arm and shoved me into the next room away from the others. "I wouldn't want you to embarrass yourself."

In the dining room, I ripped my arm away from her. "Does Griff know you're here? We had a plan." I kept my voice quiet so Kat wouldn't discover I was the real traitor in her house. "I'm supposed to have three more days."

"Griff is out on business and I have a better plan." Her eyes looked past me to the library. "Do exactly as I say or Kat will pay the price. Now, where's Rochelle?"

"Omaha, with Kinley and her aunt the TCI agent." I hoped the truth would scare Molly enough to give me some room for bargaining. "You don't want to be here when they get home."

"Don't worry. We won't be." She gave me her sweetest smile. "Go pack your bag while I verify Rochelle isn't upstairs." Before I could protest, she held a hand up in front of me. "Help with my plan and I won't take Kat out of Maibe."

I didn't want to cooperate with her, but both guys accompanying Molly were bigger than me, and my arm was still in a sling.

"Don't forget the pendant Griff assured me you'll bring home." She squeezed my injured shoulder until I took a backward step toward the basement. "It's funny how your attitude changed when he asked for it."

The muscles in my chest clenched so tight they ached. "I'll walk out of here with you and do whatever you want if you just leave Kat alone. She has nothing to do with this."

"You're in no position to negotiate." Molly smiled and shoved me toward the stairs. "Go get your stuff. You're leaving today."

Mumbling under my breath, I trudged downstairs to grab my bag. It was surreal that convincing Lareina to give me a pendant had been my biggest worry only minutes earlier. I looked around my room for anything I could use as a weapon, but of course, I had nothing to fight off two guys with only one usable arm. Frustrated, I kicked the footboard of my bed and the silent house erupted in a cacophony of shouting.

Overhead, furniture screeched across the floor. "Charlie." Kat screamed and several sets of footsteps pounded through the house above me.

Throwing my bag over my shoulder, I ran to the stairs and

made it up two before Kat let out a terrified scream followed by a thump and Kat herself tumbling down the stairs. Her head and shoulder slammed against the wall and she lay at my feet, groaning.

"Kat?" I dropped to my knees and brushed her hair back from her face. "You're all right. Tell me you're okay."

Eyes brimming with tears, she shook her head. "I want Rochelle."

Heavy footsteps stomped toward us. The guy who had been holding Kat stood on the landing with Tommy behind him.

Kat pulled herself halfway up and wrapped her arms around me. "I don't want to die. Don't let them take me."

I swallowed back the pain from her head smacking my collarbone and circled my arm around her. "It'll be okay."

"She bit me." He glared at us, holding one hand in the other. "That little—"

"Hey." It was hard to express anger without jostling Kat's head lolling against my chest. "Watch what you say about her. You should have let her go when I told you to."

"And why would I take orders from you?" His hands clenched at his sides and he descended a few steps.

"Because I'll be second in command when we get back to Kansas City."

"He's right, Alec." Tommy thrust his arm in front of Alec to prevent him from getting closer. "Charlie and Griff are like brothers, and he's been in The Defiance far longer than you. We can trust him. He won't let anyone get in our way." They both frowned at me, cradling Kat as she whimpered.

"She's not in our way. And Molly is going to flip her lid when she finds out about this." I emphasized each word, never breaking eye contact with Alec. There had to be a way I could gain some control over the situation for Kat's sake.

"What about me?" Molly appeared on the landing. "What happened here?"

"Alec shoved Kat down the stairs." I didn't yet understand the dynamic between Molly and the others, but if I learned it, I could use it to my advantage. "You're the one who knows Rochelle so well. Is she going to join you if you kill her sister?"

"Alec, come here." Molly waited until he stood in front of her at attention. "I told you to hold on to her and keep her quiet." She slapped him hard across the face. "Next time, follow orders. Go wait for us outside."

Alec glared at me, eyes dark with hatred, but he retreated, rubbing the side of his face.

"Enough playing around." Molly sauntered down the stairs and sat on the step above Kat and me. "Time to toughen up." She lifted Kat's chin with two fingers. "You'll be fine."

Kat held a hand to the side of her head and shook in my arms.

Molly sighed and rolled her eyes. "Tommy, take her to the car."

"The car?" I watched helplessly as he pulled her away from me and hoisted her into his arms. "You said you wouldn't take her out of Maibe."

"We're not going far." Molly took my arm and forced me to my feet. "It's best to meet with Rochelle in a place we can be in control, and she won't come to the meeting unless I have something she wants. Funny, I spent ten years thinking Kat was just a waste of space."

"Rochelle's aunt isn't going to let her meet with you." I clutched the strap on my bag. "Just leave Kat and I'll . . ."

"Don't worry. We both know she won't ask for permission." Molly gripped my shoulder, digging her fingers into the space above my collarbone. "Are you with us or against us? Think carefully about your answer, because it affects everyone who lives in this house."

Her victorious smirk told me things could get far worse for all of us if I made the wrong choice. A dream-like numbness enveloped me. Just like a month earlier when I'd left Rochelle with Molly, there was nothing I could do. "I'm with you."

"That's better. Do you have the pendant?"

Cooperating with Molly would provide my only chance to protect Kat and Rochelle. I reached into my pocket and inched it out until it was visible to both of us between my fingers.

"Good." She took my arm, and I slid the pendant back into hiding. "Say goodbye to all of this." She laughed as we ascended the stairs. "You and I are part of the same family now."

CHAPTER 33

ROCHELLE

December 28, 2090

"Rochelle will love attending the Accelerated Education Institute." Audrie sat next to me in the back seat of Alexander's truck as he drove us from the train station to the house. As much as Kinley had tried to discourage her from coming back to Maibe, Audrie had been adamant about discussing our situation as an entire family. "All of the students there have gone through a thorough screening process and passed rigorous tests to get in." Lunch had been civil. Audrie's partner, Sid, had joined us but remained in Omaha to finish some work on one of his cases. "Essentially, they've been recruited by the TCI because they have useful skills."

Kinley stared through the windshield. They had been arguing about Audrie's intentions for my future since we got on the train. "I don't want Rochelle training to be some TCI agent. She's already on track to be a doctor, or a teacher, or anything normal."

"There's no requirement for her to become a TCI agent." Audrie spoke in a reassuring tone. "She'll get a top-notch education and learn some real-world survival skills like all of the other students, but many of those students don't become TCI agents. Very few of them have what it takes in the end."

"What about the screening and the test?" I clutched one hand in the other. Kinley and Emma had kept me up on my studies, but I felt unprepared to compete with the rigorous standards of a place called the Accelerated Education Institute.

"No worries." Audrie patted my shoulder. "I'll vouch for all of the screening stuff, and if you're a little behind academically, we'll get you caught up."

"She won't be behind." I wished my cousin would stop defending my abilities when Audrie meant no insult to either of us, but her in-depth questioning had given me an idea of my potential future.

I would live in a dorm room with a roommate. Academic classes went from eight until two, and skill-based classes continued for an hour or two after that. I would be allowed to write as many letters as I wanted and make phone calls on Sundays, but I wouldn't be permitted to leave except for an occasional weekend with Audrie, and no visitors would be allowed.

"I know you're nervous about letting her go." Audrie sighed and crossed one leg over the other. "But I guarantee Rochelle will be safe and well cared for."

Alexander turned onto our street and gestured toward two police cars parked in front of my house. "What's going on now?" He swung the truck into the driveway.

Kinley sprang out of the truck before he even had it in park and ran toward the back door. I followed closely behind, trying not to imagine any terrible scenarios until I knew what had actually happened. Inside, the kitchen table had been shoved to the other side of the room and two of the chairs were toppled onto the floor. All of the mail and kitchen utensils had been swept off the counter nearest the door. A soft murmur of voices drifted in from the next room.

My cousin turned to me, wide eyes mirroring the panic gripping my chest. She took my hand, and we walked into the dining room where Emma and Todd sat across the table from two of Maibe's new police officers.

"What's going on?" Kinley's voice came out weak and shaky. "Where are Kat and Charlie?"

"That's what we're trying to figure out, ma'am." The cop who spoke nodded in our direction.

Todd's eyes met mine, and he shook his head. I didn't have to read his mind to understand he believed the worst-case scenario had caught us unprepared.

"Kinley, I'm sorry." Emma stood. "I came over to check on them and found the kitchen like that. I don't know how long they've been gone."

"I'll take things from here." Audrie strode into the room, holding out her credentials for the police officers to see. "TCI. Is the house clear?"

"Yes." The two officers spoke at the same time, half standing and half sitting, enthralled by my aunt's claim to authority.

"Kinley and Rochelle, go upstairs and stay there." Audrie took a step toward us when we didn't move. "Right now. I need to know you're safe so I can concentrate on finding Kat."

"And Charlie?" Kinley didn't move.

"I'll do my best." Our aunt pulled out her phone. "Now go."

My whirling mind told me I had to stay and be part of the investigation, but if I didn't obey Audrie, she wouldn't find Kat. Needing to escape all of the apprehensive eyes, I looped my arm around Kinley's waist and, without feeling my feet, walked her to the stairs. "It'll be okay." I repeated those words but still didn't believe them by the time we entered my room. "We can't panic yet." It took every ounce of my willpower to keep my voice steady. "We don't even know that something bad has happened. Maybe they just went to the library or the grocery store."

"Of course it's something bad. They wouldn't just disappear. Kat wouldn't leave the kitchen a mess." She paced the few feet between my bed and the wall with her hand pressed to her forehead. "This is what I've been afraid of. This is . . . I should have sent all of you away, right after . . ." She collapsed onto the bed. "I was selfish, Rochelle. I was too selfish to let you go because I wanted you here with me."

"That's not selfish." I sat down and rested my head on her shoulder. "You're the most unselfish person I know. This is my fault, not yours."

"It's not your fault you got caught up in this mess." Kinley sighed and slid her head against mine. "I wish I could fix this for you. For all of us. But I don't know how."

I studied us in the mirror over my dresser. Our slender figures melted together, gravity pulling us toward the floor, faces pale and defeated. Above our reflections, in the top corner, hung the sketch Todd had given me for Christmas. Directly below it, a folded piece of notebook paper stuck in the right angle of the mirror's frame.

Wriggling away from my cousin, I walked to the unfamiliar paper, pulled like a nail to a magnet. With a shaking hand, I plucked it out of place and unfolded it.

Rochelle—

I need another chance to explain why we have to work together. Kat is with me. I knew you wouldn't come unless I gave you a good reason. Meet me at the junkyard we went to with Max and Todd when we were kids. Come alone. Leave your aunt and the authorities out of it, or you won't see your sister again. You have until sunset.

—Molly

"Rochelle, what is that?" Kinley's reflection pleaded for hope.

Only a few months earlier, I would have told her it was nothing, then snuck out to save my sister. But the past few weeks of confiding in Kinley had rekindled our friendship and our trust.

"Promise not to panic?" I sank next to my cousin and held out the note for her to read. "I have to go."

"No, Rochelle." Kinley's face drained of color before she even finished reading. "This is a trap. Just like the last time."

Accepting the answer I expected from my cousin, I stood. "Then I have to go tell Audrie so she can fix this."

"Wait." She grasped my hand. "If Audrie doesn't let you confront Molly, we won't ever see Kat again."

"Kinley, the sun sets in less than an hour. We can tell Audrie or I can deal with Molly myself, but we have to decide now."

"Will Molly keep her word?" Her wide eyes met mine.

I nodded. "She'll let Kat go. But she'll also want me to go with her."

"I'm not trading one of you for the other." She rubbed her forehead. "I'm not willing to lose either of you."

"You won't have to." My hand closed around the locket Max had given me, hanging against my turtleneck sweater. "Because I have this."

My cousin looked at me as if I'd told her the snow outside would be tropical sand by morning.

"It's a tracker. I can agree to go with Molly, she'll let Kat go, and then Audrie can come and get me before I'm even out of the state. Just call Max. He'll know where I am."

Kinley raised one eyebrow at the tarnished locket. "You're sure it works?"

"He showed me. You know Max is brilliant." I took a backward step toward the window. "Molly, on the other hand, is impatient, and if I bring a bunch of cops with me when she clearly stated no authorities—"

"Okay, okay," she interrupted. "But we'll have to break one rule, because I'm going with you." My cousin stood and glanced toward the hallway. "I guess we'll have to use your window exit."

"You know about that?"

Kinley zipped the coat she'd never had a chance to remove. "I know everything, Rochelle. And had you been using it to meet up with anyone other than Todd, I would have nailed it shut a long time ago."

"Good thing you didn't." Pulling my gloves from my pocket, I took a backward step toward the window. The words I needed to thank Kinley for always looking out for me, and understanding even when I thought she didn't, failed to form. I hugged her instead.

"Rochelle. What about Charlie? Why isn't his name in the note?"

Seconds ticked by as I considered how to break the news to her. "We might have to let him go for now. He made me promise not to interfere if The Defiance got to him before he could hide."

"Too bad, because I promised to keep them away from him no matter what." Kinley lunged at the window and undid the latches. "Let's go get our family back."

CHAPTER 34

CHARLIE

December 28, 2090

"I t's s-so c-cold." Kat shivered at my side. She only wore a sweater because I hadn't thought about her needing a coat on my way out the door. "Can't we g-go back to the c-car?"

"You'll survive." Molly shifted her weight on the rusted dryer she perched on like a throne. "It's not my problem your sister is taking her sweet time."

"I told you Rochelle is out of town." I shrugged off my coat and draped it over Kat's shoulders. We sat on an overturned bathtub in a junkyard of old appliances, mattresses, and discarded building materials on the western edge of town. "We should just let Kat go and get out of here before we get caught." I wanted to drive her back to the house and drop her off before leaving town, but the others would never agree to that.

"Let's ditch 'em both." Alec paced through the snow, on his constant patrol from one end of the junkyard to the other. "This guy has done nothing to prove he's one of us. I don't buy it."

"You want to try explaining that to Griff?" Molly rolled her eyes and Alec continued his patrol, crossing paths with Tommy, who covered the rest of the area.

I had considered taking Kat's hand and making a run for it when the boys were at the farthest edges and we only had Molly to contend with. But the car was parked half a mile away on a side road and Kat's fall had left her with a limp. I didn't think we'd get very far.

"Did your plan backfire?" It made me feel a little better to point out Molly wasn't as smart as she believed. "You thought telling Griff I was alive would put him on the warpath to Maibe. Now I'll be helping him make decisions, and we both agree we have no business here."

Kat shrank away from me a little. She couldn't decide if I was on her side or with Molly, and I couldn't reassure her. In order to infiltrate The Defiance and prevent them from accomplishing the worst, I had to become one of them immediately. It would have been easier without Kat next to me, reminding me of who I wanted to be and everything I was giving up.

"My plan worked perfectly." Molly stood and stomped her feet. "I'm tired of both of you, and I don't want Kat out in the open when Rochelle gets here." She pointed over my head. "Take her and stash her in that chest freezer over there."

"No. I won't be able to breathe." Kat stood and took a few shaky backward steps.

Molly caught her elbow and yanked her still.

"She's right. That's your worst idea yet." I remained sitting, ignoring her orders.

Alec and Tommy, drawn by the commotion, stopped their patrol and waited for Molly's response to my challenge.

"I didn't ask for your opinion." She spat the words at me. "She'll have plenty of air to get her through the next hour, and Rochelle should be here by then. But if you refuse, I'm sure Alec would be perfectly willing to follow orders."

"Gladly." He smiled and wrapped his hand around Kat's wrist. She recoiled and he laughed.

I sprang to my feet and ripped her from his grasp. "Go back to your surveillance."

Turning from Molly's satisfied grin and Alec's disappointed scowl, I gripped Kat's elbow and propelled her away from them toward her prison.

"You're hurting me." A tear zigzagged down her cheek. "Why are you helping them?"

"I don't have another choice." Removing my hand from her elbow, I flipped up the lid of the freezer.

"Everyone keeps saying that, but it's not true." She pulled her arms out of my reach and stumbled backward. "I'm leaving now. You have to let me warn Rochelle not to come here."

Looking over my shoulder, I realized Molly was in a deep conversation with the boys. "I'm going to get you home, but you have to trust me." Wrapping my arm around Kat, I shoved her toward the freezer.

"No. Please, Charlie. What did I ever do to you?" Her feet slid through the snow. "I want to go home now."

"Soon." Looping my arm around her waist, I looked into the freezer. An inch of slush sat on the bottom. It was the last place I wanted to leave her, but in this situation, the safest. "You have to help me. I only have one arm to lift you."

Wrinkling her nose, she jumped a little so I could hoist her onto the lip of the freezer. "You fooled me, Charlie Keppler. I thought I knew you, but I've never been so wrong in my life." Medieval torture would have been less painful than those words, but I took a deep breath and helped her into the freezer. As she sank away from me, the coat I'd given her caught on the band of Max's watch still strapped to my wrist.

"Here." I tore at the metal catch that secured it in place. After three tries and despite my opposite arm in a sling, I managed to pull it loose. "As long as you have this, Max will know where to find you. I'll take care of everything else."

She took it, blinking back tears. "A broken watch won't help. Please don't leave me here."

"It'll be okay." Not caring if the others could see, I wrapped my arms around Kat and kissed her forehead. "I promise you'll be okay."

Although I wanted to hold her forever, I pried her hands away and gently shoved her downward so her head was below the opening. She shivered in the dirty chest, legs stretched in front of her, hands gripping the watch. I wanted to tell her that I loved her, that I wanted to stay, that I'd miss her, but there wasn't time.

"I'm sorry." With a shaking hand, I lowered the lid until Kat disappeared from view. Forcing my feet to trudge back through the shin-deep snow, I flipped the hood of my sweatshirt over my head and returned to Molly, who was rubbing her gloved hands together as she watched the horizon blend dark shades of pink and blue over solid white fields.

"I can see that was hard for you, but it was for the best." She shoved her hands into her pockets, keeping her eyes on the freezer as if she expected Kat to pop out. "You have to cut your ties with the Aumonts and this entire town, or Griff is going to see right through whatever game you're playing."

"What about your game? You couldn't collaborate with the council because you wanted everything your way. You can't even see eye to eye with Rochelle. How am I supposed to believe you can work with Griff?"

"Believe it." A smile crept over her lips. "I'm ready to work with Griff and you, if I must, to accomplish our common goals. But I would really like to work with Rochelle. Just think, if we bring her along, you could take a little piece of Maibe with you. She's your favorite anyway, isn't she?"

"Rochelle isn't like us." Aware Molly was trying to manipulate me, I turned away from her. "She didn't even know about the pendant until you told her, and now I have it. What good is she to you?"

"There are plenty of other unanswered questions she can help us with." Molly sighed. "You have to understand, Rochelle had a good dad. He helped her with her homework, volunteered at our school, took her with him to run errands just so they could talk ... There's no way she could spend all of that time with him and not pick up on what was going on. We can't finish the puzzle without her."

"There is no puzzle and she's a liability." It was my last chance to convince Molly that Rochelle wasn't worth the risk. "Her aunt is TCI, she knows about my connection with The Defiance, she knows about you, and she knows there's a pendant. When they all get home and find out Kat isn't there, Audrie won't let Rochelle out of her sight, and she'll come looking for us. We have to get in that car right now and get out of here."

Molly's eyebrows slid together. "And leave Kat in the freezer?"

My chest ached as I nodded.

"Here I thought you cared about her." She laughed. "You think you know a guy."

Lunging forward, I clasped her shoulders and shook her. "I went through a lot to get my hands on this pendant without blowing my cover. Griff is the only brother I've ever known, and what we're doing here is a betrayal of his mission."

"Maybe, just maybe, I underestimated you." She raised one eyebrow, unphased by my outburst. "Time will tell."

Shoving her away from me, I closed my eyes against the long shadows spreading over the junkyard with the sun's final minutes of daylight. I had to get them to leave before Rochelle made a predictably reckless decision. Max would check the trackers and come looking when he realized mine wasn't moving, and they would all be free to carry on with their lives.

"Molly. We have two people approaching from the road," Tommy shouted as he ran toward us. "Two girls our age."

"Rochelle and Kinley, I presume. I knew she wouldn't go to the authorities. We have an understanding much deeper than that." Molly smirked at me. "Tommy, put something heavy on the freezer, then get Alec and go to the car. We'll be there momentarily." She clamped her hand over my injured shoulder. "You stay with me. Show Rochelle how easy it is to switch sides."

CHAPTER 35

ROCHELLE

December 28, 2090

A cluster of rusted appliances and piles of discarded tires rose out of the snow ahead of us.

"You used to play here?" It was the first time Kinley had spoken since we climbed down the tree in front of our house. "Did Uncle Auggie know?"

"It was just a few times. Max was looking for parts for whatever he was inventing." I realized I hadn't answered my cousin's question. "We never told anyone because we didn't want to get in trouble."

"Rochelle, we shouldn't be doing this." Kinley stopped, letting her boots sink into the snow. "This is going to give Audrie proof that I'm an irresponsible guardian."

"We can't go back now." It was bad that I was disappointing my aunt again, and worse that I was dragging Kinley into it, but dealing with Audrie felt so far off. It was a problem for another day. "I'll take all the blame and accept the consequences, but I have to get Kat before Molly hurts her." The sun dropped lower with every passing minute. "Maybe you should wait right here and I'll send Kat to you."

"No way." Kinley took my hand. "We'll do this together or not at all."

"Okay. Are you ready?"

"You're sure Max will be able to find you?"

"One hundred percent." I squeezed her hand.

"Okay." She took a breath and a step forward. "Let's get this over with."

Hand in hand, we slogged through knee-high snow drifts. The closer we got to the long shadows of the discarded junk, backlit by the setting sun, the tighter I gripped my cousin's hand.

"Rochelle, it's about time." Molly stepped out of the shadows with Keppler by her side. "Did you disobey the instructions to come alone on purpose, or did you forget how to read?"

"What do you want?" Kinley took a step toward Molly, but my grip on her hand kept her from getting too close.

Molly's eyebrows slid halfway up her forehead as I pulled my cousin back to my side. "You can't step in and fix everything this time. Rochelle has to grow up and solve her own problems, just like the rest of us."

"Kinley is just here to take Kat home." My heart was pounding out of my chest, but I had to keep everyone calm and find my sister. "Tell me where she is and I'll go with you wherever you want."

"That's what you said last time, but I remember you weren't particularly cooperative." Molly turned to Keppler, who stood with his hands in his pockets and a blank expression on his face. "Charlie proved his loyalty to The Defiance by helping me kidnap your sister and stash her somewhere with a limited supply of oxygen."

"What does that mean?" Kinley took a shuffle step back, but her eyes remained locked on Keppler. "Charlie, tell her you're not a part of this. Tell me where you put Kat."

His eyes, empty and unreadable, met mine. "I can't. It's time for me to go home."

"You would never hurt her." My cousin choked on the words. "After everything we've done for you."

Keppler's eyes dropped to his shoes, and he shook his head.

"Good choice." Molly clapped his shoulder. "Your turn, Rochelle. Prove your loyalty."

"How?" I scanned the area for clues to Kat's location, but there were footprints going in every direction and there was no guarantee they had even brought her to the junkyard. Keppler had always been against everything Molly said. I didn't understand why he was taking orders from her, especially when it involved Kat's safety.

"Tell me your dad's pass codes to get in the safe." Molly folded her arms. "And then I'll tell Kinley where to look for Kat."

"What pass codes?" I couldn't recall anything about that from our previous conversations. "You told me the pendants were the key."

"The pendants are the key to the box they built to hold the research. The pass codes get us into the safe where the box is kept." Molly rolled her eyes and tossed her hair over her shoulder. "According to my dad's records, he let Auggie set the three passcodes. He told him to enter the three things he cared about the most because he figured he already knew the answer and would still have access. Here's a little insight into your dad's final year of life: you weren't one of the three most important things in his life, and neither were Kat and Kinley. If you need a minute to process that, I suppose I have time."

"We shouldn't be here, Rochelle." Kinley's voice shook.

Ignoring my cousin, I kept my face as stony as possible. "You asked me for a pendant, which I didn't find. Now you're asking me to come up with three passcodes on the spot. I don't know, Molly."

She shook her head and tapped her foot in the snow. "I figured you could only handle one task at a time, which has turned out to be correct. It's funny you couldn't find your pendant in eight months, but Charlie found it in a few weeks when Griff asked him to."

"What are you talking about?" My eyes slid from Molly's scowl to Kinley's furrowed eyebrows, and then to Keppler's shaking head. "What is she talking about?"

"She doesn't know about any pass codes, Molly." Keppler stepped in front of her so his back was to us. "Her dad didn't leave any clues behind. I've told you over and over that she doesn't know anything. If we take her back with us, we'll have the TCI on our trail. There's nothing for us in Maibe."

Molly shoved Keppler aside. "Think really hard, Rochelle, if you ever want to see Kat alive again. What are the pass codes?"

A distant wail congealed into the rise and fall of approaching sirens.

"We have to go, Molly." Keppler stood behind her, nodding toward his raised bare wrist. "We're out of time."

"For now. But I'll come back." She didn't move. "Good luck finding Kat."

Keppler dropped his arm to his side and mouthed something I couldn't understand. "We have to go." He reached for Molly's arm and pulled her away from us.

"See you around." With Keppler's prompting, she turned and ran with him into the deepening shadows.

"Wait." Kinley's voice exploded in my ear. "What about Kat?"

Keppler turned and looked at us. For a second, I thought he would change his mind and come back, but Molly clamped her hand around his wrist and pulled him behind a pile of bricks as the sirens wailed onto the road leading to the junkyard.

Kinley darted away from me, sprinting in the direction Molly and Keppler had run. I bounded after her and swerved into her path to stop her.

"Rochelle, get out of my way." She tried to step around me, but I mirrored her movements, keeping her in place. "They have Kat.

I'll make him tell us what they did with her. We can't let them get away." Her breaths came in short, erratic gasps. "I should have . . . We didn't . . ." She collapsed to her knees, crying, shaking, fighting to catch her breath.

"He was pointing at his wrist!" I knelt in front of her and held her hands in mine. "She has the watch. We'll be able to find her."

Kinley shook her head, unable to follow my scrambled train of thought. Over her shoulder, I watched Audrie, Alexander, and two policemen run toward us.

"What were you two thinking?" Audrie dropped to the ground and wrapped one arm around me and the other around Kinley. "I told you to stay upstairs." Her frantic voice walked the edge of fear and anger.

"We're sorry." I spoke for both of us and pulled the note out of my pocket. "We had to come for Kat. There wasn't time to . . ." My eyes jumped from the note to my aunt's stern face. "How did you find us?"

Audrie snatched the folded paper from my hand. "Your friend Todd panicked when he discovered you snuck out. He told me about Max and the trackers."

The last police officer escorted Max onto the scene. He held the old phone in his hand, shoulders stiff, and head bent forward. A dull ache throbbed in my chest as I processed what it meant for the police to know about his illegal use of technology. Despite his predicament, Max's familiar grin spread across his face when he spotted me. "Rochelle, it worked!"

Kinley choked back sobs. "We didn't . . . get Kat . . . and Charlie . . . She brainwashed him . . . or something . . ."

Alexander stepped forward, lifted Kinley to her feet, and held her close to him without a word.

Max helped me up and showed me his screen. "According to this, Keppler is still here."

"He gave Kat his tracker," I whispered, not wanting to reveal anything the authorities didn't yet know about Max's activities.

He nodded and looped his arm through mine. "I'm not going to run." Max took a cautious step away from the police officer and led me between two towers of mattresses and around a pile of broken concrete blocks. "You guys were right. I think I'm in a lot of trouble." He whispered so the others, following a few feet behind, wouldn't hear.

"It'll be okay," I whispered back before we stopped in front of an old chest freezer with a row of concrete foundation blocks piled on top. "In there?"

Max nodded, and together we started lugging off the blocks. "Rochelle, where's Keppler? What did Kinley mean when she said they brainwashed him?"

"He helped Molly kidnap Kat." My chest ached and my stomach twisted into a hundred knots. "It looked like he was working for her, or with her."

"I'm sure it's more complicated than that." Max glanced over his shoulder. "Let's just find Kat. If she has the tracker, you'll know he was actually trying to protect her."

His hand trembled as he reached for the lid, but he mustered the courage to open it.

My sister blinked up at us, sitting in an inch of slushy water, shivering so violently she couldn't speak. She wore Keppler's coat and clutched his broken watch in her hands.

"She's okay." Max shoved the phone into my hands. "Come on. I'll get you out of there." He helped Kat to her feet and lifted her out of the freezer.

Her legs wobbled and she crashed into me, taking us both down to the snowy ground. I wrapped my arms around her and she huddled against me. Soon Kinley's arms encircled both of us, and I looked up at a circle of grim faces—Audrie, Alexander, two policemen, and Max.

"Ch-Charlie w-was h-helping them," my sister whimpered in the most heartbroken voice I had ever heard.

Audrie pulled out her phone. "I'll get Sid up here for backup. Alexander, why don't you drive the girls to the hospital to get Kat checked out. Fill Kinley in on the Charlie situation, and I'll be there to conduct interviews as soon as I can."

"What is the Charlie situation?" Kinley held firmly to Kat and me. "What is she talking about?"

"I'll explain after Kat sees a doctor." Alexander scooped my sister into his arms. "Come on, Rochelle."

Max fell into step beside me, but we only made it a few steps before the police officer cleared his throat. "Not you, Max. We have a long night of contacting your parents and discussing the consequences of your actions."

"I'll tell Audrie you're a hero. She'll fix this." I handed him the phone and pulled him into a hug. "Thank you."

He squeezed me tight, and I knew he was afraid. "Don't worry about me. Go take care of Kat and Alexander. I have a feeling Kinley isn't going to like his explanation."

"Rochelle, hurry up," Kinley yelled from the truck.

I took a step back from Max, feeling a deep dread that neither of our lives would ever be the same, then turned and ran toward my family.

CHAPTER 36
ROCHELLE

December 29, 2090

66 ❚ 've seen Kinley get mad at Alexander before, but not like this." I didn't know what else to say. Todd and I had passed the afternoon sitting shoulder to shoulder in the hallway outside Kat's bedroom. I wanted to be close in case she needed me. The silence was only interrupted by bursts of thought I voiced out loud.

At the hospital, Alexander had told my cousin about the papers he signed that gave Audrie temporary custody of Keppler and allowed him to work as an informant for the TCI. Kinley had wavered between angry shouting and desperate crying as she stammered phrases like "We were supposed to make these decisions together" and "How could you lie to me about something so important?"

I squeezed my eyes shut so I wouldn't cry. "She made him leave. She told him she never wanted to see him again." Keppler was gone. Max was in deep trouble. And Kinley had kicked Alexander out of our lives. My whole world had been turned upside down and shaken.

Todd sighed. "He told me. When he left the hospital, he came to my house and told Emma she would have to give you guys a ride home in the morning."

Kinley and I had spent the night in Kat's hospital room. She was bruised everywhere from tumbling down the stairs, but the doctor was more concerned about the lump on her head and mild hypothermia, so he kept her for observation. She was released before lunch with directions to get plenty of rest and apply ice to anything that hurt. Emma and Todd had brought us home, and we'd just finished lunch when Audrie arrived.

A murmur of controlled arguing drifted up the stairs. I couldn't hear the debate between my aunt and Kinley, but I knew they were fighting for control of my fate. "How long have they been at it?"

Todd looked at his watch before realizing it was just the broken tracker. "At least an hour." He dropped his arm to his side. "How much trouble do you think Max is in?"

"Audrie said her partner is working with the local authorities on that." I drew my knees up in front of me. We had all grown up hearing about severe consequences and reform school for kids who used unauthorized technology. "I'm not sure what that means, but I hope Sid can get him off the hook."

"I can't believe I sold him out." Todd rested his head back against the wall. "After everything that's happened, I just panicked."

"None of this is your fault. It's mine. As always, I got myself in over my head, and I'm so lucky I have you guys to bail me out." My head slid to his shoulder. "And Keppler knew we would find Kat. He wouldn't hurt her. He had no choice but to play along with them." Every time I convinced myself he had done everything he could to protect all of us, the doubts crept in. Why hadn't he told me about his plan with Audrie? From what Kat overheard, it sounded like he had spoken to Griff. What else had he kept from me?

"He told me a few days ago that if The Defiance showed up he would stand in their way. That's probably what he was trying to do."

"Why would he let me believe he was going to follow Kinley's plan if he knew he was going back to The Defiance the entire time?"

"Maybe he thought you were safer that way." Todd took a breath and squeezed my hand. "I'll run downstairs, see if Emma has overheard anything, and get some fresh ice packs in case Kat wakes up."

I nodded and sat up. He had been restless since Audrie arrived. We were both worried my departure had been bumped up when I was supposed to have another week in Maibe. After Todd disappeared down the stairs, the quiet hum of the hall was shattered by Kat's scream.

Startled, I sprang to my feet and rushed into my sister's room. She sat in the middle of her bed, crying. "It's okay. You're safe." Sliding in next to her, I folded her into my arms.

"Where were you? I kept yelling for you and Kinley, but neither of you would come."

"It must have been a bad dream." I pulled a wad of tissues from the box on the nightstand and dried her tears.

She sniffled and shook her head. "Promise you'll tell Audrie you won't go with her. She can't make you."

"You'll be better off with me gone. Just me being here puts everyone in danger, and going with Audrie is my only chance to make up for it." I had convinced myself that Audrie was right and I had some memory locked away that would help the TCI get ahead in the pendant race. That would be the only way I could ever redeem myself.

"That's not true." She cleared her throat and stiffly lowered herself back against her pillows. "We never should have kept Charlie. That was our only mistake."

I couldn't blame Keppler for what Molly had done. After all, he had been the one who gave us a way to find Kat. At least, I hoped that had been his plan.

"Hey, everything okay?" Todd peeked his head around the doorframe. "I brought new ice packs."

"You can come in." Kat wiped the rest of her tears away with the sleeve of her shirt.

"Audrie and Kinley are still closed up in the library." Todd handed me the ice packs, each wrapped in a washcloth.

I took them and turned to my sister. "Where does it hurt the most?"

"My shoulder and my head." It had been her answer since Kinley's initial exam on the way to the hospital. "Can you open the curtain just a little?"

A single lamp in the corner lit the room for the sake of Kat's head. I helped my sister place the ice packs while Todd slid the curtains apart a few inches to let in some of the winter sunlight.

"Thank you, Todd." She laid back on the pillow so the left side of her head rested next to the ice.

Todd crossed the room, pulled a chair close to the bed, and sat down just as voices exploded at the bottom of the stairs.

"There has to be a way we can work this out." I'd never heard Kinley plead with anyone. "I need more time to get her ready. I need more time to say goodbye."

"She isn't safe here, Kinley." Audrie's calm was an absolute contradiction to my cousin's desperation. "The best thing you can do for Rochelle is sign these papers."

Kat bolted upright and wrapped her arms around me. "Don't go with her. Please."

Todd froze, eyes helplessly locked with mine, as the voices reached the hallway.

"Please, Audrie." Kinley paused in the doorway with her back to us. "I'll do better. I can keep her safe."

"For the past six months, you've been insisting that you're an adult. That you're perfectly capable of raising teenagers who are only a few years younger than you. And then yesterday, you made the reckless decision to take Rochelle and walk right into a trap."

My cousin turned to me, eyes puffy from crying. "Rochelle, I'm so sorry."

I didn't know what she was apologizing for, but I couldn't let her take the blame for my decisions. "It was my fault, Aunt Audrie. I said we had to hurry. I didn't give her time to think."

My aunt stood in the hallway, shaking her head and glaring at Todd.

He took Kinley's arm and walked her to the bed, where she sat down beside me. He patted my knee and then slipped out of the room.

"I know you love them, Kinley. I've never doubted that." Audrie approached us with a clipboard under her arm. "But you're so young for all of this responsibility, and you're in over your head."

My cousin squeezed my hand so tightly I couldn't feel my fingers. "She wants to take you back with her right now."

"No." Kat hugged me.

"If it helps, Sid worked some things out for your friend Max." Audrie smiled at me, ignoring my sister and cousin. "Instead of reform school, we're taking him back to the Accelerated Education Institute with us. He has some impressive skills we could utilize with the appropriate training."

When I'd talked with her at the hospital, Audrie had promised to do everything possible to help Max, and she had come through in her own way. He would be developing his skills instead of being locked up with kids who had been involved in far more dangerous activities, but he would still be leaving.

"Listen to me, Rochelle." She sat in the chair Todd had occupied earlier. "As long as Molly believes you have the information she wants, and knows where to find you, none of you are safe. We have to get you to a place where she can't manipulate you.

Starting tomorrow there will be an undercover TCI agent posted in Maibe to watch over Kat and Kinley. I'm going to make sure you're all safe."

During my interview, I had told Audrie everything Molly said except the part about Keppler having a pendant. That part didn't make sense, and when I asked my aunt about my dad's pendant she confirmed it was safely locked away in a TCI safe. She was especially interested in the pass codes Molly had mentioned, although I couldn't help her with that information any more than I could help Molly.

"Sid is on his way over here with Max right now." Audrie tapped her finger on the clipboard. "This is the perfect time to get you out of here. Before The Defiance has a chance to regroup. Before they come looking for you again. Do you understand?"

I didn't want to leave so soon, but every time I chose to face Molly, I hurt my family in one way or another and I couldn't put them through that any more. I had spent too long trying to deal with her on my own, and I needed Audrie's help. "Yes. I understand." Squeezing my eyes shut, I forced myself to breathe. "Kinley, it's the only choice we have right now."

My cousin's hand released mine and when I opened my eyes, she had the clipboard on her lap. "This is temporary, right?" Her pen hovered over the signature line. A tear dripped onto the document. "When this is over, I'll get her back?"

"When the danger has passed, I'll bring her home." The way Audrie phrased it gave me the impression she didn't expect the danger to pass anytime soon.

"No, Kinley. Don't." Kat lunged for the pen, but I caught her and held her. "If you send Rochelle away, I'll never forgive you."

"Shhh. It'll be okay." I rocked her gently back and forth. "We can still talk. I'll write to you so much it'll be like I never left."

"It's not the same." She fought to free herself from my bear hug, but I wouldn't let her go. "If you leave, I don't want to talk to you anymore."

Her words pinched my heart as Kinley's hand scrawled her signature across the paper and handed it back to our aunt.

"You've made the right decision." Audrie stood. "Rochelle, you have five minutes to get some things together. Pack light. We can buy anything that isn't provided by the school."

I let go of Kat as Audrie left the room. Tears streaking her face, my sister sank back into her pillow and turned away from me. If I stopped to think, I would cry, so I forced myself to move.

"I'm so sorry." Kinley couldn't meet my eyes. "I really thought I could keep you safe. I never thought Charlie would betray us like that. I'll do better if I ever get you back."

"You didn't do anything wrong." Ignoring her tears, I hugged Kinley, trying to memorize the comfort so I could take it with me. "I love you. I'll call you as soon as I can."

"I love you too." She held onto my hand even when I stood. "Have a safe trip and don't be afraid. Everything will be okay."

Nodding, I rested my hand on Kat's shoulder. "I love you. Even if you never speak to me again." Leaning forward, I kissed the top of her head, but she didn't respond.

"I'll stay with them, Rochelle." Emma wrapped her arms around me and I was thankful for her steady calm, how she was always there when we needed her.

As if walking through a dream, I crossed the hall to my room and mindlessly tossed clothes into my duffel bag. The only time I'd been away from home for more than a night had been almost a year earlier when I went to Omaha with Kinley, and she had done most of the packing for me. It was the trip I'd cut short to come home and help Keppler. I believed that was the reason we'd met in the first place. We were supposed to help each other because nothing happened by chance. I didn't have time to think about where that left me now.

What did I need if I wouldn't be home for months or even years? Scanning my room, I selected Todd's last drawing from my mirror and the last Aumont family picture, before the fever, from my dresser. On final thought, I opened my dresser drawer and pulled out the hummingbird charm bracelet my dad had given me before going to the hospital for the last time.

I tucked all of it into the side pocket of my bag, zipped it shut, and carried it into the hallway. Emma's soothing voice comforted Kat and Kinley as I walked away, unsure when I would see them again.

Todd sat on the landing and pulled himself to his feet as I descended the first set of stairs. "I know you have to go. Do you still promise to write every day?"

Dropping my bag, I threw my arms around him. "Twice a day." A few of my tears soaked into his shirt before I could pull myself together. "Will you look after them for me?"

"I'll check in on them every day." He kissed the top of my head. "Don't forget about me while you're away. I love you, Rochelle."

"I could never forget about you." Holding his face in my hands, I brushed a tear from his cheek with my thumb. "I love you no matter where I am, and that will never change."

"Rochelle," Audrie called. "Time to go."

Without another word, Todd picked up my bag and walked me through the house to the back door. There, I put on my coat and shoes, Sid took my bag, and I walked with him and Audrie to the car parked in the driveway.

Sid opened the back door for me and I slid in next to Max.

"Are you okay?" He rubbed his eye with the back of his hand, but I couldn't tell if he had been crying.

I shook my head, and the tears I had fought to hide from Kinley and Todd rushed to my eyes. "It's all happening too fast."

"I know." Max held his arms open and I leaned into his embrace. "At least we'll be together. I was a little afraid before, but now that I have my best friend and the only person brave enough to be my assistant with me, I'm kind of excited." He glanced out the window where Audrie and Sid were in deep conversation. "You know we're going to spy school, right?"

Despite my tears, I laughed because he said it like a little kid on his way to get ice cream after school. At least I had Max, unlike Keppler out there with The Defiance. Whatever lies he told himself, he didn't belong with them and didn't deserve to be miserable.

Sid and Audrie got into the car, and Max squeezed my hand as we backed out of the driveway. In the kitchen window, Todd waved and I waved back, not sure whether he could see me or not. Then I watched the only home I'd ever known fade behind me.

CHAPTER 37
CHARLIE

December 29, 2090

"**D**id you ever stop calling Rochelle and Max by their last names?" Molly sat back in her chair and crossed one leg over the other.

"Nope." I sat in the chair next to hers in Griff's office and stared at his unoccupied desk. When I had left The Defiance camp, he hadn't had an office and I never imagined I'd be sitting in one waiting to meet with him.

"You don't do that with anyone else. Why them?"

Molly had peppered me with nonstop questions during our half-hour wait. I wasn't in the mood to talk, and I wished Griff would just show up already. We had spent half the night driving to Kansas City, taking all gravel roads to avoid any authorities or TCI agents looking for us. When we arrived, I had trudged to my old room, which, as Griff had claimed, was exactly as I had left it. Exhausted, I crawled into bed and waited for the sweet escape of sleep, but every time I had closed my eyes, I heard Kat pleading with me not to leave her in the freezer and saw the betrayed look on Kinley's face. So I spent the rest of the night staring at the ceiling.

When the first light had slanted through my window, I was startled by a knock at the door. I had opened it to a tray of breakfast on the floor and a note inviting me to a meeting with Griff at ten.

"Well? What's with Aumont and Delgado?" Molly's relentless questions broke into my thoughts.

"Everyone I've ever met in my life has been suspicious of my intentions." If the truth would shut her up, she could have it. "Even my own family sensed something dark in me, but not Rochelle and Max. The first time I met them, we were practically in a scene from a murder movie, and they were chatting with me like I was their old pal." That chance meeting on a dark road felt like it had happened ten years ago. "So I had to be the one to distance myself. I knew this day would eventually come."

"Did you?" Molly turned to me. "Did you really think Griff would invite you back, or were you afraid he would find you and kill you?"

"What's the difference?" I slumped and stretched my legs out in front of me. "None of it matters anymore." The door creaked open behind me, but I didn't turn.

"Hey, kid. Welcome home." Griff's voice boomed and his hand clamped over my shoulder. "I didn't expect to see you for a few more days."

"I was just as surprised when Molly showed up and said, 'Change of plans.'"

"That's what I heard from Tommy." Griff walked around his desk and plopped into his chair. "Molly, didn't we just have a talk about conducting unauthorized business? I thought we were in agreement that you'd clear it with me first."

"You were out of town," she snapped. "It was my best chance to catch the Aumonts off guard, and I couldn't pass it up."

"And what do you have to show for it?" Griff's voice remained even and his muscles stayed relaxed. "The TCI out looking for you? How many times do I have to tell you that town and that Aumont girl are dead ends?"

"She knows the pass codes, Griff." Molly stood and placed her hands on her hips. "I could see it on her face."

Griff sighed and shook his head. I'd never seen him have a

polite disagreement with anyone. "Charlie was our inside guy. What's the verdict, kid? Do any of the Aumonts know anything useful?"

"They didn't even know they were connected to all of this until Molly clued Rochelle in." I sat up straight. "They're not worth our time."

"He doesn't know anything." Molly's voice rose to a screech. "The way Rochelle reacted to my comment about him finding the pendant makes me think his isn't even real. I'll bet he made a fake just to save his butt."

I slid the pendant from around my neck and tossed it onto Griff's desk. "It's the real thing. Unlike Molly, I keep my word."

Griff held his hands up. "The three of us are a team from now on, whether you two like it or not." He picked up the pendant and smiled as he examined it. "Molly, it's about time you put the past behind you."

"Fine." She rolled her eyes.

"Come on. Don't be mad." Shoving it in his pocket, he winked at her. "I'll take you to lunch. Go get ready and I'll be at your door in half an hour."

"Whatever." She turned and strode across the room. "Don't be late like you were for this meeting."

Griff chuckled and shook his head as her heels clicked in the hallway. "I've known her since we were little kids. Our families would vacation together twice a year." He wore a lovesick expression I'd never expected to see on his face. "She's always been a spitfire."

My stomach churned and I thought I would throw up. "Are you two..."

"It's complicated." Griff stood and brushed imaginary dust from the pocket of his suit jacket.

"She'll stab you in the back the first chance she gets." It was my immediate instinct to let them destroy each other, but Molly was so much smarter than Griff. She reached into people's hearts and ripped out whatever emotions she could use to manipulate them. The only thing worse than Griff leading The Defiance would be Molly leading The Defiance.

"I can handle her." He looked me up and down. "Starting in the new year, your role with The Defiance will be twofold. First, you'll accompany me for all business related to the pendant, and for that you'll need better clothes. I set your appointment with the tailor for Wednesday. How much longer are you in the sling?"

Head spinning, I tried to focus. "Uh, three or four more weeks."

He nodded. "We have two doctors on our payroll. I'll have one come in and give us an updated prognosis."

"Great." I didn't want to see a tailor or a doctor. I wanted to call my family and make sure Kat was safe. I wanted to go home. But I couldn't do either of those things ever again. Rochelle, Kat, Kinley, and the others in Maibe were worth protecting. I would sacrifice everything good in my life so they would be safe, so they could have a future, so they would never have to live in a country under Defiance control.

"Charlie? You okay?" Griff leaned back on his desk, arms folded in front of him.

"Yeah. Fine."

"You're upset about Molly interfering with our plans." He sighed and ran a hand over his short hair. "It's for the best. Your second responsibility might cheer you up. After I read your writing, I realized your talent is exactly what we need to publish our own newsletter and distribute it as we expand. You know, let other kids like us know we have a place for them." His eyes narrowed. "Make them understand we're their only hope, and the future will be incredible if they stick with us. If I get the printing equipment, you can spread our message. Right?"

"I guess I can try, but what about the TCI? They'll come looking for us." Arguing with Griff would have been pointless, and I had to get a handle on everything pendant related in order to prevent any more progress.

Griff laughed. "Don't tell Molly, but we don't have to worry about the TCI. Between you and me, we have an inside guy. I know all of their moves ahead of time, and they have no intention of getting anywhere near here."

My stomach twisted but I swallowed back the nausea. It didn't surprise me that the TCI was corrupt—Lareina had warned me about that—but I didn't expect an affiliation with The Defiance. If Griff was telling the truth, I had to assume Audrie was unaware of the leak in her organization. If I worked with her as an informant, would Griff be notified by his informant?

I stood and paced the room, trying not to look like I was about to throw up. "And where are we at with the pendants?"

"We have four of them. Thanks to you." He patted his pocket. "According to my informant, the TCI has at least two. We'll deal with that later. For now, I want to track down Brandon Davis. His last known address was in Denver, Colorado. That was a year ago, but I have some leads. The guy's on the run and we're going to catch up."

"Of course." The image of autumn leaves and blue sky on the day Griff spoke with Roger Zimmer flashed through my mind, along with the article describing Zimmer's murder. "Is Molly right? Do we really need pass codes before the pendants even matter?"

Griff waved a hand. "That's a recently discovered setback, but I'm hoping Davis can give us some insight. He was more closely aligned with Auggie's beliefs, so they probably shared information. Far more likely he knows the codes than Auggie's kids." He shook his head. "I love having Molly around, but she can be so illogical and stubborn when she sets her mind to something. Anyway . . ." He crossed the room and stepped in front of me. "Those are problems for tomorrow. My brother's home, and we should celebrate. Dinner tonight? You choose the place and I'll buy."

"Sounds great." I hadn't been able to eat anything since leaving Kat, and I doubted tonight would be any different.

Griff walked me to the door. "All right. Meet me up here at six. Until then, get some rest. You look like you haven't slept in weeks."

"Sure thing." I shuffled to the door then turned around. "Hey, Griff, you said even when you thought I betrayed you, you wouldn't have killed me. If I hadn't escaped, what would have happened?"

He stuffed his hands in his pockets. "I felt rotten after I beat you up, and the longer I thought about it the more I doubted Shane's accusations. You must have taken off minutes before I came down to talk to you and let you out."

I wanted to believe his story. After everything I'd given up, I needed the comfort of knowing at least one person cared, even if it was in his own twisted way. "You've been looking for me this whole time?"

"I didn't have a clue where to begin, but I had everyone keeping their eyes and ears open." He rubbed the side of his face. "Then Molly mentioned a Charlie Keppler arriving in Maibe and staying with the Aumont family. I took that as a sign, like it was all meant to be. Even our little skirmish put you in a position to carry out another step of our mission."

"Right." I nodded. Only Griff could call it "a little skirmish" when he'd beaten me to the point I could barely walk. But he was right about the rest. After everything I'd been through, how could I believe any moment of my life occurred at random? No matter what happened to me, serendipitous miracles or ominous disasters, they all led back to the pendants because *nothing happened by chance.*

ABOUT THE AUTHOR

Vanessa Lafleur is a high school English teacher and coach of various school activities. She lives in Nebraska where she enjoys spending summer days outside and winter days writing. Vanessa loves discussing literature with her students and helping them discover their writing talents. When she isn't teaching, she spends her time reading, writing, surprising her students with homemade treats, and counting down the days to the next speech season.

Prepare for the Worst is the third book in the *Hope for the Best* series. Find out more about Vanessa Lafleur at www.vanessalafleur. com and follow her on Facebook @vanessalafleurauthor and Instagram @vlafleurauthor.

OTHER BOOKS IN THE HOPE FOR THE BEST SERIES

Seventeen-year-old Lareina has no family, no home, and no last name. What she does have is an oddly shaped pendant and Detective Russ Galloway who would follow her across the country to take it from her.

Through her own resilience and wit, Lareina has survived her teenage years in a chaotic and crumbling world by stealing what she needs. Hoping to escape the detective and discover the truth about her pendant, Lareina flees the city.

On her journey she meets Nick and Aaron who remind her how much she has missed feeling a connection to other people. Together they learn survival is impossible unless they can learn to trust each other. With every mile they travel, Lareina races to escape the past and discover the truth.

The brand burned into Charlie's arm is a constant reminder that family doesn't exist, people only care about their own selfish interests, and a handful of pendants, if united, could lead to negative consequences for the entire world. All he wants is to escape his perilous past and the people who want him dead. By accident, he arrives in the small town of Maibe, Nebraska where he has the chance to change his life and start over.

Rochelle is trying to pick up the pieces and move forward after a year filled with loss and illness. She just wants to take care of her family, prevent her home from becoming a ghost town, and save the world if she has time. When an old friend shares secret information about pendants that could save millions of lives, she finds herself and everyone she loves plunged into a world more dangerous than she could ever imagine.

As it becomes clear that nothing happens by chance, Charlie and Rochelle must face the trauma of their pasts and work together to ensure tomorrow will be better for everyone.